THE GOSPEL OF THE BAPTIST

CHRISTOPHER LAURENT

The Gospel of the Baptist

Published by Red Penguin Books

Bellerose Village, New York

Library of Congress Control Number: 2021915112

ISBN

Softcover 978-1-63777-120-4

Hardcover 978-1-63777-128-0

Digital 978-1-63777-121-1

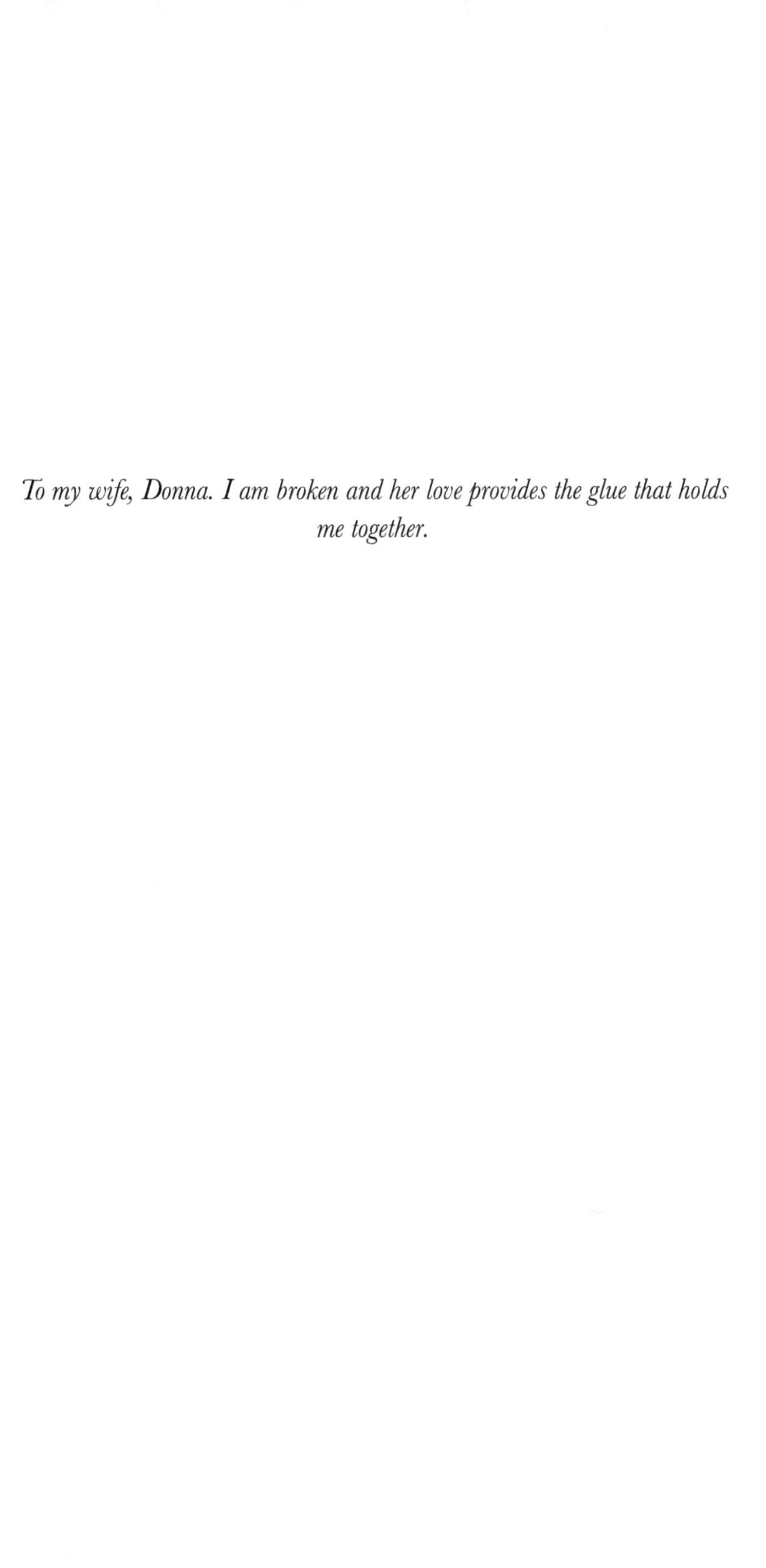

To my wife, Donna. I am broken and her love provides the glue that holds me together.

CONTENTS

CHAPTER 1

The Jerusalem sun beat down hard on Jonathan and Saul as they walked the dusty street to the Antiquities Commission. The wind blew gently to cool the beads of sweat that had appeared on their foreheads from heat. As the wind blew sand stuck to their faces and spread out across the stoned street. The sand from the street mixed with the sand on their boots from the latest dig. The walk seemed longer each time as with each new dig came new relics and information that required "approval" of the Antiquities Commission. Jonathan and Saul had been in Jerusalem for three years on this archeological expedition. For most of the first thirty months, they found nothing worthwhile so this trip was not necessary. But six months ago when they discovered what appeared to be the façade of a dwelling about twelve meters beneath the surface, these walks to the Antiquities Commission had become more frequent.

Antiquities Commission was a bit of a stretch. The "Commission" consisted of one man. A fat bureaucrat, who had little to no knowledge of archeology, made up the "Commission." He sat behind a desk too large for the room with piles of requests in his in basket and little work in the out basket. His balding head always seemed to have a sore or two as if he constantly was bumping into things. His name was Mr. Goldman and he expected to be called "Mr. Goldman." His glasses, too small for his round head, always were at the tip of his nose and when he talked he constantly was pushing them up. He wore the same white cotton suit that was wrinkled as if he slept in it every night. There was also the thin black tie that contained similar wrinkles and was never really tied. He sat there with fat fingers that showed the stains of the tiny cigarillos that he constantly smoked and fanned himself from the heat.

Jonathan and Saul finally reached the steps of the Antiquities Commission. Their requests to continue to dig, as always, had not been answered. The same routine each time, submit and request and be ignored.

"Do you have enough money?" Jonathan asked Saul.

After three years Jonathan and Saul were well acquainted with the routine. Submit the request to continue to dig, wait the two weeks, go see Mr. Goldman, listen to his lies about not having a request, his arguments about the Jerusalem artifacts, paying the bribe, and the request miraculously approved the next day. Nothing in Jonathan and Saul's training prepared them for these real bureaucratic workings of archeological exploration.

Jonathan and Saul had met at the University five years earlier. Saul was a professor of Ancient Hebrew and Jonathan joined the staff as an Associate Professor in the same department. Neither seemed suited to the life of academia. Saul was tall, thin, with long straight hair that curled at the ends and was thinning on top. The fine wisps of thin hair on top frequently swayed in the wind as he moved his head from side to side. His beard was equally unkempt and both showed the salt and pepper color of a man that was in his mid-fifties. His walk was that of a man of urgency, but with long strides reflective of his six foot frame. Amazingly his eyesight was not impaired; even after years of study, research, and teaching Saul did not require glasses, something he inherited from his Mother's side of the family. She passed at 103 years old, still reading the paper without glasses. Saul always wore the same colored brown canvas trousers, light colored shirt, and a jacket that showed the years of fondness with the patches at each elbow. Under his arms were stacks of papers, old ancient books, and a paper bag with a tuna on rye sandwich and apple for dessert inside. In fact, that was how Jonathan first met the man who would become his mentor.

Jonathan was late for a meeting with the Professor. He was rushing around the corner of the building, not realizing that Saul had forgotten the appointment. Jonathan collided with Saul, sending the contents under Saul's arm flying across the sidewalk and Jonathan down hard on his backside. Saul squinted, frustrated with the young man, and then turned to retrieve his papers, books, and most importantly his lunch. Saul looked everywhere for his lunch without success. His eyes then landed on where Jonathan remained seated on the sidewalk. Without speaking, Saul walked over to Jonathan and reached out his hand. Jonathan graciously took the hand and allowed Saul to pull him to his feet.

"Hmmph," Saul snorted as he saw the flattened sandwich, "guess there's applesauce there now."

Saul stooped to pick up the flattened bag and Jonathan adjusted his large round glasses. He immediately recognized the Professor.

"Professor Harkman, I am so very sorry," Jonathan sheepishly said.

"What?" Saul said, a bit stunned at the familiarity with which the young man addressed him.

"Professor Harkman, I am your new associate Professor, Jonathan Weiztman." Jonathan responded and stuck out his hand to shake the Professor's.

Saul just stood glaring at the young man. He certainly was not what Saul expected. But then, Saul was not sure what he expected as he had never had an Associate Professor before. There before him stood his first, Jonathan Weiztman, a prominent Jewish scholar who had lived in Israel before coming to the United States to complete his Doctorate. Dressed in a blue sportcoat and neutral "Dockers," his light blue shirt sporting a matching tie, Jonathan did not look to be almost thirty.

"More like thirteen," Saul thought to himself.

Jonathan brushed a thick lock of his black hair from his eyes and adjusted his kippah, removed his large round glasses and, with a quickness that reflected years of practice, pulled a handkerchief from his pocket and cleaned the lens before placing them back on his face. The kippah sparked Saul's memory.

"Yes," he finally said, " the Masorti Jew from Israel that has come to help me."

Jonathan could hear the sarcasm in Saul's voice and watched as Saul turned on his heels and began briskly walking away. Many Jews resented the Masorti. The Masorti are the very conservative, some might say, Orthodox, branch of Judaism. After all, "Masorti" means "traditional" in Hebrew. Jonathan wondered if Saul's sarcasm was due to a disdain for the Masorti movement, or just a disdain in general for Jonathan.

"I'm sorry, Sir," Jonathan stuttered as he tried to catch up, "I know I am late for my appointment."

Saul kept walking as if he had not heard a word Jonathan said. Finally Jonathan caught up to Saul and fell into step with the Professor. Saul looked at him again and laughed.

"Let's get started, we have a class in four minutes. You can observe, and then tomorrow you can begin teaching." Saul said with a quick, thin smile that betrayed his amusement at Jonathan's predicament.

The next day, Jonathan, without missing a beat, took over more than half of Saul's classes. After monitoring two classes, Saul realized that Jonathan was a gifted teacher and quite an academic. At the end of that first day, Saul was waiting for Jonathan after his last class.

"Well, well, who would have thought a Masorti Jew would be so well-educated," Saul said as he slapped Jonathan on the back.

Jonathan again noted the remark on his conservative background but decided to ignore it for now as he and Saul walked briskly toward Saul's office. As they went down the long hallway Jonathan eyes saw the sign next to the door.

"Saul P. Harkman, Phd,

Professor, Ancient Hebrew"

Saul walked straight into the office and Jonathan followed. Jonathan was stunned and stopped at the entrance. There in Saul's office were volumes of books stacked everywhere, many very ancient looking. On the floor, on top of a small, round table, behind the door, just about every flat surface in the room contained at least four or five books. Sticking out from the pages of each book were papers, some yellowed with age and all scribbled in ink or penciled notes, many in Hebrew that Jonathan strained to read.

"This is my office," Saul responded curtly, "yours is next door."

"Yes sir," Jonathan replied and backed out of the office.

Indeed, Jonathan's office was next door. There next to the door to his office was also a sign.

Jonathan A. Weitzman, PhD

Associate Professor, Ancient Hebrew

Jonathan slowly opened the door and found a sparsely furnished office with mismatched furniture. The desk was obviously old, as the top showed the white stains of multiple cups or glasses left sitting too long on the dark brown surface. There was a large bookcase made of lighter colored wood that did not match the desk, empty of books with a thin layer of dust present on each shelf. Behind the desk was a rather small office chair, one more befitting a secretary than an Associate Professor. Jonathan dropped his books onto the desk and a cloud of dust spread out from the four sides. He then dropped into his chair and wondered if he had made the biggest mistake of his life.

Jonathan graduated from Cambridge University " **Summa** Cum Laude" in a class of over four-hundred. He was considered a prodigy. Speeding through the undergraduate course work at an accelerated pace, he had taken time off to return to Israel and serve in the Israeli Army for two years before entering graduate school. His Master's program was boring, more of the same as undergraduate. But during his Doctorate program he became fascinated with the character of Herod Antipas, the ruler of Galilee and Persea and son of Herod the Great. Jonathan was interested in the building program of Herod Antipas and his role with the man known as Jesus of Galilee. However, the building projects of Herod Antipas were what Jonathan had written his dissertation about and brought him in contact with Saul Harkman. During Jonathan's research he read many articles written by Dr. Harkman regarding Herod Antipas and the site of Herod's dwellings in Jerusalem. To Jonathan, Dr. Harkman appeared to display the same passion about this King from the history of Judaism. Jonathan remembered how Dr. Harkman had theorized that Caesar Augustus divided Israel into three parts after Herod the Great's death to keep Herod Antipas, Herod Phillip (Antipas half-brother), and Archaelus (Antipas full brother) from uniting the country and rebelling against Roman rule. However, Dr. Harkman had also written extensively regarding the role King Herod Antipas played in the death of the man Jesus. Again, Dr. Harkman subscribed to the theory that it was King Herod Antipas who ordered the death of the prophet Jesus and, therefore, indirectly was the "Father of Christianity." Jewish scholars denounced Dr. Harkman as encouraging further anti-Semitic feelings from the Christians and Christians felt Dr. Harkman simply did not know the Christian Scriptures. Jonathan was fascinated with Dr. Harkman's theories regarding that period of time and was thrilled when he first was notified that he would be Dr. Harkman's Associate Professor.

As he sat behind his worn desk, Jonathan was not convinced that he had made a mistake, but thus far he was unimpressed with the man he had admired for so long. That all changed after the end of the semester as Saul and Jonathan began to plan together the curriculum for the next term.

CHAPTER 2

As the spring semester concluded, Dr. Harkman had notified Jonathan of the need to meet during the summer to discuss the plans for fall term, divide the schedule, and further enhance the curriculum. It was the most Jonathan heard Dr. Harkman speak to him during the past school year. Other than to discuss tests, student grades, or some other issues related to the daily work of teaching, the two rarely talked. But that all changed at their first meeting.

Jonathan entered the cluttered office of Dr. Harkman cautiously as he always did and spied Dr. Harkman sitting behind his desk, his long legs stretched upward and propped upon a stack of four books on his desk. There was a thin smile on his lips and he stroked his beard with his right hand as if to pull it from his face with each tug.

"Interesting reading," Saul said without looking up from the pages.

Jonathan's heart sank as he realized that Dr. Harkman was reading his dissertation. To Jonathan's horror, it was obvious that Dr. Harkman was almost finished with it.

Dr. Harkman finished the last page with Jonathan standing anxiously waiting.

"Sit down, Jonathan," Dr. Harkman invited.

Jonathan looked around the room for an empty chair. There were only three hard-back chairs and all were piled with books and papers.

"Just set those on the floor and sit down," Dr. Harkman barked.

Jonathan carefully walked to the chair with the smallest stack and placed them on the floor and sat down facing Dr. Harkman. It had not escaped Jonathan that Dr. Harkman called him by his first name instead of Dr. Weitzman, which was his habit. Jonathan fidgeted in his seat as Dr. Harkman looked at him though squinting eyes and continued to pull at his beard with that thin smile. Jonathan felt Dr. Harkman was trying to see through him until he finally spoke.

"Yes, Jonathan, a very interesting read," Dr. Harkman continued, "so you believe that the palace of King Herod Antipas is somewhere in the western aspect of Tiberias. Very interesting indeed."

"Yes, sir, Dr. Hark. . ." Jonathan tried to say but was interrupted.

"Call me Saul when we're in the office, Jonathan, we are going to be working together for a long time, no need for such formalities."

Jonathan sat stunned at the warm, cordial feeling from the man who essentially ignored him throughout the school term. When Jonathan did try and talk with him, Dr. Harkman seemed annoyed and always was rushing off to do something more important. Now did Jonathan hear correctly, he wanted to be called Saul.

"Yes sir, Saul," Jonathan corrected and watched as the grin widened between Saul's mustache and beard.

"You realize that Professor Hirschfield from the Hebrew University of Jerusalem, before his death, did several archeological digs and never found anything to indicate he discovered King Herod's palace," Saul countered almost as a challenge.

"The majority of Professor Hirchfield's digs were the community bath house, the marketplace, and the main street. He did discover a complex that was thought to be the capital seat of the Sanhedrin, but not King Herod's palace," Jonathan responded, feeling as if he was defending his dissertation again and thankful that the same question had been asked at his defense.

"I'm listening," Saul prodded Jonathan to continue.

"As you know, King Herod built the city at the site of the destroyed village of Rakkat and it eventually became the capital of Galilee. The Jews at first refused to live there because it was considered "unclean" due to being built atop a graveyard. King Herod forcefully moved people into the city and the Sanhedrin..." Jonathan paused as he saw the smile leaving Saul's face. "Is something wrong?"

"Jonathan, I have been a professor of Ancient Hebrew for many years and written extensively about King Herod, do you really think I need these details?" Saul sighed.

Jonathan remained silent knowing the question did not warrant an answer.

"Tell me your theories about his palace," Saul exclaimed with frustration in his voice, "Many feel Dr. Hirchfield discovered the remains of Herod's palace at the basilica digs at the seat of the Sanhedrin."

"Yes, yes, I understand, they attributed that to the marble floors as there is no natural marble in Israel. However, with King Herod's lifestyle, marrying his brother's wife, the last place King Herod would want to live is in the presence of the Sanhedrin, judges in Israel. Judges could be bribed even during King Herod's time. What better way to bribe a group than to provide marble stone for the floor. The structure is too small to be a palace. I believe the actual sight is north of the main promenade and located on the coast of Lake Galilee. This would be the "proper" site of a King with Herod's ego and it is supported by the Christian accounts of the examination of the man Jesus before Herod. I just can't see where it would be anywhere else," Jonathan was almost shouting at Saul as he spoke.

"I agree," Saul responded quietly, looking directly at Jonathan.

"What?" Jonathan asked in disbelief.

"I agree, the palace is probably at the north end of the promenade on Lake Galilee. There are numerous explanations for the marble at the seat of the Sanhedrin. To think that structure also served as King Herod's palace makes no sense," Saul stated matter of fact.

Jonathan removed his glasses and stared at Saul, "You agree?"

"I agree," Saul smiled and stood up and shook Jonathan's hand and embraced him, "I have waited for many years for someone to come and support this theory, you are truly a God-send Jonathan."

Jonathan listened as Saul with almost a frenzy moved from ancient documents, to ancient texts, and back to ancient books with maps. Saul pointed and talked, pointed and read continually to say that King Herod's palace was north of the promenade.

"Have you been there?" Saul asked Jonathan.

Jonathan just stared at the man who he thought was this reserved, studious professor as he turned into an man obsessed.

"When you were in Israel, did you go there?" Saul asked again anxiously.

"No," Jonathan said simply.

"Well, I have, at least six times, I know where to dig. I believe I know where the palace is, covered by the earthquake of 363 and just waiting to be uncovered," Saul exclaimed.

Jonathan watched as the professor was transformed into an excited little kid with a new toy. Saul rushed from stack of books to stack of books excitedly talking about a sabbatical and excavation team, taking students, almost rambling.

"Whoa, what are you talking about?" Jonathan anxiously asked.

Grabbing Jonathan by the shoulders, Saul exclaimed as if it was obvious, "I believe that the man Jesus was not 'crucified' in Jerusalem by Pilate as the Christian authors have written. As you know, I believe that Herod ordered the death of Jesus, but not by crucifixion as the custom of the Romans, but through beheading."

Jonathan sat dumbfounded as Saul expounded on his theory regarding King Herod. Saul outlined what he thought were the events leading up to the death of the man Jesus. He agreed that Jesus was brought before Pilate, and that Pilate sent him to King Herod.

"There is the key, Pilate sent him to King Herod," Saul stated emphatically. "A distance today, on the best road of 176 miles."

Jonathan just stared at Saul trying to decipher where he was going.

"Don't you see?" Saul asked, "the Christians claim that the arrest, trial, crucifixion and death of Jesus occurred in just three days!"

"But, the early Christian writers argue that Herod was in Jerusalem," Jonathan countered.

"Yes, some state that, but it is clear that Pilate sent the man Jesus to see Herod at Galilee, and it is well known that Herod's palace was in Tiberias, in Galilee."

A smile came to Jonathan's face and he realized the simplicity of the theory.

"Even if they traveled by cart, it would have taken at least three or four days to reach Tiberias," Jonathan exclaimed with building excitement.

"Yes, and three or four days to return," Saul added with a certain satisfaction as if he had argued his point to a logical conclusion.

"So, by finding King Herod's palace, you hope to find evidence to support that Herod put Jesus to death, not Pilate."

"Exactly," Saul replied, "and that the early so-called 'Christian' writers manipulated the events of the death of Jesus in order to make it appear that he fulfilled the Torah prophecies regarding the Messiah."

"If that were the case, then our assertions that the Messiah is still to come would be accurate," Jonathan added, "and that the Christian religion is based on a lie."

Saul smiled a broad smile showing all of his teeth framed by his beard. He then continued his thoughts regarding moving the class to Israel.

"Where better to teach ancient Hebrew than in Israel," Saul said, "the students will provide the workforce for the digs, learn real facts regarding the history of Judaism, and the history of Christianity."

Jonathan blinked thinking Saul looked out of focus and then remembered his glasses were in his hands. He stood in shock as Saul outlined obtaining funding, having students assist with the dig, teaching during particular hours of the day, gaining approval of the trustees, and flight arrangements. Saul was all over the place with loose associations, plans, packing.

"Stop!!!!!" Jonathan yelled, placed his glasses on his face and covered his ears.

Saul looked at him a little shocked.

"Are you crazy?" Jonathan asked, "we can't move the class to Israel, can we?"

"Why not?' Saul asked with a certain level of insult that Jonathan would challenge him, "this is the ideal educational opportunity and setting. I thought you would be thrilled with the idea. After all, that is the reason I selected you as my Associate Professor."

"Do you think that the Academic Trustees will approve such a project?" Jonathan asked.

"I've been at this University for many years, a number of the members of the Academic Trustees have privately supported my writings regarding King Herod, I think with a little politicking with those trustees regarding the purpose of the dig," Saul paused, "I mean of the educational opportunity for the students, that, yes, they will approve it."

Jonathan looked at Saul and saw a man beaming with energy and enthusiasm. Jonathan realized that if he participated in this venture and Saul was accurate that he and Saul would be remembered forever as the two archeologists who finally debunked the myths surrounding the events of the death of the man Jesus. Saul watched carefully as Jonathan looked up and directly into his eyes.

"What do you need me to do?" Jonathan asked.

"Are you in?" Saul questioned.

"Absolutely, this is the opportunity of a lifetime," Jonathan responded with glee, "let's get started."

"First thing will be the funding, then the Academic Trustees," Saul stated, "if the project is already funded and does not require the trustees to dig into the university pockets, the rest should be easy. I have a list of possible groups that might fund such a venture, will split the list and begin there."

CHAPTER 3

Saul had a list of potential contributors to such a project and handed the list to Jonathan. Jonathan reviewed the groups listed. They included the American Jewish World Service, Union of Orthodox Jewish Congregations of America, Jewish Defense League, the American Jewish Committee.

"Some of these groups are pretty radical, Saul," Jonathan observed.

The list continued with multiple Jewish organizations, many Orthodox, many radicals, some even could be considered militant. It was obvious to Jonathan that Saul was only concerned about obtaining the money and not necessarily the source. They divided the list and talked about strategies to obtain funding.

"They will need to know the purpose of the dig," Jonathan offered.

"But the purpose of the dig must be something that they can see as valuable," Saul countered, "We should formulate a statement of purpose that both of us use to ensure consistency when we talk with different groups."

Saul scurried around his office pulling books from one pile and another, moving larger stacks to different places to get to a book he needed that was at the bottom of the stack. Within these books were multiple sheets of paper, their ends curled, wrinkled, torn reflecting the abuse endured through being combined with similar books and papers. Some of the papers were yellowed, reflecting an age of some time past. Jonathan watched with interest as Saul collected these books and papers and stacked them at the end of his desk.

Leaning his hand on the stack, Saul spoke directly to Jonathan.

"This is most of the work on my theory that the man Jesus was killed by Herod in Tiberias, you better get started."

"What, you mean I should write the statement," Jonathan exclaimed, "it's your theory."

"Yes, but I'm too close to it. I need someone with an objective approach to review my work and see if the same conclusions are reached. If that is done, we can reduce the amount of holes some of the scholars will punch into the theory."

"But," Jonathan pleaded as he raised his hand to his kippah, pulled it from his head and began twisting it in his hands. His dark thick hair maintained the round shape of the kippah at the crown. "It's your theory!"

Saul ignored Jonathan as he picked up the stacks of books and walked toward Jonathan. Jonathan quickly replaced his kippah and took the stack from Saul.

"I need to work on the curriculum, compose letters to students. It will have to be voluntary, but they will need to pay something too. While you are working on the theory, I need to come up with a budget, how much it will cost. Can't go asking someone to fund a trip if we don't know what it costs. Besides, I want you to use that Orthodoxy that you are so fond of to support this theory. You know that the Masortis essentially translated the Jewish Bible and you know as much about Herod as I do."

"But, Saul, it's your theory!"

"Not anymore, it's 'our' theory. Now stop whining and get out of my office so I can work. I would think you would have plenty to do also looking at that stack of books and papers in your arms."

Saul pulled Jonathan by the arm and led him out of the office. It was clear to Jonathan that he was not going to get out of this assignment. He slowly returned to his office and placed the stack Saul had given him squarely in the center of his desk. Jonathan slumped down in his seat and glared at the stack for several moments, not sure if he was a partner with Saul, or just being used.

As Jonathan sat contemplating his misery and feeling sorry for himself, there were multiple titles, ranging from Josephus, Judaism and Christianity to a book called the Writings of Thomas Aquinas. He noticed that the two largest books were "The Holy Bible" and "Josephus." Jonathan carefully pulled these two books from the middle of the stack, avoiding making the entire stack fall as if he was playing the children's game of "Tumble Tower." These two books also seemed to have the most papers stuck between the pages. Jonathan sat each book on the desk side by side, "The Holy Bible" on the left, "Josephus" on the right.

Jonathan was certainly familiar with Flavius Josephus. The name Flavius was given to Josephus by the Roman Emperor during the siege of Jerusalem in 74 C.E. Many Orthodox Jews viewed Flavius Josephus as a traitor because of his assistance to the Romans during the destruction of Jerusalem and the temple during the Jewish Wars. However, the writings of Josephus were required reading as the only real history of the Jewish people. Jonathan really could have cared less about the politics of Josephus. Flavius Josephus was a Jew who originally wrote in Aramaic and then had his work translated into Greek and was one of the few historians of that era.

As Jonathan looked at the heavy book called "Josephus" he wondered if all four of the texts of Josephus were incorporated into this single binding. He flipped to the table of contents and saw all four books listed. *The Jewish War* that covered the Jewish revolt against Roman rule from 64 – 74 CE, *Antiquities of the Jews* which was essentially a history of the Jewish people prior to the Roman revolt. However, this was a history written from a collection of other works, including the Hebrew Bible and other writings of the period. This has led to controversy about some of the writings and Jonathan remembered that the most controversy centered on the section that he would need to review, the mention of the man Jesus by Josephus. Jonathan noted the final two texts, *Against Apion*, which is a defense of Judaism against a Roman author's attacks, and *The Life*, essentially an autobiography of Josephus. Jonathan glanced at the contents of these last two books remembering a paper he had written on the section *Against Apion*. However, he quickly dismissed all of the books except *Antiquities of the Jews* as this is where he would begin his research.

Jonathan had no trouble finding the beginnings to the text called the *Antiquities of the Jews*. That is where the trail of ragged papers started, with most of them centered around chapter eighteen. Jonathan tried to read the first page written by Saul and closed the book, tossing it on his desk.

He next picked up the other large book, "The Holy Bible", the gold lettering against the black leather binding said. Jonathan recognized this as a Christian Bible and not the *Tanakh* or Hebrew Bible. He glanced over to the stack and saw no Hebrew Bible. At first puzzled, he remembered that the part of the Christian Bible called the *Old Testament* was, with very few exceptions, essentially the *Tanakh.* Jonathan was familiar with the Christian Bible as he was required in one of his philosophy classes to read certain teachings found in what the Christian's called the *New Testament.* Jonathan could see that Saul had stuffed this Christian Bible with the most single pages with words scribbled everywhere. Jonathan lifted the book and flipped it open. He immediately saw several of the pages contained multiple passages that were underlined or highlighted, pages dogged eared, and those papers stuck between pages throughout the book.

"Makes sense," Jonathan thought to himself, "the majority of the history of Jesus would be found here."

Jonathan turned to the index and saw the familiar division of the books found in the Christian *Old Testament* just like the *Tanakh.* The *Pentateuch* was the same as the *Torah*, containing the book of creation, "Genesis," and the early laws of Moses. He recognized the books of the *Nevi'im* or Prophets and the *Keutvim* written during the Babylonian exile. He noted that the books in the Christian Bible were the same but not divided into these subheadings, with the exception of the first five books. As a Masorti Jew, Jonathan recognized that these contained only the written laws of Moses and not the oral laws passed from generation to generation found in the *Talmud*.

Jonathan turned back to the first page of notes found in the book known as "Psalms." Jonathan recalled that most were written by the great Jewish King David. Saul's paper was stuck at Psalms 22. There was scribbled in the margin the words "made lying about events easy," "see the Gospels" and other nonsensical phrases and words. Jonathan thought about beginning to read Psalms 22, but decided against it.

"This is the bulk of the work; I will start with Josephus, how much could be there."

Jonathan opened the second drawer on the left where he kept the yellow legal pads and removed one and placed it on the desk next to the text of Flavius Josephus. He removed his glasses and fumbled through his pocket to find his handkerchief to clean the lens and quickly accomplished that feat. Adjusting those same glasses on his face, he sighed out loud as he turned to the first page stuffed in the section on the *Antiquities of the Jews*. He began to read in Book 18: *From the Banishment of Archelaus to the Departure of the Jews from Babylon*, Chapter 2, Section 3.

> *And now Herod the tetrarch, who was in great favor with Tiberius, built a city of the same name with him, and called it Tiberias. He built it in the best part of Galilee, at the lake of Gennesareth. There are warm baths a little distance from it, in a village named Emmaus. Strangers came and inhabited this city; a great number of the inhabitants were Galileans also; and many were necessitated by Herod to come either out of the country belonging to him, and were by force compelled to be its inhabitants; some of them were persons of condition. He also admitted poor people, such as those that were collected from all parts, to dwell in it. Nay, some of them were not quite free-men, and these he was benefactor to, and made them free in great numbers; but obliged them not to forsake the city, by building them very good houses at his own expenses, and by giving them land also; for he was sensible, that to make this place a habitation was to transgress the Jewish ancient laws, because many sepulchers were to be here taken away in order to make room for the city Tiberias*

whereas our laws pronounce that such inhabitants are unclean for seven days.

Jonathan read the passage again and looked at Saul's notes. "Tiberias" was written in large letters and the passage *best part of Galilee* was underlined. This passage would seem to confirm the theory that Herod's palace would be in Tiberias as it supports the assertions that it was built on a graveyard and people were forced to live there. Jonathan thought for a few minutes and concluded that there was nothing profound or unknown in these passages. This simply supported that Herod built Tiberias. However, it seemed entirely reasonable to conclude that Herod would have lived there himself.

There were several other pages hand-written by Saul. Jonathan looked at each one, hoping to find some stronger evidence of clue. Most had just a single word, sometimes circled, and a reference to the passage, but little else of value.

Jonathan turned to the next dogged ear page and found again several notes hand-written by Saul and stuck between the pages. An entire passage was highlighted on the dog-eared page. Jonathan read in Book 18 again, this time Chapter 3, Section 3:

Now there was about this time Jesus, a wise man, if it be lawful to call him a man; for he was a doer of wonderful works, a teacher of such men as to receive the truth with pleasure. He drew over to him both many of the Jews and many of the Gentiles. He was [the] Christ. And when Pilate, at the suggestion of the principal men amongst us, had condemned him to the cross, those that loved him at the first did not forsake him; for he appeared to them alive again the third day; as the divine prophets had foretold these and ten thousand other wonderful

> *things concerning him. And the tribe of Christians, so named from him, are not extinct at this day.*

Jonathan was puzzled. This would seem to confirm that Pilate crucified Jesus and dispute Saul's theory. Jonathan read the passage again, *And when Pilate, at the suggestion of the principal men amongst us, had condemned him to the cross.*

"This makes no sense," Jonathan said out loud.

Frustrated, Jonathan pulled the handwritten notes from Saul from the pages surrounding this passage. He was looking for clues that he was sure were in Saul's notes because a man of Saul's intelligence would not make such an elementary mistake. The first note Jonathan came to was scrawled in large letters, "it sounds too Christian to be from Josephus."

"Just an opinion," Jonathan thought.

However, the next piece of paper had several one line notes scribbled. Some printed, some in cursive, most obviously written in a very hurried manner. They were listed and numbered.

1. In 1995 discovery indicated that Josephus' description of Jesus was similar to another writer's description.

2. Early writer Origen stated that Josephus did not believe Jesus was the Messiah.

3. Too similar to Luke

. . .

4. Entirely forged!

5. Text was altered by Greeks

Jonathan thought these were the musing of a desperate academia grasping at straws to protect their theories until he read the next page. The text was identical with one major difference, references were sighted.

1. In 1995 discovery indicated that Josephus' description of Jesus was similar to another writer's description. – Goldberg 1995

2. Early writer Origen stated that Josephus did not believe Jesus was the Messiah. – Feldman 1670

3. To similar to Luke – Goldberg 1995

4. Entirely forged! – Birdsall 1984

5. Text was altered by Greeks – Eisler 1931

Jonathan read more of the notes and found that just about all were devoted to discrediting specifically this passage. However, it was the final scrawl at the bottom of the book itself that made Jonathan stop and think.

"A later text by Origen 230CE – 250CE cites Josephus' reference to the death of James, Jesus' brother in Book 20 but makes no reference to the passage in Book 18, contrived by early Christians to further support the myth that Jesus was the Messiah."

Jonathan realized quickly that Saul essentially found that the discrepancies in Josephus Book 18 support his theory that the early Christians manipulated the text, the gospels and history to make the man Jesus out to be the Messiah. If Jonathan was going to find his answers he would have to take a look at the Christian Bible. Since the Old Testament was the same as the Hebrew Bible, the prophecies should be easy enough to find.

"I am a scholar of the Hebrew Bible,," Jonathan mused, "that should be the easy part. The difficult part will be finding where those prophecies are fulfilled in what is called by Christians, the 'New Testament.'"

CHAPTER 4

Jonathan pulled the large, black, leather bound book with the gold inscription "Holy Bible" and laid it on top of his desk. The multitude of yellow sticky notes crumpled and dog-eared pages stuck out from what seemed to be every page. Jonathan decided his first task was to ensure that he was using an accurate translation of the Christian Bible. He knew from his studies that with the numerous splits and dissensions within the Christian Church had come as many versions of the Christian Bible. He recalled from his studies some of the varied versions including the Revised Standard Version, the New International Version, the King James Version, the New King James Version, the English Bible, the American Bible, and the list goes on and on with each version different. Some of these versions were just translated from one or the other versions. Most frequently, the writers just "rewrote" the King James Version to meet their personal needs. Others were, in fact, translated from the original scrolls that had been discovered over time written in Hebrew, Aramaic, and Greek. Jonathan recalled that the "Holy Bible" in its present form is actually two different texts. These two are distinguished between those with the

Apocrypha and those without. Jonathan knew there was little dispute over the "Old Testament" because of the foundation in the Jewish history. The New Testament and the Apocrypha were and have been chronically disputed since 325 AD when the early Christian Church leaders decided what was and was not the "inspired word of God." From his studies, Jonathan knew that this was in part a response to the multitude of gnostic "gospels" that flourished during this period. These books were purported to be written by other followers of Jesus, such as Thomas or Mary, but were deemed "questionable" in authorship by these early Church leaders and therefore not included. The Apocrypha came under criticism by Martin Luther and then again by the Anglican Church, but was still included when King James' scholars wrote their translation of the "Holy Bible," just placed in the back.

"Almost like an addendum," Jonathan thought.

After the mid-1800's the King James Version and most "protestant" versions of the "Holy Bible" do not include the books. Jonathan thought this was unfortunate as the Apocrypha contains the story of the Maccabees. The Maccabees are important in Jewish history for the revolt that re-established Judaism in Israel.

"Without the Maccabees there would have been no Jewish nation in Israel for Jesus to have been born," Jonathan muttered. "Where would that leave the Christians and their Messiah?"

Jonathan had concluded in school that Christianity was in its early stages more pure, with less corruption of man. When the original Great Schism occurred in the fourth century between Rome and Constantinople, Christianity began declining into nothing more than divisions, offshoots, cults, and numerous fighting amongst themselves. Judaism, on the other hand, had remained essentially unchanged for six thousand years with the exception of Orthodox versus modern Judaism. Jonathan considered this to be more of a disagreement regarding modernization of Judaism rather than an actual division in dogma.

Armed with this knowledge of the Christian religion, Jonathan was skeptical as he opened Saul's "Holy Bible." A smile quickly ran across his mouth as he viewed the first page. There at the bottom "copyright 760 AD from the Latin Vulgate of Saint Jerome."

"An original," Jonathan thought, "unblemished by these petty Christian squabbles."

To Jonathan's delight, this version contained the Latin from the original Vulgate with the English translation beneath. This made the likelihood of error slim. Although Jonathan was fluent in Hebrew, Aramaic, and Greek, the Latin would be somewhat difficult. He recalled how he had an opportunity to take Latin as an elective and chose Greek instead. He now regretted that decision.

Jonathan removed his glasses, cleaned them and placed them high on his nose. In the Hebrew Old Testament there are over 360 prophecies of the coming of the Messiah. Hebrews and Christians alike believe that the first prophecy is found in the book of Genesis. However, Jonathan also recalled that of those 360+ prophecies, Christians assert that Jesus fulfilled 109.

"Wow, less than 30 percent," Jonathan mused, "and this is considered adequate to support a claim that Jesus was the Messiah."

This gave Jonathan an ideal for the statement of purpose for the funding that Saul wanted for the dig. Jonathan surmised that if less than 30 percent of the prophecies were fulfilled according to the Christians themselves, then there is a 70 percent chance that Jesus was not the Messiah. That leaves a lot of room to dispute the claims that Jesus was Messiah and something as simple as finding a single artifact in the temple of Herod that could be attributed to Jesus would be enough to topple the entire myth.

Jonathan feverishly wrote out his thoughts into a concise statement of purpose and hurried down the hall to show it to Saul.

Jonathan found Saul sitting behind his desk, also writing.

"Trying to put together a speech for the fund raising," Saul said as Jonathan rushed into his office.

"I've got it," Jonathan shouted excitedly, "I've got the statement of purpose."

He handed the paper to Saul, who sat up straight and read what Jonathan had written intently. Jonathan saw just the slightest smile form in the beard around Saul's mouth.

"Perfect," Saul agreed and reached out and shook Jonathan's hand vigorously, "just perfect."

Saul took the paper and began copying the words onto the pad where he had been writing.

"The Christian faith is based on the principles that the man Jesus was the Messiah foretold by the prophets of the Old Testament. Of the 360 plus prophecies, the Christian faith can only support that Jesus fulfilled thirty percent of those prophecies. To date, there has been no scientific evidence to dispute the Christian claim. However, there is hard evidence found in the Christian New Testament that will provide the evidence to dispute that claim. This will be found in the palace of King Herod."

Saul looked up from his writing.

"So, you have reviewed these prophecies," Saul asked Jonathan, looking up over the top rim of his glasses, "also the multiple discrepancies in the Christian New Testament?

Jonathan slowly shook his head to indicate a negative response. He scratched his scalp under his kippah, again adjusted his glasses, and slowly walked back to his office.

"Discrepancies?" Jonathan pondered, "what discrepancies?"

Jonathan recalled a discussion regarding the prophecies from the Old Testament but was unclear on the New Testament discrepancies. When he returned to his office he sat down and turned the pages of the Holy Bible to the New Testament. He had not noticed the number of yellow notes sticking out from these pages. The greatest number was coming from the four books known as the "Gospels." Jonathan sighed.

"First the prophecies, then the discrepancies," Jonathan decided and returned to the Old Testament.

Jonathan thought this was a waste of time. The Christians claim that the Father of Jesus was God. The Messiah would be from the tribe of Judah. All Jews understand that tribal affiliation is conferred through the birth of the father only. Jonathan compared the Old Testament passages in Number 34:14, 1:18-44 and Leviticus 24:10 to the *Torah.*

"They say the same thing," Jonathan exclaimed, "this is ridiculous."

However, Jonathan was also a scholar, so he began his review with each of the prophecies. But he decided for the sake of time he would limit his review to just the 109 that Christians claim Jesus fulfilled. There was no reason to review the others as there was no claim by Christians of the fulfillment.

Looking at it logically, Jonathan took the word "Messiah," which in Hebrew is *Mashiach*. This simply means "anointed" and generally refers to a person initiated into God's service by being anointed with oil. As a Masorti Jew and familiar with the scripture, Jonathan quickly found the passages in Exodus 29:7, I Kings 1:39, and II Kings 9:3 that describe this action. One of the central themes of Biblical prophecy for the Jews is the promise of a future age of perfection characterized by universal peace and recognition of God. Jonathan found the references to these passages marked in faded yellow highlighter from the prophets Isaiah (2:1-4; 32:15-18; 60:15-18), Zephaniah (3:9) Hosea (2:20-22), Amos (9:13-15), Micah (4:1-4), Zechariah (8:23, 14:9), and Jeremiah (31:33-34). Jonathan reviewed the passages quickly and recalled that these prophetic passages spoke of a descendant of King David who would rule Israel during the age of perfection. Jonathan made notes that Jesus certainly did not appear in an age of peace or perfection. The world, and especially Judah, at the time of Jesus was at war and full of turmoil. However, Jonathan realized that Christians argue that this will occur during the "second coming" of the Messiah. This made no sense to Jonathan as nothing in the Torah spoke of a "second coming" for the Messiah.

"These passages required a leap of faith to believe that Jesus was the Messiah," Jonathan thought, "more than a leap of faith, a leap of blind faith."

Jonathan sat back in his chair and continued the daunting task by reviewing the yellow sticky notes located in the books of Ezekiel, Isaiah, and Zechariah. Saul had scribbled, "not fulfilled" at the edges of the notes. Jonathan looked first at the passage in Ezekiel 37: 26-28.

. . .

---

26 et percutiam illis foedus pacis pactum sempiternum erit eis et fundabo eos et multiplicabo et dabo sanctificationem meam in medio eorum in perpetuum.

And I will make a covenant of peace with them, it shall be an everlasting covenant with them: and I will establish them, and will multiply them, and will set my sanctuary in the midst of them for ever.

---

27 et erit tabernaculum meum in eis et ero eis Deus et ipsi erunt mihi populus.

And my tabernacle shall be with them: and I will be their God, and they shall be my people.

---

28 et scient gentes quia ego Dominus sanctificator Israhel cum fuerit sanctificatio mea in medio eorum in perpetuum.

And the nations shall know that I am the Lord the sanctifier of Israel, when my sanctuary shall be in the midst of them for ever.

From Jonathan's studies he knew these passages prophesied that the Messiah will build the third temple. He quickly read the passages marked in Isaiah 43:5-6, the Messiah would gather all the Jews back to Israel, 2:4 usher in a world of peace ending all hatred, suffering, disease, and oppression, and Zechariah 14:9, spread universal knowledge of God. None of these prophecies were fulfilled by Jesus. Jonathan realized this was a historic fact. Christians however had always countered with the same argument, that these prophecies would be fulfilled at the second coming of Jesus.

"How can you dispute these sort of statements by Christians," Jonathan wondered, "there is no historical fact—it is an opinion and anyone could have an opinion. Who is to say who is right and who is wrong."

Jonathan thought for a moment on the concept of the second coming. This is based on the words of Jesus himself recorded in the New Testament. The Christian's viewed Jesus as a prophet.

"Jesus was not a prophet," Jonathan said under his breath.

According to the Torah, prophecy can only exist when the majority of Jews inhabit Israel. Around 300 BCE when the last prophets, Haggai, Zechariah, and Malachi died, prophecy ended. The man Jesus did not appear until around 350 years after prophecy ended, therefore he could not be a prophet and this nonsense about a second coming has no foundation in fact or truth.

Jonathan's frustration with these Christian beliefs was reaching a boiling point. He realized that you cannot dispute something that is an interpretation unless there are solid facts to support that a person's opinion is in error. Otherwise it is just one opinion against another and who is to say who is right. There is no science, just words. He reviewed the concept of the virgin birth the Christian's say is foretold in Isaiah 7:14.

---

propter hoc dabit Dominus ipse vobis signum ecce virgo concipiet et pariet filium et vocabitis nomen eius Emmanuhel.

Therefore the Lord himself shall give you a sign. Behold a virgin shall conceive, and bear a son and his name shall be called Emmanuel.

Again, Jonathan realized that this is just words. The Hebrew Torah uses the word "alma," which means "young woman." This word was replaced in the fifth century to be translated into "virgin." This was consistent with the pagan belief that mortals were impregnated by gods. Jonathan realized this was the early Christians method of bringing pagans into their ranks. This theme runs through the Christian concept of Easter, Christmas, and other Christian special days that have their foundation in pagan rituals. Jonathan recalled a quote from Gregory, a 4th century Christian leader who was called the "Bishop of Nazianzus," who wrote, "a little jargon is all that is necessary to impose on the people; the less they comprehend, the more they admire."

Jonathan shut the Saul's Holy Bible with a thud. He suddenly realized that the Christians for centuries had manipulated and mistranslated the Torah to meet the needs of their religious beliefs. Studying the prophecies was of no value. It was clear that this man Jesus did not fulfill the majority of the prophecy and the 109 claimed to be fulfilled by Christian was actually a retro-prophecy. Jonathan realized that for centuries people had attributed events that occurred to statements made by someone in the past, a fulfillment of a prophecy. No science, just words, which made reviewing the Old Testament a futile venture. Jonathan decided since so much emphasis is placed on the Christian New Testament that he should look for discrepancies and contradictions there.

"After all, the Christians claim it is the inspired word of God," Jonathan thought, "and if that is so, that the words would be perfect: no errors, no flaws."

He again pulled the heavy book of Saul's from the table, but then glanced at his watch. He had been at it for several hours, and it was now way past supper.

"I'll pick it up tomorrow," Jonathan decided as he returned the book to his desk.

Jonathan grabbed his sweater and briefcase, looked again at the array of books on his desk and headed out the door, shaking his head.

"How did this religion of Christianity ever take hold," he wondered as he started down the long hallway for the exit.

He passed Dr. Harkman's office and saw the dim light shining from underneath the shut door, indicating at least Saul was still working. Jonathan started to knock and held back. He not only did not want to disturb Dr. Harkman, but he also did not want any more assignments. Jonathan was tired, his eyes were tired and his brain was tired; tomorrow would be another day and a fresh start might bring more success.

CHAPTER 5

After multiple late night sessions, Saul had finally come up with a figure for having the classes in ancient Hebrew in Israel, and of course for the digs. He decided to take just eight students. Each student would have to apply and be interviewed by him and Jonathan. Saul estimated the cost of travel, living expenses, tools, and bribes for local officials for just one year would be right at ten million dollars. Saul then presented his ideas and thesis to the University Academic Trustees. He had given the idea a title "The Excavation and Exploration of the Palace of King Herod." With surprisingly little effort, his plan was approved with the overall support of the University President. Of course, it had not hurt his cause that the University President secretly supported his theories and was anxious to have these Jesus stories exposed as the myths they were. However, the Academic Trustees and the President were clear that all funds must be raised outside the University. The University would not be able to contribute a single dime to the venture. Saul queried about the use of the tuition of the students selected. With eight students a year and tuition per year right at 50,000 dollars, that would be almost half a million immediately. The

Trustees deferred to the President who reiterated the decision: not one dollar from the University could be used and this included the students' tuition. Saul for a moment thought about arguing that since the students would not be at the University but with him in Israel that their tuition would not be needed, but decided against it just as quickly. This University, as with others across the country, was struggling and all he really hoped for was approval, which he had.

After leaving that meeting, Saul rushed to find Jonathan. Jonathan was in his office, still pouring over the multiple Bibles and references that required review. While Saul excitedly explained about the approval of the Academic Trustees, Jonathan looked over his glasses from his desk without a word. When Saul was finished, he waited.

"Wow, I can't believe you already have approval from the Academic Trustees, but that is just for one year; it will take longer, and cost much more," Jonathan observed.

Saul was surprised and a little miffed at Jonathan's lack of faith. Saul explained to Jonathan that he knew it would take longer, but just to get started was the goal at present. He would worry about later, later.

That was three months ago and now, Saul was beginning to worry. He had delivered speeches to the "World Jewish Organization," "Christian Jews," "American Jewish Congress," and so many he had forgotten the names. Thus far, in three months, Saul had raised just over one million dollars. This was not near enough to even begin to interview students. It was now April, and he had to have the money in place no later than June. Saul was thankful that, between his studies, Jonathan was reviewing applications to select the students for interview. Thus far, the response had been overwhelming. Jonathan and Saul had received over 200 applications for the eight positions. They had decided to select the top twenty to perform interviews and then select the eight and two alternates from that group. However, those selections needed to be in place by June in order to spend the summer preparing to travel to be in Israel by September. Saul was becoming overwhelmed with everything that needed to be done when he glanced down at his watch and realized it was almost 7 pm. He had about ten minutes to get to the address for his next fundraising effort. He had been walking and thinking about everything as he frequently does and for a moment was not even sure of his location.

To get his bearing, Saul looked for a street sign and then toward the end of the street saw the sign. He recognized the Star of David with the fist inside as the symbol of the Jewish Defense League. Saul's heart began beating a little faster as he slowly walked to the entrance below the sign. Although Jewish, Saul had always been taught and believed that the Jewish Defense League (JDL) was a bad organization of hooligans and thugs. Formed in 1968 by Rabbi Meir Kahane, several acts of terrorism has been attributed to this group. Saul recalled that in 1994 JDL charter member Baruch Goldstein killed 29 Palestinians at prayer in the Cave of the Patriarchs Massacre in Hebron. Saul recalled that the JDL had openly supported these actions as a "preventative" against the killing of Israelis by Arabs. In 2001 the JDL was placed on the list of terrorist organizations by the Federal Bureau of Investigation. Jonathan was opposed to Saul soliciting funds from this group from the very start.

"Are you nuts," Jonathan had said, "these people are terrorists, we don't want their blood money."

Saul and Jonathan argued about something non-academic for the first time since meeting. Jonathan was unwavering in his belief that they should have nothing to do with this group. Saul argued that the group has as a stated goal on their website to “protect Jews from antisemitism by whatever means necessary.”

“But they are terrorists,” Jonathan had countered.

“No, they state that they unequivocally condemn terrorism and have a strict no-tolerance policy against terrorism and any other felonious acts,” Saul argued, “It states this right on their website.”

Saul was acutely aware that he was rationalizing with every bit of skill he had to convince Jonathan, and himself, that this was okay. In the end, Jonathan relented, but with reservation. He wanted to accompany Saul to the presentation, but Saul assured Jonathan he would be alright.

Saul entered the doorway and was greeted by a friendly fellow wearing a kippah and smiling broadly. He was short, but very stout, not fat, Saul observed, but definitely built thickly. He wore black pants, a white shirt with a thin black tie, and a black matching jacket. Saul noted nothing unusual and breathed a slight sigh of relief. Although, Saul felt underdressed with his khaki pants, loafers, checkered short-shirt, no tie, and a corduroy jacket.

“Too late now,” he thought.

“Welcome, Professor Harkman, we are excited to hear your presentation. I am Shelley and will escort you to the meeting. This is a pamphlet about our organizations’ values that I suggest you read before you start,” the young man stated and handed Saul the pamphlet as they began to climb the long stairway.

Saul glanced at the title, “The Five Principles of the Jewish Defense League” and kept it in sight to read later as they ascended the stairs.

At the top of the stairs, Shelley knocked on a door and said something in Hebrew that Saul could not understand. The door opened and inside the room was filled with men. Saul could not see any women. There was someone at a podium in the front of the room speaking. Shelley escorted Saul to the back of the large room and opened a door into a smaller room. Saul noticed there was a couch and a couple of chairs.

"You should wait here," Shelley instructed, "and when we are ready for you I will come for you."

Saul was left in the room and the door was shut behind him. He could hear the speaker's voice, but could not make out anything being said. Saul decided to read the pamphlet and sat down on the couch.

Saul read the title aloud, "The Five Principles of the Jewish Defense League."

"AHAVAT YISRAEL - LOVE OF JEWRY

The Jewish Defense League came into being to educate the Jewish people to the concept of Ahavat Yisrael—one Jewish people, indivisible and united, from which flows the love for and the feeling of pain of all Jews. It sees the need for a movement that is dedicated specifically to Jewish problems and that allocates its time, resources, energies and funds to Jews. It realizes that in the end–with few exceptions–the Jew can look to no one but another Jew for help and that the true solution to the Jewish problem is the peaceful liquidation of the Exile (may it come speedily, and in our days, as prophesied) and the return of all Jews to Eretz Yisrael–the land of Israel. It sees an immediate need to place Judaism over any other "ism" and ideology and calls for the use of the yardstick: "Is it good for Jews?"

HADAR - DIGNITY AND PRIDE

JDL teaches the concept of Hadar–pride in and knowledge of Jewish tradition, faith, culture, land, history, strength, pain and peoplehood. Hadar is the need to have pride in Judaism and not allow it to be disgraced and defiled by beating and desecration of Jewish honor. This is the concept that the great Jewish leader Zev Jabotinsky attempted to instill in the oppressed and degraded masses of Eastern Europe 70 years ago. The anti-Semite's hatred and contempt of the Jew is an attempt to degrade us. It is an attempt to instill within the Jew a feeling of inferiority. It is an attempt that, all too often, succeeds in promoting Jewish self-hatred and shame in an attempt to escape one's Jewishness. Hadar is pride. Hadar is self-respect. Hadar is dignity in being a Jew.

BARZEL – IRON

JDL upholds the principle of Barzel—iron—the need to both move to help Jews everywhere and to change the Jewish image through sacrifice and all necessary means—strength, force, and even violence as a last resort. The Galut image of the Jew as a weakling, as one who is easily stepped upon and who does not fight back is an image that must be changed. Not only does that image cause immediate harm to Jews but it is a self-perpetuating thing. Because a Jew runs away or because a Jew allows himself to be stepped upon, he guarantees that another Jew in the future will be attacked because of the image that he has perpetuated. JDL wants to create a physically strong, fearless and courageous Jew who fights back. We are changing an image, an image born of 2,000+ years in the Galut, an image that must be buried because it has buried us. We train ourselves for the defense of Jewish lives and Jewish rights. We learn how to fight physically, for it is better to know how and not have to, than have to and not know how.

MISHMAAT - DISCIPLINE AND UNITY

Mishmaat—discipline and dedication—creates within the Jew the knowledge that he (or she) can and will do whatever must be done, and the unity and strength of willpower to bring this into reality. It was the lack of discipline and Jewish unity that led continually to the destruction of the Jewish people. It is Jewish unity and self-discipline that will lead to the triumph of the Jewish people.

BITACHON - FAITH IN THE INDESTRUCTIBILITY OF THE JEWISH PEOPLE

Faith in the greatness and indestructibility of the Jewish people, our religion, and our Land of Israel is Bitachon. It is a faith that is built by our belief in HaShem Tzvaot—the one and only Jewish Yaweh of Hosts—and the incredible saga of Jewish history that has seen us overcome the flood of enemies that have arisen to wipe us out in every generation. It is this faith in the permanence and survival of the Jewish people that, in turn, gives faith in the ultimate success of the Jewish Defense League. No matter how difficult, no matter how impossible the task may seem—if it is a good task, if it is a holy task—it will succeed, because it must."

Saul studied the document intently. Saul could easily identify that the sources of this philosophy were founded in ancient Jewish Teachings, the Hebrew Scriptures, in the Talmud, and the teachings of Chazal. Saul recognized that these were the sources of these principles but could see the radical interpretation evident in the words. However, he rationalized to himself that there was really nothing here that could be considered terrorism or promoting terrorism. Deep in his thoughts, Saul jumped when Shelley suddenly opened the door.

“We’re ready for you,” Shelley stated and walked forward, indicating that Saul should follow.

Shelley led Saul to the stage at the front of the room. The man was still speaking but obviously wrapping up. Saul looked into the crowd of about two hundred. All men, as noted earlier, and most wearing kippahs. Saul recognized a few Orthodox Jews due to their “Pe’at.” Saul was unable to tell if these men were Haredi, Yemenite, or Hasidic Jews, as all three sects wore this distinctive style of long hair in front of their ears. As an expert in ancient Hebrew, Saul knew that this came from a verse in the Torah that states, "You shall not round off the פְּאַת Pe'at of your head.” In the Christian Bible this was Leviticus 19:27. Saul did recognize the features of some traditional Yemenite Jews due to their distinctive long and thin twisted locks, reaching to the upper arm, very neat and tidy.

“Professor Harkman… Professor Harkman,” the man at the podium stated.

Saul realized it was time to begin as the introduction was over. He heard the polite applause as he shook the hand of the man who had been speaking and took his place behind the podium.

“Thank you,” Saul remarked, sighed a little, and began his presentation.

In the past, Saul had focused his presentations on the archeology and learning aspects of his trip. For this group, he opted to discuss this, but then emphasize the potential for dismissing the man Jesus as the Messiah and discrediting the Christian religion. Saul was passionate in his delivery and comments related to these two theories received scattered applause. Saul concluded his presentation after about twenty minutes with a plea for donations and the address of the "The Excavation and Exploration of the Palace of King Herod Fund." He also offered that he would be available for questions and to receive donations after the presentation.

Again there was polite applause as Saul was escorted from the stage by Shelley and to the back of the room. The crowd mingled and there were a few attendants who stopped and made small talk with Saul, but there were no donations this day. As the last of the attendees left, Saul thanked Shelley and started for the door. Saul was somewhat discouraged, but there was still the possibility of donations through the mail. Just as Saul reached the door, he heard Shelley.

"Professor Harkman, wait," Shelley stated emphatically.

Saul stopped at the door and waited as Shelley approached. He noticed off to one side of the room the man who had been speaking just before him slipping through another door.

"Professor Harkman," Shelley began, "are you convinced that you can find evidence that this man Jesus was not the Messiah?"

Saul nodded his head affirmatively. Shelley paused for a moment then continued.

"There is someone who wishes to help you with your project, but desires to remain anonymous," Shelley stated.

Saul explained that many contributors remain anonymous and that this would not be a problem.

Shelley responded, "You don't understand, this donor wants to fund your project."

Saul could not believe what he heard, "fund the project."

"Do you mean the entire project, all funding?" Saul asked excitedly.

"Yes," was the only response from Shelley.

Saul dropped his books and papers and quickly bent down to retrieve them.

"There are conditions," Shelley added, "let's go into the back room where you waited to speak and talk."

Saul gathered his books and papers and followed Shelley into the back room once again. Saul was in a state of shock as Shelley explained the "conditions."

"First and foremost, the donor is to be anonymous. You must not try to identify this individual in any way, no questions, no inquiries," Shelley stated.

That was no problem for Saul. He listened intently to the other conditions. These included things like monthly reports and financial statements, expected items. Saul waited for the catch, the bombshell, but there was none.

"That's about it," Shelley said, "I will need the bank account number and routing number to transfer the monies into the 'The Excavation and Exploration of the Palace of King Herod Fund.'"

Saul blinked several times, "You just need the account number and routing number, nothing else?"

"That's all," Shelley responded, "Ten million will be deposited into the account tomorrow morning. That should get you started, and depending on how things go, there will be more as needed."

"I don't know what to say," Saul exclaimed, "this is a blessing from God."

Saul provided Shelley with the numbers of the fund, bank account and routing number. Shelley walked with Saul down the stairs and outside into the New York night.

"Goodnight, Professor Harkman, and good luck," Shelley stated as Saul reached the sidewalk.

Saul turned back to thank him again, but the door was closed and Shelley was gone.

To himself, Saul recited The Shehechiyanu. "Blessed are You, Lord our God, King of the universe, who has kept us alive, and sustained us, and enabled us to reach this moment," and hurried off to tell Jonathan the great news.

Although it was late, Saul found Jonathan where he had left him, studying the various ancient texts and trying to find the evidence needed to support their theories and help with the excavation. As Saul rushed into his office, he startled Jonathan, who jumped up from his desk.

"What's happened?" Jonathan shouted.

"The most amazing thing, I can't believe it myself," Saul shouted back gleefully.

Saul outlined the visit with the Jewish Defense League and his conversation with Shelley.

"The entire trip funded, unbelievable," Saul exclaimed again and began dancing around the room.

"You didn't give him the routing number and bank account number, did you?" Jonathan asked.

Saul explained again that the donor was anonymous and just wanted to transfer the money directly into the account.

"How much do we have?" Jonathan continued.

"Just a little over a million dollars," Saul replied, "Why?"

Jonathan carefully explained to Saul that now someone had access to those funds. Whoever this anonymous donor was, if he really existed, could empty the account.

"No," Saul screamed, "they are going to fund the entire expedition, I don't believe it."

"I believe you have been victimized," Jonathan stated, "First thing in the morning, we need to call the bank and put a stop on any attempts to transfer money out of the account."

Jonathan felt sorry for Saul, he looked so defeated, so hurt that he was betrayed. Saul was so sure this was real, or had he let his desire to make this trip cloud his judgment? He just slumped into a chair and sat silently.

"There is nothing to do about it till morning," Jonathan said, "I'm going home."

When Jonathan returned the next morning he found Saul still sitting in the chair, sound asleep. Jonathan quietly dialed the number to the bank.

"Bank of America, Miss Connelly," the voice said to Jonathan.

"Checking accounts please," Jonathan replied.

Jonathan explained the situation to the person in checking accounts and then asked the current balance. Jonathan dropped the phone and quickly picked it up.

"Please repeat that number," Jonathan demanded, "thank you," and hung up the phone.

Jonathan walked over to Saul.

"Wake up old man," Jonathan screamed at Saul, "we are going to Israel!"

Saul opened his eyes and looking confused asked, "What, what are you talking about."

Jonathan exclaimed, "The money, the money is there, in our account!"

"How much money?" Saul asked excitedly,

"Over 11 million dollars, you did it!, you did it!," Jonathan shouted over and over again and pulled Saul to his feet.

The two men danced around the office like school children excited on the last day of school, skipping and waving their hands in the air, hugging each other, with tears in their eyes.

"Stop!, Stop!" Saul shouted, "we have to get to work, we just have three months to put this trip together!"

Jonathan and Saul hugged again and agreed to take a break tonight for a celebratory dinner, and then back to work selecting the candidates and getting everything ready for Israel.

CHAPTER 6

Jonathan was excited. Obtaining the funding for the trip would now leave Saul to the details of planning the trip and Jonathan to focus more on his studies of the Christian New Testament. Jonathan had previously concluded that there were more than 360 prophecies in the Hebrew text regarding the coming of the Messiah. He had focused his research on the 109 that the Christians claimed Jesus fulfilled and found so many holes in these prophecies that he had given up and decided to focus on the Christian New Testament. Jonathan had a copy of the Latin Vulgate of Saint Jerome that Saul had provided. This original version was devoid of the blemishes of later years and was considered to be more true to the original text. As he opened the large, heavy book to the section entitled "New Testament" Jonathan came to the first book, "Matthew."

When Jonathan was at the University studying ancient Hebrew, he had taken courses regarding the New Testament used by Christians. He recalled that, contrary to popular belief, there was never a single time in history where a decision was made as to which books to include in the Bible.

Although the Roman Catholic Church claimed to be the authority for the Scriptures, there was little oversight for the Eastern Churches. After the Great Schism in the 4th century, Jonathan recalled there were churches in Rome, Ethiopia, and Syria, and these churches were considered equal with the Roman Church. Yet, these Churches all had separate ideas about what should be considered part of the "canon" of the Bible. Some early texts from the followers of Jesus such as Thomas and Mary had been found and were not considered "canonical" and therefore not included. In addition, Jonathan was aware of omissions such as the early Jew Saul and his earlier letter to the Colossians that is mentioned in the current "Bible" (Colossians Chapter 4 verse 16). Jonathan was confused as to how "men" could decide what the inspired "word of God" was and yet not account for this missing text, or simply just eliminate others as not being "inspired."

Jonathan scratched his head and wondered if reviewing this New Testament would be of any value at all with all the discrepancies regarding its origin. But then again, he was trying to find contradictions. Jonathan knew that Christianity had already rationalized that this text was the "divine inspired Word of God" without reservation.

"Attempts to dispute these books with science would be useless," Jonathan thought, "my goal of finding discrepancies would be of more value."

As with the numerous prophecies of the Messiah, Jonathan decided to narrow the focus of his research. He would concentrate on the first four books identified by Christians as the "Gospel." These books contained the life of the man Jesus and the narrative of his teachings, his life, his arrest, and subsequent death by crucifixion.

"That should make it somewhat easier," Jonathan mused.

Jonathan decided in order to conduct the research scientifically, he needed to know who authored the text. He recalled that Matthew and John were disciples of the man Jesus, and that Mark and Luke were just followers. Jonathan at first had been unclear about the differences between a disciple and a follower, and had asked one of his professors. The professor explained that the Christians actually used the term "apostle" to denote those men that Jesus himself chose to be part of his inner circle. This included Matthew and John. Mark and Luke were thought to be just part of the group that followed Jesus around. However, the professor had reminded Jonathan that these texts were written sometime after the death of Jesus. Jonathan also remembered that there was really not any proof as to who authored these books. However, the earliest writings were by the Jew Saul who later changed his name to Paul. These were thought to be composed sometime between 48 and 58 AD. Mark was thought to be written first between 60 -70 AD, Matthew second between 70 and 80 AD, Luke, third between 80 and 90 AD, and finally John between 90 and 100 AD. Jonathan recalled that Paul, the first writer, does not reference the other writers and it is therefore assumed that these books were written sometime after his letters. Also, Matthew, Mark, and Luke make reference to the destruction of the Jewish temple by the Romans in 90 AD. Jonathan was happy that at least some science was used to date the material. However…

"This makes no sense," Jonathan thought, "why would a book be written out of chronological order, what were these people thinking?"

Staring down at the big Vulgate Bible, Jonathan decided to just look at things in order. It was just too confusing to try and do things chronologically, although that would make more sense. He dug through several books until he found the one he was searching for, "St. Matthew" from the Catholic

Encyclopedia. New York: Robert Appleton Company. 1913. Jonathan began to skim over the pages.

"At least he was a Jew, but a tax collector," Jonathan thought, "why did someone want a low-life like that?"

Jonathan pieced together a picture of the author. Matthew was most likely born in Galilee, but worked in Capernaum as a tax collector for Herod Antipas, the tetrarch of Galilee. He most likely was literate in Aramaic and Greek. His father was Alpheus, also a tax collector. He is known in some of the other Christian writings as "Levi." According to Christian legend, he witnessed the resurrection of the man Jesus and his purported ascension into Heaven. Jonathan found that he preached Christianity for some time in Judea and traveled to Ethiopia, Macedonia, and Persia. There was no clear evidence of how Matthew died, but Christians believe he was a martyr somewhere in Ethiopian. Jonathan found a reference to the "Gospel of the Hebrew" which is another name for the Gospel of Matthew.

Jonathan reached for a copy of the Qur'an that was lying on a chair to his right. He thumbed through the index and found a reference page for "Matthew." Looking at the text, he was surprised to find that Matthew was mentioned among the disciples of Jesus but was called a "helper to the work of God."

Surprised, Jonathan returned to his book on Matthew and noted with great interest that the author's commentary on the Gospel of Matthew was simple.

"It is written by a Jew, to the Jews, about a Jew," Jonathan said out loud.

Jonathan noted that Matthew contained 28 chapters beginning with the genealogy of Jesus Christ and ending with the man Jesus directing his disciples to preach Christianity throughout the world. Jonathan also found that the famous "beatitudes" given in what has been called "Sermon on the Mount" are found in Matthew's writing. In addition, main cities in Israel such as Bethlehem, Nazareth, Galilee, Capernaum, Jerusalem and Judea are talked about frequently. Matthew gives a detailed account of the genealogy of Jesus. Jonathan knew that would be expected from a Jew writing to the Jews. Matthew also described the birth of Jesus in detailed and early years of his life, including his parent's escape to Egypt from the murderous Herod and their return to Nazareth. As did the other writers, Matthew included Jesus' years of ministry, miracles that were attributed to him, his trial, crucifixion, death, supposed resurrection, and ascension into Heaven. Jonathan found this to be the most incredible part of the stories. That a man could actually be raised from the dead was impossible. He thought it was clever of Matthew to indicate that, after the resurrection, Jesus ascended into Heaven.

"A convenient explanation to avoid having to deal with the facts," Jonathan sighed.

He completed his reading of Matthew and next turned his attention to the next book entitled "Mark." Jonathan thought it was curious that this was the first book written of the four, yet included second.

"Whatever," Jonathan moaned, and turned the pages in the Catholic Encyclopedia from Matthew until he found the chapter on Mark.

Jonathan found that Mark, although not one of the "apostles" or the original twelve called to follow the man Jesus, supposedly was one of seventy persons who saw Jesus ascend into heaven.

Jonathan paused for a minute and wrote down his thoughts on a yellow legal pad in front of him.

"If this event was so spectacular, the resurrection and ascension, why would someone who wanted to start a new order only reveal these incredible events to a select few people. You would think that a large audience to provide support for these supernatural events would have been of more value." Jonathan wrote at the top of the paper, "Lack of Proof" and continued to read.

Jonathan continued to read in the Catholic Encyclopedia and saw a reference to a book by Eusebius of Caesarea. He had seen that book in the stacks of books in Saul's office. Jonathan went down the hall and entered Saul's office and looked at the books stacked everywhere.

"With a little luck," Jonathan stated with optimism and began looking for the book he wanted.

After only about twenty minutes of searching, Jonathan found it: "Ecclesiastical History" by Eusebius.

"This would be better," as Jonathan pulled the book from the stack on the floor behind Saul's desk.

He glanced at the pages and felt he had a more original source than the Catholic Encyclopedia. Jonathan did not have to look far, and by the second chapter he found reference to Mark. Jonathan read that in the second year of Emperor Claudius,a man named Peter, who is mentioned prominently in the Christian New Testament, arrived in Rome with a travelling companion named "Mark." Peter used Mark as an interpreter while in Rome. Accordingly, Mark also served as Peter's scribe, writing down the teachings of Peter, which eventually became the Gospel of Mark. According to Eusebius, Mark traveled to Alexandria and founded the Church of Alexandria.

Jonathan thought for a moment, "I believe that is Coptic," he said to himself and jotted the same on his legal pad.

Jonathan continued to read Eusebius. Mark was succeeded by Annianus as the bishop of Alexandria in the eighth year of Nero due to the impending death of Mark. Jonathan could only find in Eusebius that Mark was killed. Curious, he went to another text and found another story of supernatural events.

Jonathan could not suppress his laughter as he read the story of Mark, being dragged through the streets of Alexandria by "pagans," and God appearing to him, and then his death. As these "pagans" were going to burn Mark's body, there was a severe hailstorm and earthquake that scared everyone away and Mark's followers spirited his body away.

Jonathan laughed aloud, not at the fate, but at another unbelievable tale about a follower of Jesus.

Satisfied with the history, Jonathan turned his attention to the Gospel of Mark itself. As he began reading, Jonathan felt as if he was reading an eyewitness account of the events as they were occurring. Jonathan thought this was odd, as most of his readings indicated that he was a companion of Peter and that his writings were just transcriptions of Peter's words and teachings.

"What an idiot I am," Jonathan stated, "Peter was supposed to be the right hand man of Jesus; Mark is writing the eye witness accounts of Peter.

Jonathan noted that Mark just passes over the story about the genealogy of Jesus, the birth, conception, the birth of this man John the Baptist, the birth of Jesus, etc, recorded by Matthew. Instead, Jonathan noted, Mark seems more interested in the things Jesus did and what he said to his followers. Jonathan saw that, in the very first chapter, Mark recorded three miracles attributed to Jesus: his casting out of an unclean spirit, the cure of Peter's mother-in-law, and the healing of a man with leprosy. Jonathan found a total of 15 miracles in just the first eight chapters. But Jonathan also found conflicts in the information and each time jotted down notes on his yellow legal pad. He flipped back to Matthew to confirm his suspicions and then would write down the discrepancy. Between that, to Jonathan, it seemed that Mark paid special attention to the human feelings and emotions of Jesus and to the effects produced by the miracles upon the people following him. Jonathan notes that the twelve chosen followers seem weak, more humanistic in the description afforded by Mark. Mark begins with the teaching of Jesus and the miracles that he performed. Jonathan summarizes that Mark wanted to make a case for Jesus being the Messiah and at one point even has Jesus declare the same. Mark has Jesus going from synagogue to synagogue and gathering more and more followers. While in Jerusalem, Jesus declared himself to be the Messiah to his followers. Jonathan finds that Mark makes sure that Jesus fulfills some of the prophecies, including his arrival in Jerusalem as a hero at the Feast of the Passover. Jonathan is annoyed that he again must read about the trail, crucifixion, and resurrection of Jesus in Mark's gospel as well. He was, however, surprised that Mark was so short, only sixteen chapters.

Jonathan began to review his notes. He had recorded over 25 contradictions between Matthew and Mark. Many were just really semantics and were of little consequence. In Matthew 1:13, Matthew states that Jesus was tempted during the 40 days in the wilderness, Mark 4:2, 3 indicated that the temptation occured after the wilderness. In the description of the baptism of Jesus, Mark stated that the baptism of Jesus was with the Holy Ghost, Mark 1:8; while Matthew added "fire," Matthew 3:11. Jonathan noted that Matthew stated that Jesus healed Simon Peter's mother-in-law after he cleansed the leper, Matthew 8:1-15; while Mark stated that it was before he cleansed the leper, Mark 1:30-42.

"Who cares about these," Jonathan thought, "they mean nothing."

He glanced through the remainder of his notes. There was an interesting discrepancy regarding divorce. In Matthew 5:32 it is stated that divorce, except for unfaithfulness, is wrong, while Mark asserted in chapter 10:11,12 that divorce is wrong for any reason. Jonathan had listed multiple disagreements between Matthew and Mark regarding the trail, crucifixion and resurrection. During the trail, Matthew portrayed Jesus as evasive and uncooperative while Mark depicts Jesus as more straightforward. When questioned regarding whether he was the son of God, in Matthew 26:64, Jesus states "You said it, not me." However, Mark indicates Jesus responded with a definite "I am," Mark 14:62. Matthew indicated that Jesus did not answer any of the charges, Matthew 27:12-14; while Mark contends that Jesus answered some of the charges, Mark 14:61,62.

"There's still not any real contradiction of the authors at this time, at least not anything to make an argument about," Jonathan thought.

He continued looking at his notes, as there was an issue regarding the stone in front of the tomb. Jonathan recalled hearing Christian's stating that this huge stone had been miraculously removed.

"Not according to Matthew 28:1,2." Jonathan saw he had written "stone still in place" beside this verse and the verse noted in Mark 16:4 that the stone had been removed.

"That may be an important contradiction," Jonathan observed, and he starred this verse.

As Jonathan finished reading his comments regarding Mark compared to Matthew, he yawned and looked at his watch and jumped up. It was almost midnight. Just reading and reviewing these first two books had taken all day and into the night. Jonathan was shocked that he had lost track of time. He had not even eaten anything except a small lunch around noon. Jonathan felt his stomach growl and wondered where he would find something to eat this late.

Jonathan closed the Vulgate Bible, but not before marking his place at "Luke." He had to admit, he found the study of these two men fascinating and he was anxious to see what Luke had to say about some of the events. However, he was also realistic and understood how these two men could easily have their lives updated and be classified as superheroes today.

"Well, at least they try to build a case that Jesus was the Messiah," Jonathan observed as he turned the light out and headed down the hallway and outside into the night air.

Outside the building that housed his and Saul's office, Jonathan gazed upward into the sky. Even with the light pollution, the stars filled the darkness in every direction. Jonathan thought about God, and the Messiah.

Silently he dreamed, "It would be something if it turned out this man Jesus was the Messiah."

As he walked, he quickly changed his thoughts to tomorrow. He and Saul had to interview students for the trip. Luke would have to wait.

CHAPTER 7

As usual, Jonathan was running late when he finally arrived at Saul's office the next morning. Saul was feverish looking through stacks of papers on his desk and shuffling them back and forth into piles.

"We have over 200 applicants for eight positions," Saul said, exasperated, "How are we going to sort through all of these, and where have you been?"

"Slow down!" Jonathan responded, "this will all come together."

It had been a little over a year since Jonathan and Saul had started working on the project. The funding was in place, the research was moving forward and Jonathan felt the pace was good. However, he knew Saul was anxious to get to Israel and begin the excavation as soon as possible. Jonathan joined Saul at his desk and looked over the stack of applications.

"First, let's just divide the stack and eliminate those that are definitely not going to qualify," Jonathan suggested.

Saul queried him on criteria and Jonathan suggested that first, only sophomores and juniors be considered. Jonathan explained that freshmen did not have the experience or maturity and seniors would be too involved with graduation. Saul liked that idea but asked about graduate students. Jonathan countered that those applicants could be considered separately. Saul handed Jonathan about half of the applications and they began the first sorting process.

Within minutes, the stack of 200 was narrowed to a manageable pile. Jonathan quickly thumbed through the applications, counting them, and now there were only fifty-eight eligible applicants. Of those, Jonathan suggested that transfer students be eliminated. He had noted at least one or two applicants that were juniors that had attended college elsewhere the first two years. Saul agreed and added that the cumulative GPA (grade point average) should be at least 3.5. Jonathan thought that number was high and wanted to cut it off at 3.0. Saul countered that the dig would need students who could apply themselves in difficult situations and challenges. Jonathan countered that there needed to be some personality and "realness" with the brains. After some back and forth, a GPA of 3.2 was agreed upon.

Saul divided the fifty-eight applications and again went through them with the new criteria. With only fifty-eight, Saul and Jonathan quickly pared down the applicants to an even more manageable twenty-three.

"These are the finalists," Saul exclaimed, "these are the ones we will interview.

Jonathan took the applications and reviewed each one carefully to make sure there were no errors. He next took the discarded applications and reviewed them a second time. Jonathan wanted to make sure there were no mistakes, no errors. Satisfied that the twenty-three selected met their criteria, Jonathan walked into the hallway down to the Dean's office and handed the applications to the secretary.

"Please put together a rejection letter for these students for Dr. Harkman to sign," Jonathan requested.

The secretary looked up and took the applications. She would compose a rejection letter for Dr. Harkman to sign and mail it to each student rejected.

"What about the students selected?" the secretary asked as Jonathan was leaving the office.

Jonathan turned and explained to her that he and Dr. Harkman would call each student individually and set up an interview. After the interview process, Dr. Harkman would notify those selected.

"You better hurry," the secretary countered, "there is not much time left in this year."

Jonathan nodded in agreement and was aware that the next semester started in just six months. He and Dr. Harkman would need to hurry and set up the interviews and make the selections quickly.

As Jonathan returned to Saul's office, the professor was busily reading another of his reference books.

"How are you doing on your research?" Saul asked.

Jonathan felt his stomach grumble, looked at his watch and realized it was lunch time. He suggested that Saul join him for lunch and he could go over the details. He then urged Saul to begin calling the twenty three students to set up interviews.

"We should be ready to begin by next school year," Jonathan advised.

Saul's face lit up with the prospect of starting in the fall.

"Really, you think we can be ready?" Saul asked with the glee of a child.

Jonathan reassured Saul that, once the students were selected, they could begin helping with the planning and purchasing of supplies and that fall was very realistic. Saul grabbed his coat and hat, took Jonathan by the arm and pulled him out of his office.

"Let's hurry then and eat, I want to hear how far the research has come and get back here and set up the appointments," Saul spoke hurriedly as he pulled Jonathan down the hall toward the direction of the cafeteria.

Saul quickly made his selections and sat down at the table, waiting for Jonathan. Jonathan was much slower and finally set down. Saul immediately started peppering him with questions, while Jonathan had barely sat down. He surveyed Saul's tray.

"That's all you're eating?" Jonathan questioned.

Saul's tray contained an apple and a small salad.

"It's all I need, now tell me about what you've learned," Saul stated dismissively.

Jonathan looked at how thin Saul was with his long, thin, straight hair. Jonathan sat with two sandwiches, a side of potato salad, and a dessert. Jonathan removed his glasses and cleaned the lens with his handkerchief, adjusted his kippah and silently murmured a prayer of thanks. As he completed his prayer he noted that Saul looked annoyed, but did not say anything. After all this time, Saul had finally adjusted to Jonathan's conservatism in all things Jewish.

"Thank goodness they serve kosher food here," Saul quipped.

"It's a Hebrew University," Jonathan responded and they both laughed at the absurdity of the statement.

As soon as Jonathan started to eat, Saul started with the questions about what he had learned. Jonathan explained that he had only completed Matthew and Mark.

"Did you find the discrepancies?" Saul questioned.

Jonathan went into detail that the differences between the two writers were not significant. With the exception of the reasons for divorce, many of the differences were insignificant and not strong enough to bring question to the documents.

"What about Herod and his palace?" Saul questioned.

Jonathan knew that Saul had read the text and was surprised by the questions. He asked Saul about this and Saul explained that he had read these texts over two years ago and wanted a "second opinion." Jonathan explained that in Matthew and Mark there is mention of Herod the Great and Herod Antipas. Herod the Great only appears in the book by Matthew in relation to the great massacre. Jonathan explained that according to Matthew, after the birth of Jesus, wise men visited Herod to inquire the whereabouts of Jesus because they had seen his star in the east and therefore wanted to pay him homage. Herod the Great, as King of the Jews, was alarmed at the prospect of a new king not understanding the prophecies of the Torah. According to Matthew, Herod assembled the chief priests and scribes of the people and asked them where Jesus was to be born. Referring to the prophets, he was told Bethlehem. Herod sent the wise men to Bethlehem, instructing them to search for the child and, after they had found Jesus, to return and tell him his whereabouts. Matthew claims that, after they had found Jesus, the wise men were warned in a dream not to report back to Herod. Similarly, Joseph was warned in a dream that Herod intended to kill Jesus, so he and his family fled to Egypt. When Herod realized he had been outwitted, he gave orders to kill all boys of the age of two and under in Bethlehem and its vicinity. Joseph and his family stayed in Egypt until Herod's death, then moved to Nazareth in Galilee in order to avoid living under Herod's son Archelaus. Jonathan pointed out that Josephus writes about Herod the Great but does not mention any massacre of children at this time. There is no other historical evidence to support that this event actually occurred. The only facts are that Herod the Great was King of Judea and Samaria and was a Jewish convert.

"Josephus is very detailed about Herod the Great," Jonathan offered, "but he is only mentioned by Matthew.

"No, no," Saul exclaimed, "I don't care about Herod the Great, it is Herod Antipas that I am interested in, what did you learn about him from these books?"

Jonathan explained that the major emphasis by Matthew and Mark regarding Herod Antipas was in relation to the man known as "John the Baptist." Jonathan explained that Matthew and Mark indicated that this man John was a Jew who was the predecessor to the man Jesus.

"In fact, according to both Matthew and Mark, this John the Baptist baptized Jesus," Jonathan stated.

Saul looked perplexed and Jonathan explained that baptism was a Christian method of "washing away sins" or a rebirth through immersion of the person in water. Jonathan further stated it was like the purification rites in Jewish laws and tradition, called Tvilah. The "Tvilah" is the act of immersion in natural sourced water, called a "Mikvah" in which the immersion in water for ritual purification was established for restoration to a condition of "ritual purity" in specific circumstances. For example, Jews who became ritually defiled by contact with a corpse had to use the mikvah before being allowed to participate in the Holy Temple. Immersion is required for converts to Judaism as part of their conversion. Immersion in the mikvah represents a change in status in regards to purification, restoration, and qualification for full religious participation in the life of the community, ensuring that the cleansed person will not impose uncleanness on property or its owners. This change of status by the mikvah could be obtained repeatedly. Jonathan pointed out that John was Jewish and that Jesus was Jewish so this may have been a Tvilah and then the Christian just adopted this Jewish law. However, unlike in Judaism, where Tvilah can occur repeatedly, in the Christian religion this is a one-time occurrence.

Saul was beginning to regret having a Masorti Jew as an assistant. All of these details were not answering his questions. However, he had learned over the years to be patient with Jonathan.

"Anything more about Herod Antipas," Saul asked again.

Jonathan realized Saul was becoming inpatient, but he reminded him that all he had time to review were Matthew and Mark. Both confirmed the death of John the Baptist. Jonathan explained that, early in his reign, Antipas had married the daughter of King Aretas IV of Nabatea. However, on a visit to Rome he stayed with his half-brother Herod Philip I and there fell in love with Philip's wife, Herodias, and the two agreed to marry each other, after Herod Antipas had divorced his wife. Both Matthew and Mark report that John attacked Herod's marriage as contrary to Jewish . Herod had John imprisoned. Jonathan pointed out that Josephus supports all of these accounts except that the man John was imprisoned due to fear of starting a rebellion. According to Matthew and Mark, Herod was at first reluctant to order John's death but was compelled by Herodias' daughter to whom he had promised any reward she chose in exchange for her dancing.

"Yes, yes," a frustrated Saul stated, "but what about him and Jesus."

Jonathan explained that Jesus increased his teachings and followers after John's death. According to both Matthew and Mark, this led Herod Antipas to believe that John had been raised from the dead.

"Okay, but what about the trial?" Saul asked.

"Nothing about a trial," Jonathan responded, "it must be in Luke or John."

Saul expressed his frustration with Jonathan's lack of progress. He was disappointed that there was no evidence found to discredit the Christian New Testament, but he was more disappointed about the lack of information regarding the trail.

"It's in the book called Luke," Saul muttered.

"The book is called Luke?" Jonathan asked.

Saul explained that the account regarding Jesus' trial was in the text in the book of Luke, possibly John but he could not remember. He also felt there were major discrepancies present in the text. Saul was puzzled that there was not more about Herod Antipas in Matthew and Mark.

"We need to get back to work," Saul ordered Jonathan.

"But I'm not finished eating," Jonathan exclaimed.

Saul ignored Jonathan's plea and stood up, holding his tray. He told Jonathan he would meet him back at the office.

"But hurry," Saul chided, "I want you to start on Luke ASAP!"

Saul left with Jonathan only half finished with his lunch. Jonathan sighed as he realized that he had spent most of his time talking instead of eating. He also was feeling a bit of pressure. Thus far, the reading and review of this New Testament had been interesting, but had not really provided anything of value. Historically, Herod of Antipas existed. This is documented in numerous historical texts besides Josephus. However, Jonathan understood, in order to support their thesis, they had to discredit the Christian account of the events.

Jonathan looked down at his half-eaten lunch and realized he no longer had an appetite.

"There is too much work to be done," Jonathan thought, stood up and took his tray to dispose of his lunch and quickly tried to catch up to Saul.

Jonathan caught up with Saul just as he reached their office building. He suggested that Saul contact the twenty three students selected for interviews and he would return to his review of the books Luke and John. Saul agreed and offered that Jonathan should focus on this research until the first appointment. Saul stated that he would set up four or five appointments a day so the interviews would only take a week. Jonathan agreed and, as they entered the building, Jonathan went to his office to tackle the two remaining books. As he entered the office, he saw the Vulgate Bible sitting prominently on his desk, as if waiting for him to return. John exhaled slowly, found the bookmark and opened the book to Luke.

CHAPTER 8

Jonathan stared down at the first three lines of the first Chapter of the Book of Luke.

---

1 quoniam quidem multi conati sunt ordinare narrationem quae in nobis conpletae sunt rerum

---

2 sicut tradiderunt nobis qui ab initio ipsi viderunt et ministri fuerunt sermonis

---

3 visum est et mihi adsecuto a principio omnibus diligenter ex ordine tibi scribere optime Theophile

---

Jonathan quickly translated the Latin to English:

---

1 Forasmuch as many have taken in hand to set forth in order a narration of the things that have been accomplished among us,

---

2 According as they have delivered them unto us, who from the beginning were eyewitnesses and ministers of the word:

---

3 It seemed good to me also, having diligently attained to all things from the beginning, to write to thee in order, most excellent Theophilus

---

Jonathan stared at the pages, "Who is Theophilus?" he thought, "for that matter, who is Luke?"

Jonathan did not recall any mention of a "Theophilus" in Mark, nor a Luke as one of those chosen by Jesus. Furthermore, according to these first words, Luke was writing what he had been told from "eyewitnesses," not what he had seen himself. He looked around his desk and found the Catholic Encyclopedia and learned that Theophilus was Greek for "friend of God," the conclusion being that the author Luke wrote to a large generalized audience. However, Jonathan noticed that the Latin indicated the words "most excellent Theophilus," which would imply that this was a real person. In order to determine the identity of this Theophilus, Jonathan decided to determine just who this person Luke was as he was never mentioned before.

Jonathan searched his desk; he had seen a dusty, old book somewhere that had been in Saul's office that contained the word "Luke." He recalled bringing it to this office but could not remember where he had placed it. After a thorough moving around of the books on his desk without finding it,

Jonathan began searching the room. There was a stack of old books on a chair in the corner.

"Perhaps there," Jonathan thought as he walked across his office to the chair.

There were at least ten books stacked carefully, and the first one was a text about Luke, but not the one Jonathan wanted. However, Jonathan quickly worked his way down through the references on Luke until he found it, *New Testament Studies. I. Luke the Physician: The Author of the Third Gospel, Adolf von Harnack, 1907.*

"Perfect," Jonathan commented to no one in particular, took the book over to his desk, and began the read.

Luke was reportedly a physician. The Jewish writer, Paul refers to him frequently in his letters later in the New Testament. He was from Antioch in Syria, which would have been one of the seven original Christian churches. There is speculation that most likely Luke was not Jewish. This is based on a letter written by his friend Paul in which Paul differentiates between Luke and his "uncircumcised" colleagues. This was interesting to Jonathan as that would make Luke the only non-Jew writing in the Christian New Testament and may be of value in the future. Luke was apparently a companion of the Jewish writer Paul, as in Luke's second book called the "Acts of the Apostles" the term "we" is used. In addition, at one point Paul wrote in one his letters that Luke was with him, and this was in a letter of another follower named Timothy. Jonathan made a note to himself that when he finished with Luke and John he should just read the "Acts of the Apostles." Jonathan also noted that, according to his research, this book was also written by Luke and sent to the same person, Theophilus. Therefore, Jonathan concluded, Theophilus must be a real person.

Jonathan further found that Luke is often considered one of the "seventy" followers that reportedly was present when this man Jesus, after his death and resurrection, "ascended" into Heaven. Jonathan found these portions of the story of Jesus to be the most incredible of all, not so much the death, but that after death, Jesus came to life again and then was taken into Heaven. Jonathan felt that if seventy people witnessed this event that there would be more writings and more references to it in other non-Christian historical documents. However, the only accounts of this ascension were recorded in the books that the Christians use to support their religion.

"How convenient," Jonathan murmured.

It did not make sense to Jonathan that the person Luke would be part of those seventy because Luke himself stated that he was not an eyewitness. If Luke had been one of these seventy at this ascension, he would have been an eye-witness. Jonathan dismissed the idea that Luke was one of the "seventy." However, Jonathan deduced that, if Luke were considered part of this group, then he would have been alive around the time this event was said to have occurred 33 – 34 AD. According to his research, Jonathan learned Luke died at the age of eighty-four. From the letters written by Paul indicating that Luke was a companion and Luke implying that he is writing from eyewitness accounts, Jonathan determined that Luke must have written this book somewhere between 50 – 70 AD. Jonathan went back to the books on the stack of chairs and found *A. T. Robertson, Luke the Historian*, which supported this theory and actually dated the book of Luke at around 59 – 60 AD.

That did not really provide any additional information and Jonathan was frustrated at his lack of information regarding Theophilus. Jonathan was sure that knowing who this person was would be helpful in understanding the text.

"The library," Jonathan thought.

He looked at his watch and it was almost five o'clock. There was not enough time to go to the library tonight. He would go in the morning.

Jonathan returned to the office the next morning after spending most of the morning at the library. He had found a book, *Richard H. Anderson, Who are Theophilus and Johanna? The Irony of the Intended Audience* that was very interesting and explained the person Theophilus.

Jonathan was fascinated as he had read that Theophilus was most likely the High Priest Theophilus ben Ananus. This Theophilus was High Priest of the Temple in Jerusalem from 37 – 41 AD. As Theophilus was appointed by the Romans, he would have been titled "most excellent" for that period. Theophilus would have been a Sadducee, son of Annas, and brother-in-law of Caiaphas. Jonathan recalled that these two men, Annas and Caiaphas, were involved in the trial of Jesus. Jonathan felt this was a very well supported argument and would make sense. From Jonathan's knowledge of ancient Hebrew, he felt that a Jew, unless he was royalty or another Priest, would not have written a letter to a Jewish High Priest. Therefore, Luke must have been a Gentile or non-Jew. As a physician, Luke would have been well-respected, and intelligent. If Luke felt that the man Jesus was unfairly treated by the High Priest with his trial and execution, then a letter to the High Priest outlining the events of Jesus' life would seem logical.

Based on his research, Jonathan felt satisfied that Luke had written this book called the "Gospel of Luke" to the High Priest in Jerusalem, Theophilus, in order to point out that Jesus, as an innocent man, was falsely convicted of crimes he did not commit and was executed unjustly.

Jonathan was now ready to tackle the "Gospel of Luke." He felt that he had the background information that would help him to understand what the writer was trying to say. Judging from the thickness of the pages, Jonathan realized that Luke must be the longest of the Gospels. "Perhaps this will be of more value," Jonathan thought.

He felt that a non-Jew writing to a High Priest might provide some insights or a different perspective from the other two writers. Jonathan settled back in his chair with the "Vulgate" in his lap and started reading the book again.

Jonathan first noticed that a time frame was established. Luke cites the fifteenth year of the reign of Tiberius Caesar, Pontius Pilate as governor of Judea, and Herod as the tetrarch of Galilee and Phillip, Herod's brother, as tetrarch of Iturea. This was consistent with historical accounts of when Jesus supposedly lived. Interesting to Jonathan was that Luke spent some time on the man John known as the Baptist. While Matthew and Mark talked about John and his role in the baptism of Jesus, Luke discusses John's parents, birth, and his role in Jesus's life even from the womb. Jonathan made some notes and continued to read. Jonathan noted that, according to Luke, Jesus began his recruitment of his disciples after he performed miracles. According to Mark, Jonathan recalled, he recruited the first disciples before any miracles occurred.

"That's interesting," was Jonathan's only observation.

Jonathan noted that Luke had a tendency to have Jesus take on the Jewish leaders in the synagogue of the day. There is more emphasis on women as playing important roles among Jesus' followers. Jonathan found it interesting that women such as Mary Magdalene, Martha, and Mary of Bethany are discussed and that only Luke contained a spiritual announcement of the birth of Jesus to his mother Mary. There was an additional mention of a female prophet named

"Anna," and prominent discussion was given to the lives of Elizabeth, the mother of John, the one called the Baptist, and of Mary, the mother of Jesus. Jonathan would have thought this to be unusual if Luke had been Jewish. However, since Luke was not Jewish, then a discussion of these females would be customary if their role was important to the story.

As Jonathan continued to read, he discovered that Luke, when compared to Matthew and Mark, treated the meal between Jesus and his disciples as an "institution" to be repeated by his followers. At first Jonathan thought this was a major deviation from either Matthew or Mark, but he recalled that Mark supported a theme that the meal was symbolic for atoning death and Luke most likely just elaborated the concept into an institution.

"Not a big deal," Jonathan mused.

Jonathan continued to read and found the passages that had started the entire journey. In Luke 23:6-12 was the description of the man Jesus sent by Pontius Pilate to Herod for judgment.

---

[6] Pilatus autem audiens Galilaeam interrogavit si homo Galilaeus esset

But Pilate, hearing Galilee, asked if the man were of Galilee

---

[7] et ut cognovit quod de Herodis potestate esset remisit eum ad Herodem qui et ipse Hierosolymis erat illis diebus

And when he understood that he was of Herod's jurisdiction, he sent him away to Herod, who was also himself at Jerusalem in those days.

---

8 Herodes autem viso Iesu gavisus est valde erat enim cupiens ex multo tempore videre eum eo quod audiret multa de illo et sperabat signum aliquod videre ab eo fieri

And Herod, seeing Jesus, was very glad: for he was desirous of a long time to see him, because he had heard many things of him; and he hoped to see some sign wrought by him.

---

9 interrogabat autem illum multis sermonibus at ipse nihil illi respondebat

And he questioned him in many words. But he answered him with nothing.

---

10 stabant etiam principes sacerdotum et scribae constanter accusantes eum

And the chief priests and the scribes stood by, earnestly accusing him.

---

11 sprevit autem illum Herodes cum exercitu suo et inlusit indutum veste alba et remisit ad Pilatum

And Herod with his army set him at nought and mocked him, putting on him a white garment: and sent him back to Pilate.

---

12 et facti sunt amici Herodes et Pilatus in ipsa die nam antea inimici erant ad invicem

And Herod and Pilate were made friends, that same day: for before they were enemies to one another.

Jonathan was stunned.

"How could this mistake have been made," he thought, "This clearly states that Herod was in Jerusalem."

Jonathan could not believe what he was reading. He referred back to Matthew and Mark. He had not seen anything about Herod participating in the trail.

"But Luke is not an eyewitness account, he is simply writing what he has been told," Jonathan rationalized.

Jonathan felt beads of sweat on his forehead. He removed his round glasses and cleaned them, trying to organize his thoughts to save this disaster. He furiously made notes on his pad and starred several related to these passages so he could question Saul regarding these statements.

"Perhaps there is something else major, some other 'error,' that can discredit Luke," Jonathan pondered and continued to read.

As Jonathan entered into the trial and execution phase of Luke's writing, he began to have a sense that there was a huge difference between the description by Matthew and Mark and that of Luke. Luke emphasized that Jesus was innocent of any crime, and this is confirmed by a thief executed with him. Jonathan saw two issues: Luke clearly laid the blame for the execution of Jesus at the feet of the Jews, primarily the High Priest, and the confirmation of this, the thief, is not mentioned anywhere else. Luke has an entire conversation regarding a thief who supports Jesus' innocence that is not spoken of in Matthew or Mark. To make sure, Jonathan went back to Matthew first, Chapter 27: 41-44:

---

[41] similiter et principes sacerdotum inludentes cum scribis et senioribus dicentes

In like manner also the chief priests, with the scribes and ancients, mocking said:

---

[42] alios salvos fecit se ipsum non potest salvum facere si rex Israhel est descendat nunc de cruce et credemus ei

He saved others: himself he cannot save. If he be the king of Israel, let him now come down from the cross: and we will believe him.

---

[43] confidet in Deo liberet nunc eum si vult dixit enim quia Dei Filius sum

He trusted in God: let him now deliver him if he will have him. For he said: I am the Son of God.

---

[44] id ipsum autem et latrones qui fixi erant cum eo inproperabant ei

And the selfsame thing the thieves also that were crucified with him reproached him with.

Jonathan noted that Matthew clearly indicated that both thieves that were executed mock Jesus and "reproached" him with the same words as the priest and the scribes. Jonathan next reviewed Mark Chapter 15:29-32:

---

[29] et praetereuntes blasphemabant eum moventes capita sua et dicentes va qui destruit templum et in tribus diebus aedificat

And they that passed by blasphemed him, wagging their heads and saying: Vah, thou that destroyest the temple of God and in three days buildest it up again:

---

30 salvum fac temet ipsum descendens de cruce

Save thyself, coming down from the cross.

---

31 similiter et summi sacerdotes ludentes ad alterutrum cum scribis dicebant alios salvos fecit se ipsum non potest salvum facere

In like manner also the chief priests, mocking, said with the scribes one to another: He saved others; himself he cannot save.

---

32 Christus rex Israhel descendat nunc de cruce ut videamus et credamus et qui cum eo crucifixi erant conviciabantur ei

Let Christ the king of Israel come down now from the cross, that we may see and believe. And they that were crucified with him, reviled him

---

Jonathan now was intrigued and excited.

"How could this be?" he wondered aloud.

Jonathan knew that this was a key point of many Christian stories and "lessons" about the two thieves. He needed to check the next book to see if this discrepancy held there as well. He went ahead to "The Gospel of John" and skimmed the pages until he found the account of the trial and execution of Jesus.

"This is interesting," Jonathan observed and began making notes, "John does not mention this at all, just that two thieves were executed with Jesus."

Jonathan was now unsure of the facts. This was certainly a major discrepancy. Mark was reportedly an eyewitness account and conflicts with Luke, who basically wrote his account from the discussions with eyewitnesses. As he had not researched John, he was unable to determine if this was the one that was called the Baptist or the John called by Jesus or some other person. If it was either of the first two, then it would also be an eyewitness account. Jonathan wrote several more notes regarding his findings on his yellow legal pad. He was more frustrated than excited about what he had found. Jonathan no longer was sure of what was actually true. Luke seemed to provide almost a different story of this man Jesus than Matthew and Mark. If John were more consistent with Matthew and Mark, that would leave Luke as the one with the different story. In addition, Jonathan knew that Matthew and Mark were eyewitnesses to the events. He was not yet sure about John. However, he knew John was one of the men selected to follow Jesus and assumed that John was an eyewitness.

"This will probably make Luke's story suspect," Jonathan muttered to himself, not really convinced.

Jonathan finished Luke and noted that Luke's description of the appearances of Jesus after the supposed resurrection was also different from Matthew or Mark. Luke stated that after Jesus died he appeared on the road to Emmaus to the eleven remaining followers. Jonathan noted that there were only eleven because the man accused of being a traitor had committed suicide. Luke made the point very vividly that the man Jesus appeared in flesh and blood and not as a ghost or spirit. Again, Jonathan was confused, as Luke was not an eyewitness. However, Luke was reportedly writing from eyewitness accounts. Jonathan now was beginning to feel that Luke was a good storyteller, maybe embellishing facts for some other purpose. If Theophilus was a Jewish High Priest, this Luke may have been trying to write a convincing argument that the Jews had executed an innocent man. To do so, Luke must have played loose with the facts.

Jonathan made several more notes regarding the book written by Luke. Jonathan felt that clearly there were some major issues with his account. Jonathan considered what would be a reason for these different stories, especially the ones that have been so important in Christian teachings such as the thieves on the cross and the appearance of Jesus after his death.

"After all," Jonathan thought, "without these appearances of Jesus after death, he was just another prophet or Holy man, just like so many others, and there goes the basis for the Christian religion."

Jonathan grabbed Josephus and looked up the references to Jesus. He was stunned to find that Josephus also supported that Jesus was seen after his death:

"Now there was about this time Jesus, a wise man, if it be lawful to call him a man; for he was a doer of wonderful works, a teacher of such men as to receive the truth with pleasure. He drew over to him both many of the Jews and many of the Gentiles. He was [the] Christ. And when Pilate, at the suggestion of the principal men among us, had condemned him to the cross, those that loved him at the first did not forsake him; for he appeared to them alive again the third day, as the divine prophets had foretold these and ten thousand other wonderful things concerning him. And the tribe of Christians, so named for him, are not extinct at this day."

"Amazing," was Jonathan's only comment.

He closed Josephus and closed the Vulgate Bible. Standing to stretch, he wondered how Saul was doing with contacting the students. Jonathan knew he would have to question Saul regarding the statement that Herod was in Jerusalem. Without some valid explanation, the excavation of Herod's palace really had no purpose. He would check with him in the morning before starting "The Gospel of John." He reached down and re-opened the Vulgate to the Book of John.

"*Evangelium Secundum Ioannem,*" Jonathan read out loud, "The Gospel according to John.

Jonathan was tempted to begin reading. However, he knew he would not stop and his stomach was growling for supper. He again closed the Vulgate and walked to the door of his office. He looked back at this desk one last time and turned out the light.

"Tomorrow," he whispered as he felt a level of excitement about this next book.

CHAPTER 9

Saul was just hanging up the phone when Jonathan entered his office. Saul did not even look up from his desk and Jonathan walked to the front of it. Jonathan adjusted his kippah, removed his glasses, and pulled the ever present handkerchief from his pocket and cleaned the lens as he had done thousands of times. It was a nervous habit he had developed and he seemed to repeat the same motions each time before he began a conversation or was in a situation for which he was apprehensive about the outcome. Jonathan cleared his throat, but Saul did not look up.

"There might be a problem," Jonathan stammered out.

Not looking up, Saul made a grunting sound and indicated that Jonathan should continue. Jonathan began explaining that he had almost concluded his research and came upon a passage that might be a problem for Saul's theory. He outlined the preliminary information about Jesus and the High Priest and slowly began to point out the "problem."

"It states that Pilate sent Jesus to Herod who was also in Jerusalem that day, not in Galilee," Jonathan offered hesitantly.

"Yes," Saul responded as if there were more.

"But your theory argues that Herod was at his palace in Tiberias, in Galilee, and the Christian Bible states that Herod was in Jerusalem. You don't see this as a problem?"

Jonathan was becoming more anxious as he pressed the points. He felt that this was a major issue and that Saul did not understand the significance of this finding. Saul just sat shuffling through papers on his desk, stacking and restacking the papers. Jonathan's hand went to his kippah again and he removed his glasses.

"You just cleaned those," Saul commented without looking up.

Jonathan quickly stuffed the handkerchief back in his pocket and replaced his glasses on his face.

"Did you finish all of the first four books?" Saul inquired again without looking up.

Jonathan did not answer.

"Of course that is what was written, you must be reading Luke," Saul finally looked up and addressed Jonathan.

Jonathan nodded affirmatively.

"Don't you remember, we went over this. You yourself said that the early Christian writers had argued that Herod was in Jerusalem," Saul reminded Jonathan.

Jonathan thought back and could not recall such a conversation. He noted that Saul seemed a bit hurt at the revelation that Jonathan had provided.

"Do you think I am such a poor academic that I would miss such a detail?"

Saul proceeded to talk to Jonathan as he would a student. He explained that he knew that Luke had made that statement. However, he questioned Jonathan about the other writers, Matthew, Mark, and John. Jonathan explained that he had not read John, but that neither Matthew nor Mark made any such statements.

"Exactly," Saul said with some frustration, "and did you find any other discrepancies in Luke, I mean big discrepancies."

Jonathan thought for a moment. He related that the supper Jesus had was described by Luke to be an institution and then he blurted out the issues with the two men who were executed with him. There were other issues too, but Jonathan started with those.

"Luke was an anti-Semitic, a non-Jew," Saul commented.

Saul continued that Luke obviously wrote from a different perspective. Luke clearly lays the blame for the execution of Jesus with the Jews and makes that argument in the text. Saul then offered that, in order for Luke to support this argument, he had to have Herod in Jerusalem.

"This writer Luke went so far as to claim that after this event Herod and Pilate became good friends. The entire story written by Luke is different from any of the other writers. And. . ." Saul paused to emphasize this point, "Luke was writing from second and third hand reportedly eyewitness accounts."

Saul stood up as he finished his last statement and slammed his hands on his desk, obviously frustrated. Jonathan blushed crimson as he realized that he had been foolish and sloppy—foolish to doubt Saul and sloppy in his research. Jonathan mumbled an apology, removed his kippah and reached for his glasses.

Jonathan had slept poorly that night fretting over the issue of Herod being in Jerusalem for the trail. Saul had dismissed the issue and seemed more upset about the lack of understanding Jonathan displayed. Jonathan realized he had made a rookie mistake and felt he had been taken to task by the Professor like a new graduate student in his first research class. Saul's conclusions and logic were right in front of Jonathan. Jonathan just did not allow his mind to be open to the obvious.

"One other thing you should know," Saul said to Jonathan, "I also believe that the man known as John the Baptist and Jesus may have been the same person. "

Jonathan sat down in one of the chairs in front of Saul's desk. This was new information and Jonathan listened intently as Saul explained that he believed that the execution of John the Baptist may have actually been the death of Jesus also. Saul stated that he believed the "Christian" writers took some of the facts about John and expanded them into a Messiah in the form of the man named Jesus. He reminded Jonathan that he believed that Jesus was beheaded by Herod the same way that reportedly John the Baptist was beheaded. Saul explained that he believed that Herod convicted Jesus at Tiberius and then shipped him to Machaerus in the north east area of the Dead Sea for execution. Saul stated that Jesus was very popular in and around Tiberius as Jesus traveled and spoke in Cana, Capernaum, and Nazareth. If he was as popular as the Christians believed, Herod would have been fearful to put him in prison in Tiberius where his followers were numerous.

"Machaerus is where Josephus writes that the execution of John the Baptist took place," Saul said in conclusion.

Jonathan was aware that Josephus provided a detailed description of John the Baptist. He needed to find the reference as his memory of the passages was fuzzy. However, Jonathan did recall that Josephus described John the Baptist much in the same way as these early Christian writers described Jesus.

"One in the same," Jonathan thought silently and made a mental note that when he returned to his office he needed to review Josephus.

"So we dig at Tiberius and find evidence of Jesus there, what about Machaerus?" Jonathan asked.

Saul explained that Machaerus had undergone multiple excavations over the past half century. The archaeological excavation of Machaerus was begun in 1968 by Jerry Vardaman from some Christian university.

"I believe they are called 'Baptist.'" Saul muttered.

He continued to explain that in 1973, the German scholar, August Strobel, identified and studied the wall by which the Romans encircled the defenders within the fortress. However, it was not until 1981, when excavations carried out by Virgilio Corbo, Stanislao Loffreda and Michele Piccirillo, that anything significant was found. These archeologists found within the ruins of Herod's palace, including rooms, a large courtyard, and an elaborate bath, with fragments of the floor mosaic. From this point further down the eastern slope of the hill were other walls and towers, representing the lower tower that Josephus speaks on. Saul stated that the digs at Machaerus had thus far only proven that Herod's palace was there, but many historians had already indicated that Herod used this palace primarily in the summer. Saul also pointed out that these archeologists were all Christians and were only searching for evidence to support the writings of the New

Testament. Saul reminded Jonathan that their goal is to dispute the writings. Saul felt that there was little to find a Machaerus.

"Luke is so fraught with errors and discrepancies, it is hard to see how anyone would believe what he has written," Saul said emphatically, moving the subject back to the original discussion.

Jonathan had recalled reading these theories of Saul that John the Baptist and Jesus were the same man. This had been the source of much ridicule from the Christain community and he had thought Saul had given up on this notion. However, it appeared that he had just learned to choose who he would talk with about it. Jonathan knew that this was far-fetched and had caused problems for Saul in the past, which is probably why he had not mentioned it before, and why Saul did not use it in his fund-raising speeches. The prospect of not only discrediting the Christian accounts based on logical logistic evidence, but to actually claim that Jesus and John were the same made Jonathan very nervous. He felt beads of sweat on his forehead and upper lip. Jonathan again reached to adjust his kippah and removed his glasses.

"Don't you clean those glasses again," Saul ordered, "now we have some work to do with these applicants and you need to finish the author John."

Saul showed Jonathan the schedule to interview the twenty applicants. It was Tuesday and they would interview two a day through Friday and finish on Monday. The interviews were scheduled for two hours each. Saul hoped that Jonathan would be able to finish his work on John during the times when there were no interviews. Saul caught Jonathan off guard when he pointed out that the first interview was in about an hour. Jonathan realized that would give him time to review Josephus regarding John the Baptist, or at least to find the passage.

Jonathan told Saul he would be back in time for the interview at ten and went to his office. The copy of Josephus was buried under the Vulgate and several other reference books. He opened the book to the marked, ragged pages in chapter 18 that he had looked at before in reference to Jesus. He saw a faded yellow tab with the words "John, Baptist" written in Saul's hand. Jonathan sighed as he realized he had missed this part of the puzzle. But then, Saul had not been forthcoming about the "John and Jesus the same man" theory. Jonathan began to read:

About this time Aretas, the king of the Arabian city Petra, and Herod Antipas had a quarrel. Herod the tetrarch had married the daughter of Aretas [called Phasaelis], and had lived with her a great while. But when he was once at Rome, he lodged with Herod, who was his brother indeed, but not by the same mother (this Herod was the son of the high priest Sireoh's daughter). Here, he fell in love with Herodias, this other Herod's wife, who was the daughter of Aristobulus, their brother, and the sister of Agrippa the Great. Antipas ventured to talk to her about a marriage between them; when she admitted, an agreement was made for her to change her habitation and come to him as soon as he should return from Rome: one article of this marriage also was that he should divorce Aretas' daughter.

So Antipas made this agreement and returned home again. But his wife had discovered the agreement he had made before he had been able to tell her about it. She asked him to send her to Macherus, which is a place in the borders of the dominions of Aretas and Herod, without informing him of her intentions. So, Herod sent her thither, unaware that his wife had perceived something.

Earlier, she had been sent to Macherus, and all things necessary for her journey were already prepared for her by a general of Aretas' army. Consequently, she soon arrived in Arabia, under the conduct of several generals, who carried her from one to another successively. She met her father, and told him of Herod's intentions. So Aretas made this the first occasion of the enmity between him and Herod, who had also some quarrel with him about their limits near Gamala.

So both sides raised armies, prepared for war, and sent their generals to fight. When they joined battle, Herod's army was completely destroyed by the treachery of some fugitives, who, though they were from the tetrarchy of Philip, had joined Aretas' army. So Herod wrote about these affairs to the emperor Tiberius, who became very angry at the attempt made by Aretas, and wrote to Lucius Vitellius, the governor of Syria, to make war upon him, and either to take him alive and bring him to him in bonds or to kill him and send him his head. This was the charge that Tiberius gave to the governor of Syria.

Now some of the Jews thought that the destruction of Herod's army came from God as a just punishment of what Herod had done against John, who was called the Baptist. For Herod had killed this good man, who had commanded the Jews to exercise virtue, righteousness towards one another and piety towards God. For only thus, in John's opinion, would the baptism he administered be acceptable to God, namely, if they used it to obtain not pardon for some sins but rather the cleansing of their bodies, inasmuch as it was taken for granted that their souls had already been purified by justice.

Now many people came in crowds to him, for they were greatly moved by his words. Herod, who feared that the great influence John had over the masses might put them into his power and enable him to raise a rebellion (for they seemed ready to do anything he should advise), thought it best to put him to death. In this way, he might prevent any mischief John might cause, and not bring himself into difficulties by sparing a man who might make him repent of it when it would be too late.

> *Accordingly, John was sent as a prisoner, out of Herod's suspicious temper, to Macherus, the castle I already mentioned, and was put to death. Now the Jews thought that the destruction of his army was sent as a punishment upon Herod, and a mark of God's displeasure with him.*

As Jonathan read these passages, he realized that Josephus was describing John in the same manner as Matthew, Mark, and Luke described Jesus. John, as described by Josephus, was a "good man, who had commanded the Jews to exercise virtue, righteousness towards one another and piety towards God." In addition, John advocated baptism as an acceptable means to remove one's sins before God, essentially the same message conveyed reportedly by Jesus.

"Maybe there is some truth to the "one in the same" theory," Jonathan pondered as he closed the book and glanced at his watch.

Jonathan jumped up and rushed to Saul's office and arrived just as the first student arrived. Saul had set up chairs in front of his desk in a crude circle in which to conduct the interviews. Everyone was standing as Saul introduced everyone.

"This is Professor Weitzman," pointing at Jonathan, "I am Professor Harkman," Saul said to the student, "let's all sit down."

With those brief introductions, the interview process started for the day. Saul and Jonathan peppered the student with questions about their past educational experiences, their current educational experiences, their families, and other small, assorted talk of no real value until Saul popped the loaded question.

"What are your beliefs regarding the figure in Christian history named 'Jesus.'"

More such questions followed.

"Do you believe in the Messiah?"

"Do you believe in God?"

"Explain the political state of Israel between 4 BC and 40 AD."

"Name the first four writers of the Christian New Testament."

"Why do you want to be involved in this project?"

And so on and so on with Saul and Jonathan taking turns in an unscripted interview that demonstrated the consistency of thought of the two men. Both listened intently to the answers to the questions and took notes on each student. For each interview the questions were essentially the same, perhaps in a different order, or phrased differently, but for the most part the same. Some students did very well, some not so well.

The interviews concluded on Monday and Saul and Jonathan reviewed their notes for each candidate. Interestingly, they both had eliminated the same six students at the very beginning without any real argument. That left fourteen, with only eight eligible to go to Israel. Saul and Jonathan both agreed to go home and think about each of the fourteen remaining, order them from one to fourteen, and return in the morning and make the selections.

On Tuesday morning, Jonathan brought his list to Saul, numbered and ordered. Saul had done the same. The first five names were identical, which left only three positions. Jonathan suggested that they add the numbers they each had selected and chose the top three. Saul agreed and the selections were done. Jonathan and Saul reviewed the list. First was Judah, a sophomore, locally from New York. He was rather large and rotund and very jovial with thick black hair. He was also a Masorti Jew and had been the first choice of both Jonathan and Saul. Their second choice was Emma, a junior from upstate New York. Her long red hair and piercing green eyes appealed to Jonathan, while her liberal views regarding Judaism interested Saul. Saul's only concern was her size—she was tiny, only about 54 inches, and very thin. He was concerned about the rigors of a daily dig but she assured him that would not be a problem. Besides, she had a 4.0 average and was very knowledgeable about Christian history.

The third student chosen was Simon, another junior and another Masorti Jew. However, Jonathan noted he did not wear a kippah and, when questioned, Simon responded that he only did so during Jewish celebrations or synagogue. The fourth and fifth students that both Saul and Jonathan agreed on were Joseph, a junior and Orthodox Jew, and Rachel. Rachel was a sophomore and was shy but obviously very smart about Jewish history. She impressed Jonathan and Saul with her calmness in the interview process and her detailed responses to the questions. The sixth student selected was Joshua. He had been sixth on Saul's list and ninth on Jonathan's list. Jonathan had not been that impressed with Joshua. He was an Orthodox Jew whose last name was "Cohen." He spent a great deal of time emphasizing that he was a direct descendant from Aaron, Moses' brother. However, he also was large for a Jew at six feet and looked to be very strong and would be valuable in Israel. He had grown up in Philadelphia. The next selection was Sarah, a "reformed" Jew who was a junior. She had dark brown hair and very large breasts that Jonathan had to keep reminding himself not to stare at when talking with her. She was dressed somewhat provocatively for an interview with a short skirt, heels and a shirt that accented her physical features. When

Jonathan commented about the physical features to Saul, he acted as if he had not noticed and instead focused on her knowledge of ancient Jewish history, her major.

The final selection was unusual for both Jonathan and Saul. He was a sophomore, but he was a "Christian Jew." Michael was from Boston and about one year before entering the university had converted to Christianity. Jonathan had him last on his list and Saul listed him as eight. Saul argued that Michael's knowledge of Christianity combined with his Jewish heritage would be an asset. Jonathan agreed and Michael, a Christian Jew, became the final selection.

Saul and Jonathan looked at the list: five men, three women. They felt that they had a strong group that would work as a team. Saul took the list to his secretary and advised her to send all the twelve not selected a letter of regret, but to indicate that they were each alternates. The secretary was to send to these eight, Judah, Emma, Simon, Joseph, Rachel, Joshua, Sarah, and Michael letters of acceptance and details regarding the trip to Israel. The date of departure was set for the 8th of August. Within the letter contained details of what to bring, money needed, travel dates, times, and places that the group would be staying. Each of the eight had five days from the date of the letter to accept the invitation or decline. If no acceptance was received within five days, this would be viewed as a decline and an alternate would be selected. It was May and in just three months, Jonathan and Saul, along with the eight students, would be on their way to Israel to begin their archeological digs and to study ancient Jewish history up close and personal.

Saul had a lot of work to do and planned to go to Israel in July to have everything ready for the students when they arrived. Between the interviews, Jonathan had been working on John.

CHAPTER 10

Jonathan found the pace difficult. He would do an interview, return to his office and continue his review of John, then rush back to another interview. He felt that this was somewhat disjointed as he did not have the consecutive time he had spent on the other four books.

Just as he had done with the previous books, Jonathan tried to find out something about the author. This was difficult as the author was not stated except in the title. After some research, he learned that the author identified himself later as the "beloved disciple," referencing John. From Matthew, Mark and Luke, Jonathan learned that John was the younger brother of another disciple called "James." His father was Zebedee and his mother was Salome, reportedly the younger sister of Mary, the Mother of Jesus. This would have made John the cousin of Jesus. He was a fisherman by trade and, along with his brother, was a follower of John the Baptist. According to the other writers, John witnessed the scene in which this man Jesus reportedly appeared with Moses and the prophet Elijah. He also witnessed Jesus' arrest in Gethsemane. Jonathan found that John was frequently linked to Peter, another disciple. According to his research, John was born shortly after Jesus in 6 BC. Most interesting to Jonathan is that John lived around one hundred years, which was unheard of during that period of time. During that period, he taught a man named Polycarp, who eventually wrote some of the sayings of John, and was head of the Church that John reportedly created. For the most part, Jonathan could find nothing about John outside of the Christian Bible. He did find a reference to John the Apostle surviving being boiled in oil in the second century Christian writer Tertullian, who references this event in his book *The Prescription Against Heretics*. Jonathan concluded from the references that John was a disciple of the man Jesus and must have witnessed the events he had written. This would make John and Matthew the only eyewitnesses to the events in the life of Jesus.

As Jonathan opened the Vulgate and began to read the words of John, he was fascinated that the opening passages were very different from the other three writers. In these opening words, the author declares the man Jesus to be the *Logos* or the External Word of God and takes precedence over all other messengers including the prophets, angels, or any others mentioned before. Jonathan recognized this concept from Greek philosophy, meaning the principles of cosmic reasoning. This was similar to the Hebrew philosophy regarding Wisdom, God's companion and intimate helper in creation. Jonathan recalled from his studies in graduate school that a Hellenistic Jewish philosopher called Philo had merged these Greek and Jewish philosophies. Jonathan noted that Philo believed that literal interpretations of the Torah would stifle mankind's view and perception of a God too complex to be understood in literal human terms. In these first lines written, Jonathan realized that John was assigning those characteristics to the man Jesus and indicating that he was the incarnate of the "Word."

"This is pretty incredible," Jonathan thought.

As he continued to read, Jonathan noted a pattern developing fairly quickly. This author John had placed a tremendous emphasis on the divinity of the man Jesus. There is no record of the birth of Jesus as is in the other authors' stories, and it seems to jump right into the role of the man called John. Jonathan notes that this author does not refer to this John as "the Baptist" and established through the man's own words that he is not the Christ. Jonathan noted that there were no stories of exorcisms as are in the previous three books, although he also recorded "miracles." He also noted that John provided much more historical documentation that could be validated by secular historians in regards to events. Jonathan found that, based on John's description, the teaching of Jesus lasted between two and three years. Jonathan found that John makes reference to at least three "Passover" meals within the text. The first is at the beginning of Jesus' teachings when John stated that Jesus was at the Passover in Jerusalem. The second was in Galilee and the final Passover was at the death of Jesus. This would account for three years in which the previous books of Matthew, Mark, and Luke have no such reference points.

Jonathan is fascinated by the prose used by John and the style of writing. Although he is frequently interrupted to conduct interviews, Jonathan finds that he does not lose interest and finds the author John to tell a fascinating story that is completely different from the previous three writers. Even with the interruptions, Jonathan made numerous notes and comments to check on the references. He realized quickly that, as an eye witness and with the attention to details of time, John provided a much more accurate historical account of the man Jesus than the other three writers.

Jonathan finally concluded his reading of John's "Gospel" with only two interviews left. While Saul sorted through the copious notes from the interview that Jonathan provided on each applicant, Jonathan reviewed his notes on John and did some cross checking with the other three writers.

Jonathan was most interested in the fact that this author John did not really address that Jesus performed miracles. John actually referred to them as signs and recorded only seven. Jonathan found each (1) turning water into wine, (2) healing the rich woman's son, (3) healing the man at Bethesda, (4) feeding the 5,000, (5) walking on water, (6) healing the blind man, and (7) raising Lazarus from the dead. Jonathan also noted that John describes in much greater detail the resurrection of the man Jesus from the dead. Also, Jonathan found in his notes that Jesus referred to himself as the Messiah, or the Christ in statements that begin with the phrase "I am." As early as the sixth chapter, John indicated that Jesus said "I am the bread of life." Just two chapters later, Jesus was quoted as stating "I am the Light of the World," and then "Before Abraham was, I AM." Jonathan concluded that this was definitely an admission by the man Jesus that he was God. Recalling Moses at the burning bush when asking which god is sending him, the bush replies אהיה, which means "I am that I am." Jonathan suddenly realized that this is the Hebrew *hayah* or Yahweh, the name for God.

"There is no question that the man Jesus is claiming to be God, just from this passage alone," Jonathan murmured.

The other quotes attributed to Jesus included "I am the Good Shepherd," "I am the Resurrection and the Life," "I am the Way, the Truth, and the Life," and finally, "I am the True Vine." Jonathan was clear that John was trying to establish the divinity of this man Jesus with Jesus' own words.

Most interesting for Jonathan was the discussion of the Passover meal that Jesus was reported to have made with his followers just before his death. Jonathan recalled that Mark had indicated that Jesus, just before his death, took the Passover meal with his followers. Mark then stated that Joseph of Arimathea bought a shroud for Jesus on Good Friday. Jonathan knew as a student of ancient Hebrew that would have been impossible on a festival day. Also, Jonathan knew that, in the Jewish calendar, each day runs from sunset to sunset. Therefore, the last meal that Jesus took with his followers would have been on Thursday evening and Jesus's execution on Friday afternoon. This would mean that, in accordance with the Jewish calendar, the events technically occurred on the same day. The writer John stated this day was the 14th of Nisan in the Jewish calendar, that day in the afternoon of which the Passover victims were sacrificed in the Temple. Jonathan knew that this was called the *Day of Preparation.* Jonathan quickly concluded based on John's dates that the Passover meal itself would have been eaten on the Friday evening, which would have been a Sabbath. Jonathan was very familiar with the Jewish rites of Passover and the laws of ancient Hebrew. Matthew, Mark, and Luke all asserted that the last meal of Jesus, the trial, and the execution occurred with some symbolic representation of the Passover lamb. In ancient Hebrew, a formal trial before the Sandhedrin as described by Matthew and Mark would have been on a festival day and historically impossible.

"So Jesus's execution could not be as accounted for by these other three," Jonathan decided.

He then began another search through a stack of books, looking for a reference to the date of the execution of Jesus. Jonathan was sure he had seen it with the stack of books about John. Finally he located the book entitled *The Mystery of the Last Supper: Reconstructing the Final Days of Jesus*, by

Humphreys Collins. This was a relatively new book that Jonathan had found just recently in the library. He quickly thumbed through the pages and found the evidence. John indicated an informal investigation by Caiphas and Annas without any witnesses. Historically, this is possible in an emergency on the day before a festival. This would have indicated that Jesus was in fact executed on the Day of Preparation for the Passover. Jonathan looked for the astronomical reconstruction of the Jewish Lunar calendar and found that the only year during the governorship of Pilate when the 15th Nisan is calculated as falling on a Wednesday/Thursday was 27 AD. However, Jonathan found that the 14th of Nisan described by John fell on a Thursday/Friday in both 30 AD and 33 AD. Jonathan concluded with some excitement that John basically indicates that the other three writers are inaccurate or concocted their stories and, most importantly, Jesus may have been sent to Herod and held for three years before returning.

Jonathan looked at the notes he had made regarding Jesus driving the money changers from the temple. Matthew, Mark, and Luke clearly indicate that this occurred just prior to the arrest of Jesus. However, John indicated that this took place at the beginning of Jesus's teachings. Jonathan noted that the other three writer's claimed that the temple authorities did not arrest Jesus because of the popularity of John the Baptist. Jonathan shook his head at this inconsistency. According to their own writings, John the Baptist would have already been dead by the time Jesus was executed. John clearly is the more accurate historian.

Jonathan had multiple other notes but knew that the bottom line was that John, from a historical and chronological aspect, presented a more accurate account of this man Jesus. As Luke and Mark relied on others' "eyewitness" accounts, their errors could be overlooked, but Matthew was an eyewitness and part of the inner circle. There is no explanation for his lack of attention to detail.

"Very sloppy," Jonathan thought.

He also had another thought formulating, but glanced at his watch and knew he had to join Saul for the final interview. He quickly made some notes on a pad and took it with him to discuss with Saul afterwards.

With the interview concluded, John and Saul were going to begin narrowing down the group of twenty to eight. Jonathan asked Saul to wait on the selection as he was anxious to discuss some thoughts with him. Saul sat down behind his desk with Jonathan across from him. Jonathan adjusted his kippah, took off his glasses and cleaned them, placed them back on his face while Saul waited patiently.

Jonathan then began to explain that he found the four books interesting, but most interesting was the last book, "The Gospel of John." Jonathan outlined for Saul the arguments that John made for the divinity of the man Jesus. Saul admonished Jonathan that he had read the text and was aware that all four writers made the same argument.

"Then the man Jesus would have to be perfect?" Jonathan asserted.

"Yes," Saul replied, frustrated that is what the Christians believe, that he was perfect. "What is your point?"

Jonathan began to explain to Saul that, with the accounts of the four writers of the man Jesus, he found several "human" characteristics that would indicate someone less than perfect. Saul was intrigued and urged Jonathan to continue. Jonathan explained that Jesus was deceptive and in some cases an argument could be made that he actually lied about being the Messiah or the Christ.

"He even kept his followers in the dark and was deceptive with them," Jonathan argued.

Next, Jonathan asserted that this "perfect" man demonstrated anger.

"Anger?" Saul asked.

Jonathan relayed the events in the temple with the money changers. He explained how there are different accounts, but basically the concept is the same. The man Jesus found a weapon and drove these people from the temple, shouting and threatening them.

"A 'perfect' man who lies and threatens others," Jonathan said sarcastically, "I don't think so."

Saul thought Jonathan's conclusion to be somewhat elementary, but good arguments against this Jesus being the Messiah or the Christ. Jonathan further explained that there is good reason to believe based on John that Jesus and John the Baptist were the same man, or at least could have been. In addition, with the historical dating that John provided in his story, it is also plausible that Jesus was sent to Tiberius to see Herod and remained there for a period of three years before being returned to Jerusalem for execution. Jonathan acknowledged that it was a stretch, but that, with the discrepancies and now armed with the historical dating provided by the fourth author, there was a good chance that their thesis would be validated. Jonathan was now even more sure that Jesus was not the Messiah or the Christ and that the four books he had read supported that this was most likely an incredible tale based on the man John the Baptist in order to meet the criteria of the Hebrew Prophets for a Messiah.

"These writers just took the teachings of John the Baptist and expanded them to meet the criteria of the prophets for a Messiah," Jonathan said with passion.

Saul looked at Jonathan and a large smile came to his face. He had been waiting for the young assistant professor to show the same passion he felt in finally putting an end to this myth of Jesus. Saul stood up from behind his desk and walked over to Jonathan. Jonathan stood up as Saul approached. Jonathan was unsure of what Saul was going to do—he saw the large smile but was confused. Saul took hold of Jonathan and placed him in a big bear hug and whispered in his ear.

"This is why I wanted you to read and study these books, so you could see that their own words do not support this man Jesus as the Messiah."

As Saul released Jonathan he exclaimed, "I am so happy."

The rest of that day Saul and Jonathan selected the eight students that would be fortunate enough to accompany them to Israel. Saul proceeded to have the secretary send out letters of selection/rejection. Jonathan returned to his office. He had left the Vulgate opened to the last chapter of John. Jonathan read the last sentences again:

Sunt autem et alia multa quae fecit Iesus quae si scribantur per singula nec ipsum arbitror mundum capere eos qui scribendi sunt libros amen

But there are also many other things which Jesus did which, if they were written every one, the world itself, I think, would not be able to contain the books that should be written.

Jonathan closed the Vulgate, stacked the books neatly, placed his notes inside a folder marked "The Book of John," and started to leave his office. He wondered, if this man Jesus had been the Christ, the Messiah, why would he come in such a harsh period of history without the modern method of communication today? He recalled with a chuckle the words from the rock opera *Jesus Christ Superstar*. Jonathan had been dragged to the performance while in graduate school by a friend who thought it would "convert" him. Jonathan began to sing to himself the words as he remembered the lines: "If you'd come today you could have reached a whole nation. Israel in 4 BC had no mass communication." He began humming the song as he flipped out the light and started for home.

Outside in the parking lot, he ran into Saul getting into his car.

"A good day," Jonathan said,

"A good day, indeed," was Saul's reply as he got into his car.

Jonathan sighed heavily, realizing that the real work would begin when they finally arrived in Israel. For now, Jonathan decided he would enjoy the fact that this man Jesus was not what the Christians believe him to be and that the writers of the four books known as Gospels knew this all along. Jonathan was convinced that the archeological proof would be found in Israel and was anxious to get started.

CHAPTER 11

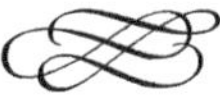

"I don't have any request," Mr. Goldman said again, annoyed that it seemed that the two men were not paying attention.

"Mr. Weitzman, did you hear me?" Mr. Goldman repeated.

Mr. Goldman put out the cigarillo he was smoking and immediately took another one from the pack sitting on his desk and searched for the lighter. He shuffled the papers on his desk, picking up some here and there. Jonathan watched, seemingly dazed as Mr. Goldman searched for the lighter as if he were searching for a gold nugget and finally found it. He quickly lit the cigarillo, inhaled slowly and forced the smoke from his nose.

"As you can see, I am very busy," Mr. Goldman stated to Jonathan and Saul, "and I have no request."

Jonathan and Saul waited for the lecture and were not disappointed. Mr. Goldman informed them that the artifacts belonged to the country of Israel. He again argued that it was criminal that any of these relics were allowed to be taken out of the country. He complained about how busy his department was and that there were always multiple digs for artifacts, especially during this time of year. Mr. Goldman assured Jonathan and Saul that no such request to continue the dig at Tiberia had ever crossed his desk. Finally he came to a stop.

"The fact that you two are still here is criminal in itself," Mr. Goldman chided both Jonathan and Saul, "you've found nothing except some interesting stones and metals and most of your help has left you."

The words stung Jonathan's ears as Jonathan thought back to the day they arrived in Israel, three years ago. The group of ten, Jonathan, Saul and the eight students, had arrived together at the Ben Gurion Airport in Tel Aviv with such idealism and promise. Saul had made arrangements for the group to be housed on a Kibbutz. Not just any Kibbutz, but the Degaina Bet, which was the first Kibbutz founded in 1909 by immigrants from the Second Aliyah. On the flight over, Jonathan and Saul had taught their eight assistants that the Aliyah referred to the immigration of Jews into the country of Israel, at the time Palestine. The Second Aliyah took place between 1904 and 1914 with approximately 40,000 Jews immigrating into Ottoman Palestine. Jonathan had pointed out that the majority of these Jews were from the Russian Empire and the stimulus was the growing anti-Semitism. Saul told the students that the Second Aliyah were primarily idealists who sought to create a communal agricultural settlement system in Palestine. The commune was called Kibbutz. Jonathan also added that the Second Aliyah is largely credited with the revival of the Hebrew language and the establishment of the Hebrew language for Jews in Israel. Jonathan had a copy of the first modern Hebrew dictionary that was created during the Second Aliyah. Saul felt, and Jonathan agreed, that for students from the United States to experience a Kibbutz while doing the archeological digs at Tiberia would just add to the learning experiences for them.

Jonathan, from living in Israel, knew the story of the Degaina Bet Kibbutz well. The Degaina Bet was abandoned in 1920, but the settlement was re-established in 1936. Jonathan had told the students that the Degaina Bet contained a dairy farm, almond orchards, banana, date, and avocado plantations. Most importantly, another communal project is "kibbutz cottages", which are an important tourist accommodation and where the group would be staying. The Degaina Bet Country Lodge would be the home for the professors and the students during their stay in Israel. As the Degaina Bet is located on the southern shores of the Sea of Galilee, it is in close proximity to the excavation site at Tiberias.

After arrival at the airport, the group had taken the train to Haifa and then boarded a bus to Tiberias. From Tiberias, another bus was used to get to the Degaina Bet Kibbutz cottages. The students had questioned both Jonathan and Saul as to why they were not staying at the Aviv Hotel in modern Tiberias. Saul had explained that it was the cost, and he wanted the students to have the experience of the kibbutz. The students were satisfied with this explanation and seemed excited as they boarded the bus for Degaina Bet.

Jonathan recalled how awkward the living arrangements that Saul had made were on their first arrival. The cottages were set up for double occupancy and Saul had basically put Rachel in a room with Joshua. Rachel, being shy, was mortified, and Joshua thought it was a great plan. Saul did not see the issue, but Jonathan arranged for a roll-away-bed and housed Rachel with Sarah and Emma. Another roll-away was placed in the room Joseph and Simon occupied and this is where Joshua was assigned to sleep. Jonathan recalled that no one was happy with the situation except for Judah and

Michael, who continued to have just two to a room. Jonathan and Saul roomed together. The rooms were not bad; each was equipped with a kitchenette, refrigerator, air conditioner, and TV. In addition, there was limited internet access. After being settled, a meeting had been arranged by Saul in the main forum of the lodge to make arrangements for getting started the next day. Saul also announced that all of the equipment had arrived and been unloaded at the site of Tiberias.

"Do you have something for me," Mr. Goldman inquired of Jonathan and Saul as he held out his hand.

Jonathan looked at Saul, a bit embarrassed that he was caught daydreaming. Saul took an envelope from his pocket and handed it to Mr. Goldman. Jonathan knew it contained two thousand Isareli shekel, which was about five-hundred forty US dollars.

"Perhaps this could pay a staff member to find our request," Saul directed at Mr. Goldman as he handed him the envelope.

Mr. Goldman reached out with his fat fingers and took the envelope. He never looked inside, but instead opened a side drawer of his desk and stuck the envelope inside. He wiped his fingers on his jacket as if to wipe the unspoken bribe and cleanse his hands from it.

"I'm sure we will find the request, come back tomorrow," Mr. Goldman responded.

Jonathan watched in disgust as ashes fell from the end of Mr. Goldman's cigarillo onto the papers on the desk. With one hand, Mr. Goldman brushed the ashes away while with the other hand his fingers picked at a sore on his scalp. Mr. Goldman pushed his glass from the tip of his nose, back on his face, and stood up, putting out the cigarillo in the ashtray while fumbling in his pocket for another. He escorted Jonathan and Saul to the door and repeated his assurances that everything would be ready tomorrow. For three years, Jonathan and Saul had endured the same process in order to get the necessary permits to continue their digs.

As Saul opened the door to the Antiquities Commission to the outside street of Jerusalem, the hot air hit him and Jonathan in the face and the beads of sweat immediately began to form. The trips to the Antiquities Commission had been rare until recently. In the past six months, Jonathan and Saul had located what appeared to be a dwelling about twelve meters beneath the surface. They had found a few coins, a piece of a broken sword, a couple of brass chains used for oil lamps, but nothing of any significance. It was somewhat discouraging as the excavations of the Hebrew University of Jerusalem under the direction of Dr. Katia Cytryn-Silverman were nearby and this group had made several discoveries. When they had first arrived in Tiberias, Saul, Jonathan, and their students were not allowed to dig for almost two weeks. Saul was required to negotiate with the Hebrew University of Jerusalem because of Dr. Cytryn-Silverman's work. The Hebrew University finally agreed with Saul when he assured them that his digs would be just outside the borders of the ancient city, as Dr. Cytryn-Silverman's excavations focused at the center of the ancient city. Dr. Cytryn-Silverman's excavations had produced a mosaic floor, a large water cistern, Arabic inscriptions, oil lamps, figurines, brass chains, and hundreds of coins. In addition, this group from the Hebrew University was well-funded, the students and participants paid for the privilege to work at the sites, and they had ten times the number of workers. This group had uncovered a bath house and the foundations for a temple. Saul and Jonathan had just watched as their excavation produced little until six months ago. Saul had dated the facade of the building to about 25 C.E., which, if accurate and could be proven, would be a significant find.

"Do you want to get something to eat before we go to the hotel?" Saul asked Jonathan.

Each trip to Jerusalem involved an overnight stay while waiting for the "request" to be found and approved. It made no sense to go back to the excavation site and return the next day. Jonathan and Saul generally stayed at the Alcazar Hotel. It was only fifteen minutes from the Damascus Gate and a ten minute walk from the old city where the Antiquities Commission was located. It was located in the Arab section of town and a bit run down, but very clean and the staff was exceptional. In addition, the price was right at less than a hundred US dollars a night. Jonathan and Saul had left their vehicle at the hotel and walked to the Antiquities Commission. Money had become an issue this past year when the contribution from the Jewish Defense League had been dramatically reduced. After two years of spending millions and finding nothing, the anonymous donor from the Jewish Defense League had sent Shelley to find Jonathan and Saul in Tiberias. The message from Shelley was simple: funding was to be reduced to bare essentials until something of significance was found and Jonathan and Saul would only be funded for one more year if nothing was found. Shelley had pointed to the Land Rover Saul had purchased on arrival as an example of how the anonymous donor felt his money was being wasted. Saul had argued that a vehicle was needed, but Shelley really was not interested in an argument or an expense account. The message from the anonymous donor was not a discussion; it was the way it would be. Shelley delivered the message and left the same day without displaying any remorse for delivering bad news or accepting Saul's offer to tour the excavation site.

"Jonathan," Saul shouted, "do you want to get something to eat?"

Jonathan nodded in the affirmative and stepped out onto the streets in the heat and walked quietly beside Saul. So much had transpired in such a short time. Jonathan, Saul and the eight students had started with such idealism and enthusiasm. Now only one student remained, Michael, the "Christian Jew." One by one the students left, either quitting due to the tediousness of the work or graduating and moving on. Emma was the first to leave, which was no surprise. Saul had been concerned about her size and the ability to endure the early days. The group generally started around five in the morning and quit around one o'clock in the afternoon. Judah and Rachel began having a love affair and eventually married in Jerusalem and returned to the states. This was just in the first nine months. After the first year Joseph applied and was accepted at the Hebrew University of Jerusalem. Occasionally Saul and Jonathan would see him at the other excavation site. Within six months, Joshua had followed Joseph and transferred to the Hebrew University of Jerusalem. However, neither Saul nor Jonathan had seen Joshua since he left. Simon had stayed through his junior and senior year. However, he learned that he was not going to have enough credits to graduate and left Israel to return home at the end of the second year. He was very upset and promised Saul and Jonathan he would return when he graduated, but thus far he had not come back to their knowledge. Sarah was sent home by Saul just at the end of the first year. She would go to the excavation site frequently wearing extremely short shots and skin-tight tee shirts that showed off her ample breasts. Sarah always was a distraction and frequently had a large following of other students from around Tiberias gathering to talk or to watch her. Saul commented that she was like a female dog in heat and every "male dog within smelling radius" was hoping to mate with her. Jonathan was not sure if Saul realized how prophetic his words actually were. With Emma and Rachel both gone, there was always a steady flow of male visitors to

Sarah's room at the cottages. Saul had finally had enough when he went to her room when she was late for the bus to the excavation site and knocked until she finally opened the door. She was wearing just a robe, which was not a problem, but Saul could see the two men in her bed through the opening in the door. Jonathan recalled that Saul sent her home the next day without much of an explanation other than it was just not working it out. Sarah did not seem at all upset. This left only Michael, the Christian Jew. Michael had somehow managed to graduate and stay in Israel with Jonathan and Saul. Saul was keenly aware that Michael's desire to stay had ulterior motives. Every break, every winter, anytime there was "down" time, Michael was off touring Israel and the "Holy Lands," as he called them. Michael had stayed home for the last semester in order to graduate, but as soon as graduation was over, he was back at Tiberias. He now helped with the excavation about two or three days a week, which did provide some assistance. Jonathan had listened politely to Michael's naiveté in relating the stories of the Christian Bible. Jonathan was not the type of person to destroy Michael's passion, but it sometimes took a great deal of restraint as things Michael would quote were obviously in error. Jonathan almost bit through his lips during one discussion when Michael indicated there were no contradictions in the Christian Bible. In addition to visiting different historical sites, Michael frequently tried to evangelize in Jerusalem. On two occasions, Saul was required to bail Michael out of a Jerusalem jail. Michael regarded the experiences as the same as what the early Christian Jew Paul experienced and laughed it off. However, after the second time, Saul strongly advised Michael to be more careful that he and Jonathan may not always be around or have the resources to help him. This became even more true when Shelley had informed Jonathan and Saul that their funding was reduced. When Saul broke the news to Michael he again urged Michael to avoid jail at all costs. Since that time, Michael had toned down the evangelizing and remained a little closed to the Degania Bet cottages. He found that there were plenty of Jews to evangelize there, which markedly reduced risks.

Jonathan smiled through dinner as he recalled the adventures with the students the past three years. He and Saul now laughed at the mis-steps and miscues and tried to focus on the positives. As dinner finished, Jonathan asked Saul if he was sure that they were close to a major discovery. Saul explained to Jonathan that from his research he was fairly certain that the excavation site was underneath the site of Herod's palace. Saul supported this by some of the artifacts found, some of the iron rings and chains. It was known that Herod kept stables under his palace in addition to his dungeon. Saul explained that the dating of the coins and the location of the façade at that depth meant that it was almost certainly from the same era. Jonathan questioned Saul on his hypothesis.

"I think it is either the entrance to the stables or the dungeon," Saul replied with confidence.

"What would be the significance of this find?" Jonathan asked.

"That the Hebrew University of Jerusalem is digging in the wrong place," Saul replied with a chuckle.

Jonathan laughed also and agreed with Saul that would be significant. But Jonathan wanted to know how this would help their hypothesis regarding the man Jesus. Saul explained to Jonathan that if they could find the dungeon and then evidence of the same, that would be enough. Jonathan asked what it would mean if they found the stables.

"That the dungeon is nearby," Saul responded.

Jonathan felt somewhat deflated as that left a lot to be desired in terms of providing some certainty. However, the first thing was to get the approval to continue the dig from Mr. Goldman in the morning.

Jonathan and Saul arrived back at the hotel. The next day, they drove to the Antiquities Commission and amazingly Mr. Goldman had their request to continue the excavation approved. He explained how he had found it just after Jonathan and Saul left and had tried to catch them so they would not have to return. Saul and Jonathan both knew these were just lies. With their renewed approval to continue the excavation, Saul and Jonathan hurried to the Land Rover to make the one hundred seventy five mile trip back to Tiberias. Depending on traffic they should be back in about three and a half hours.

As the Land Rover sputtered and headed out for the highway with Saul driving, Jonathan felt some hope that they may find something soon. Saul seemed certain. Jonathan wished he shared Saul's conviction, but to him, it just looked like another wall, just like all the other walls that had been uncovered at various excavation sites all over the city of Tiberias. However, it would be grand if what Saul had said was true.

Jonathan smiled and thought, "maybe they are digging in the wrong place, just like 'Raiders of the Lost Ark.'" Jonathan began humming the theme to that Steven Spielberg classic film "da ta da da, ta da," as the Land Rover bounced down the road taking them back to Tiberias.

CHAPTER 12

Jonathan and Saul arrived back at Degaina Bet Kibbutz. As the Land Rover bounced along the dirt road toward their cottage, Michael came running out of his cottage to greet them. He stood on the edge of the road as the Land Rover rolled to a stop. He was on Jonathan's side of the vehicle.

"Professor Weitzman," Michael exclaimed, "you should see it, you should see it now."

Jonathan could see that Michael was very excited but was unsure of the cause of all the excitement. Saul was unimpressed as he had become immune to Michael's excitable state.

"Oh God," Saul moaned to no one in particular, "what new treasure has he seen now?"

Jonathan laughed as he knew Saul was right. Being a "born again" Christian and a Jew, Michael had become excited at every new discovery. As Michael had toured the "Holy Lands," he had been excited about being at the Sea of

Galilee. Next, it was Cana, then the pools at Bathsheba, and Jonathan did not want to think anything about the week that Michael went to Jerusalem and retraced the steps of Jesus through the city.

"Yes, Michael was an excitable man," Jonathan thought to himself.

As Saul and Jonathan exited the Land Rover, Michael rushed up to both of them. Saul held his hand up and shook his head to dismiss Michael. This had generally worked and Michael would turn his attention to Jonathan. But, this time, Michael was emphatic that he needed to talk to both of them.

"Professor Harkman, Professor Weitzman, you have to listen to me now, it is about the dig, I have found something I think is important," Michael rushed the words out as Saul was walking away.

Saul stopped and slowly walked back to where Michael was standing with Jonathan. He folded his arms over his chest and stared at Michael. A small smile ran across Jonathan lips as he could see the aggravation building in Saul.

Saul pulled at his beard, which was now very gray, and squinted through his eyes, "well!" he shouted at Michael.

Michael jumped at first and then began to speak rapidly about digging yesterday, and hauling out buckets of dirt, and how hot it was, and that the students from the other dig came over. His rapid speech and excited manner made most of what he was saying sound like gibberish to both Saul and Jonathan. Jonathan could see the color of red forming in Saul's face as his frustration was reaching a level that his patience would not be able to contain. Jonathan held up his hand to stop Michael and patted Saul on the shoulder.

"Let's get out of the sun," Jonathan offered to Michael and Saul, "and you can tell us your story inside."

Michael sighed, frustrated to have to wait longer to tell his big news. Saul sighed in relief that he now had a reprieve from Michael's incessant jabbering without a purpose. Saul had not wanted to select this "Christian Jew" for this project three years ago, but Jonathan had convinced him that Michael would be an asset. He had been a strong and consistent worker, when he worked. Most importantly, Saul did give Michael credit for still being around after three years, especially since all the other students had departed or been asked to leave. As the three walked toward the cottage Jonathan and Saul had lived in for three years, Saul became more relaxed. He had lived through many of these periods of excitement before with Michael. Saul knew that once Michael got his story out, then his excitement would be over and things would return to normal.

The three entered Saul and Jonathan's cottage. As always, the cottage looked like the inside of a neglected library that had been used as an equipment storage facility. The small living room was cluttered with books stacked as high as they could be without toppling over and papers were scattered in multiple directions. The mounds of books, papers and pamphlets stretched into every room, including the bathroom. Scattered among the make-shift library were tools for digging. There were shovels, buckets, sifters, small trowels, large trowels, rakes, gloves, and other assorted digging tools, large and small. On top of all the furniture was a thin layer of fine dirt. In the hallway was a closet that was filled with dirty clothes to the point that the doors would not shut. Jonathan pointed to a couch covered in papers and told Michael to sit down. He and Saul went to their respective bedrooms to deposit their briefcases and make a quick check for messages. Saul's bedroom had a small trail with walls of books on either side to the bed; another trail off to the left led to a small desk with a computer sitting on top of several books. Jonathan's room was not much better, but the books were stacked against a wall and there was more visible floor. The bedroom closet had maybe one or two pairs of trousers hanging, but the remainder of the clothes were in scattered piles on the floor of the closet. The clothes were somewhat folded, but in neater piles than in Saul's closet. In the closet on the shelf were three kippahs in addition to the one still on Jonathan's head. Jonathan checked his email and he could hear Saul urinating in the bathroom between their two bedrooms. There were no messages and Jonathan glanced out the window. He noticed that the sun was setting and the day was almost over. As it was Thursday, the Shabbat would not start until tomorrow. Jonathan continued to practice his Hebrew faith every weekend, much to the displeasure of Saul. However, no one worked anywhere during the Shabbat, so Saul used that time to write and tend to the business of being a Professor at a University. Although Jewish, Saul did not practice his Jewish faith, at least not with the same consistency as Jonathan.

Jonathan recalled that Michael was waiting and shouted at Saul that he would meet him in the living room. Jonathan entered the living room and asked Michael if he wanted something to drink. Jonathan noticed that Michael was sitting on the edge of the couch, hands clasped together and slightly rocking back and forth. Jonathan had not seen Michael this excited since Michael had visited the Mount of Olives. Saul entered the room just as Jonathan brought in three bottles of water. Saul sat down in the recliner and Jonathan pulled a chair from the kitchen. Michael now had both professors undivided attention.

"Okay, Michael," Jonathan started, "tell us what you have found, but try to speak slowly."

Michael drew a deep breath and began. He explained how he had nothing to do yesterday after Jonathan and Saul left for Jerusalem so he decided to work at the excavation site. Michael stated that working alone he could sort through his thoughts and that he found the digging to be peaceful, sort of like yoga.

"Back to the point, Michael," Saul admonished.

Again Michael sighed. Michael related how he was digging around the wall that Saul had found earlier when he struck something metal.

Saul now leaned forward in the recliner. Jonathan remained unmoved; sitting in the chair, he leaned back, sipping his water.

Michael continued to reveal that he carefully removed the dirt from around the metal object and found it to be a large bar that was vertical. He stated that he continued to dig horizontally from that bar and, after about 15 centimeters, he struck another bar.

Now Jonathan sat down his water and leaned forward. He adjusted his kippah, removed his glasses and cleaned the lens and placed them back on his face. He glanced at Saul, who was moving his lips slowly, the lower lip across the upper lip as if tasting something.

"What did you find?" Saul exclaimed as Michael just paused.

"Another bar," Michael blurted out excitedly.

Michael then described how he continued to dig horizontally from the second bar and found a connecting wall.

"How much farther down?" Saul questioned in a demanding tone.

Again, Jonathan adjusted his kippah, removed his glasses and cleaned them, but this time just held them for a moment.

"No more than a centimeter or two deeper," Michael replied, somewhat subdued.

Michael had expected more excitement from the news. He felt that Professor Harkman and Professor Weitzman were not that impressed.

"Perhaps," Michael stated softly, "this is not that big a deal."

Saul rose from his chair and knelt beside Michael and asked him to again explain what he had found and where. Jonathan replaced his glasses and leaned forward to insure that he did not miss a single word. Michael explained about the two bars and the wall.

"How do you know it is a connecting wall?" Saul demanded.

Michael explained that the second wall was at a ninety degree angle from the first wall. Although only one to two centimeters of dirt had been removed from around the bars and the walls, there was no question that these were two walls.

"I believe the bars are part of the dungeon," Michael blurted out.

Saul sat in disbelief. The top part of the wall they had discovered had been excavated about 25 centimeters, but was just a façade of a wall. There had been no back of the wall. The length of the wall was only about two meters. Now, a former student, a "Christian Jew," may have made the most remarkable discovery of all. Suddenly, Saul jumped up.

"We need to go to the site," he said to Jonathan, "Michael, you need to show us now."

Saul was out the door before Jonathan and Michael were completely standing. Michael looked at Jonathan, confused.

"You did good," Jonathan replied and motioned for Michael to leave the cottage. Saul was already in the Land Rover with it started, waiting on Jonathan and Michael. Jonathan shut the door to the cottage and walked quickly to catch up to Michael. Michael climbed into the back seat and Jonathan took his place up front. Saul drove quickly to the dig site without saying a word. Jonathan glanced at the sun, almost gone, and glanced at his watch. He knew it would be dark soon.

Saul slowed the Land Rover as they approached the site outside of the city of their excavation. There was no one to be seen. The students from the Hebrew University of Jerusalem were all gone for the day. There was some activity of residents milling about, but nothing significant. Saul directed Michael to descend the ladder down to the level of their discovery of the façade. There were two tiers and Michael quickly climbed down the first six meters, walked over about a half a meter and descended the remaining six meters to the site of Saul's façade that had been found six months earlier. Jonathan and Saul were closely behind. When all three were at the site of the dig, Saul directed Michael to show them his discovery. Michael led Saul and Jonathan to the area where he had been digging the previous day. Saul knelt down, as did Jonathan, and brushed away some more of the dirt from around the two iron bars. There were only the two centimeters of metal sticking up, but there was no doubt that these were definitely iron bars. Saul traced the edge of the wall to the end and saw the beginning of the second wall at a right angle to the first, just as Michael described it.

"It's a room," Saul exclaimed as he jumped up, "It's a room," he shouted again as he turned toward Jonathan, "this is great news!"

Saul began shouting orders to Jonathan and Michael to get this tool, this bucket, to start digging more here, no wait, over there. Jonathan laughed as Saul now sounded just like Michael did when they first arrived. Saul stopped and realized how he sounded and began laughing too.

"So this is good?" Michael asked.

Saul hugged Michael hard. This was the first time Saul had displayed any sort of emotion to Michael in all the time that he had been with the two professors. Jonathan slapped him on the back and told him that he just made their day.

Saul knelt down again with a small trowel in his hand and began removing dirt horizontally in the opposite direction from the corner of the wall. He quickly found the beginnings of a third bar, then a fourth bar, each bar about 14 – 15 centimeters apart. There was now no question that this was a cell and most likely part of the dungeon underneath Herod's palace. Jonathan and Michael began moving dirt from the second wall as Saul found the beginnings of more bars. The sun was fading fast and the light was at a dusk-like level down in the large excavation site where all three were now digging.

"We need lanterns," Saul finally said when it became too dark to see.

Their group had never been digging after dark and Jonathan reminded Saul that there were no lanterns.

"Where can we get some tonight?" Saul asked as he started for the ladder.

Jonathan and Michael stood up and dropped their digging tools. Jonathan explained to Saul that there was not anywhere to purchase lanterns now. Saul was insistent and finally Michael spoke up.

"If we dig at night,won't that raise suspicions?" Michael asked.

Jonathan agreed with Michael and convinced Saul to wait until morning. The three exited the excavation site, climbed into the Land Rover and headed back to their cottages for the night. No one said a word. Jonathan glanced at Saul and could see the gears turning in his head. Saul was deep in thought, planning, forecasting. Jonathan hoped this would not be another disappointment.

Saul did not sleep that night and therefore neither did Jonathan. Jonathan could hear Saul pacing, working on his computer, digging through his text, reviewing and re-reviewing all of his notes. Jonathan was trying very hard not to get caught up in the excitement of their discovery. It was very hard. They had worked so long, and so diligently. They had endured the scorn of the students and faculty of the Hebrew University of Jerusalem and the disappointment of their own university. Just about everyone had lost confidence in their ability to find anything, including their financial backer, the Jewish Defense League. Jonathan was so hopeful that this was what they were looking for and prayed quietly that there was not another disappointment lying beneath the dirt. His prayers were interrupted by a quiet knock on his door from the adjoining bathroom.

"Jonathan, are you awake?"

It was Saul, which was no surprise.

"Yes, come on in," Jonathan replied.

Saul looked weary in the dim glow of a night light that was plugged in beside Jonathan's desk. He looked concerned.

"What is it Saul?"

Saul explained that he was almost certain that this was a very significant finding and was worried about what to do about this news. Jonathan was puzzled and cautioned Saul that nothing had been found except a wall and the beginnings of some iron bars. Saul waved Jonathan off from these comments. He wanted Jonathan to agree to not reveal the findings to anyone, not yet anyway. This was easy for Jonathan as he was not sure there was anything to report at this juncture. This seemed to make Saul feel better and he left the room muttering words that Jonathan could not understand. Forgetting where he was in his prayers, Jonathan said "Amen" and finally dozed for what seemed to be only minutes before Saul was standing beside his bed.

"Get up, the sun is up, we can resume the dig now, get up!" Saul was announcing.

Jonathan rubbed his eyes. He had slept in his clothes so there was no need to change. He took his glasses from the bedside table, cleaned them and put them up. He pulled his boots on over the socks he slept in and grabbed his kippah for his head as he followed Saul into the kitchen. Jonathan glanced at his watch and it was just a little after five o'clock in the morning. In over three years, this was the earliest by at least three hours that Saul had wanted to start digging. At least Saul had made coffee, and he handed Jonathan a cup.

"You awake?" Saul asked.

Jonathan moaned and nodded in the affirmative.

"Let's drink our coffee on the way to the site," Saul offered and started for the door.

Jonathan realized it was going to be a long day and he hoped not a disappointing day. As they arrived at the Land Rover, Jonathan started to ask Saul if he wanted to wake up Michael.

Jonathan chuckled when he saw Michael already sitting in the back of the Land Rover, ready to go.

"Maybe not such a long day after all," Jonathan said to himself as he climbed into the Land Rover for the short trip to the excavation site.

CHAPTER 13

Jonathan, Saul, and Michael quickly descended the two ladders to the site of their find. Everything was just as they left it, tools lying eschewed, buckets half full of dirt, a sifter half filled. No one said a word as each grabbed a small trowel and started working on a different portion of the two walls that were found. Progress was slow, but steady. By mid-morning Saul had unearthed the beginning of three additional bars bringing the total to six. Jonathan and Michael had been disappointed as the second wall appeared to end after about one and half meters. Saul found no additional bars, at least not at the same two centimeter level as the previous six. The work was slow as all three began to dig vertically now around their previous finds. Jonathan and Michael worked at one end of the wall where the two walls connected and Saul worked at the site of the last three bars, moving downward very slowly.

As lunch approached, all three men had dug down about three meters along most of the two walls. Saul stopped the digging to evaluate what they had unearthed to this point. The connecting wall that Michael had found earlier appeared to be a solid wall. Movement horizontally revealed that the wall was broken or just deteriorated as a jagged edge was discovered at the three meter mark, extending the wall further horizontally. The section of the other wall revealed that the bars continued downward. Saul had noted that the bars were very brittle and obviously pitted from centuries of wear. He and Jonathan had removed dirt from about two meters on both sides of the bars. No additional bars had been found yet by Saul and he feared that this might be the only section of the wall remaining. The three talked and the decision was made to dig out two meters from each wall on both sides and then to resume digging vertically. Saul reasoned that this would give room to work around the walls and move dirt upward and out as the downward momentum continued. The digging was made slower by the meticulous attention paid by each man to each bucket of dirt before it was discarded. The bucket would be filled three-quarters full with dirt, then dumped into a sifter and sifted over another large box to make sure no artifacts were contained in the dirt. Then the box was emptied into a bucket and the bucket was emptied at another site. Each find, the right angle of the two walls, the deterioration of the second wall and each bar were tagged and marked. Saul would periodically stop and take digital photographs of the artifacts, the identification tags and the dig site.

As the sun rose, the work was slow. Jonathan was thankful that it was late April and the weather was not too harsh. It was 22 degrees, which was somewhat warm but not too bad for this time of year. Jonathan quickly translated the Celsius to 72 degrees Fahrenheit in his head. The nights were still cool, which was a blessing when trying to sleep. By late afternoon there had been about another meter of progress, but the sifting of buckets of dirt had revealed no artifacts. In addition, Saul had moved horizontally more distance and gone down about three meters without finding any additional bars. It was getting late for the Shabbat and Jonathan kept checking his watch. This was the fourth Friday in April and, according to his reference site, the Shabbat started at 1847 hours tonight; it was now 1610 hours. Jonathan did not want to stop, but it was the Shabbat.

"Saul, we need to stop," Jonathan finally said at 1630 hours.

"What?" Saul responded, "why?"

Jonathan explained that it was the Shabbat and that the Shabbat began at 1847 hours. Saul did not look pleased. Michael had stopped working and was watching the interchange. Jonathan explained to Saul that they had stopped every Friday for the Shabbat and, although Saul did not participate, the digging still stopped.

"But we have not found anything as important," Saul stated argumentatively.

Jonathan did not budge. He felt it was even more important to celebrate the Shabbat given the importance of the findings.

"We should offer prayers," Jonathan countered.

Saul looked at Michael, then at Jonathan. He knew that the site would be unchanged by Sunday morning when they returned. He just did not want to wait to continue the dig. He finally relented, with the agreement that the three of them would take the time to cover what they had done. Saul was afraid that if anyone saw the fruits of their efforts it would either be sabotaged or taken away from them. Michael asked if he could join them and Jonathan agreed. It took about thirty minutes to cover and secure everything to Saul's satisfaction. They quickly loaded into the Land Rover and headed to Jonathan and Saul's cottage.

When they returned to their cottages, Michael quickly went to his to change into what little formal wear he had for the ceremony. Jonathan removed a loaf of challah and a container of chicken soup from the refrigerator. He placed the challah in the oven to warm and the chicken soup on the stove to warm for their Shabbat meal. He then went into his bedroom and to his closet. The only clothes hanging were his dress pants and, after he removed his working clothes, he showered and quickly dressed in this more formal attire. By the time he was finished dressing, the loaf of challah was warm, as was the chicken soup. Jonathan left the chicken soup on the stove and placed the challah on the tables. He found the two candles and candlesticks where they had been left at the last Shabbat and placed them on the table along with the goblet for the wine. Saul joined Jonathan and offered to say the Kiddush. The Kiddush was a blessing recited over a cup of wine expressing the sanctity of the Shabbat and was generally done by the head of a household. As Saul was Jonathan's only family, it seemed appropriate for Saul to recite the blessing. With two minutes to spare, Michael knocked on the door. Jonathan waited until exactly eighteen minutes before sunset and lit the Shabbat candles. After the candles were lit, Saul recited a blessing for the day and the day's findings. As they were not in the synagogue, the three began to sing the L'cha dodi in Hebrew.

Lecho dodi, likras kaloh penei shabbos nekabeloh

Shomor vezochor bedibur echod hishmi'anu El hameyuchod

Hashem echod ush'mo echod leshem ulesif'eres ve-li-sehiloh

Lecho dodi...

Likras shabbos lechu v'nel-choh ki hi mekor hab'rochoh

merosh mikedem nesuchoh sof ma'aseh b'mach'shovoh techiloh

Lecho dodi...

Mik'dash melech ir meluchoh kumi tze'i mitoch hahafechah

rav loch sheves be'emek habochoh ve'hu yachamol olaich chem'loh

Lecho dodi...

Hisna'ari me'afar kumi liv'shi biYawehei sif-artech ami

al yad ben Yishai beis halach'mi korvah el nafshi ge-oloh

Lecho dodi...

Hisoreri, hisoreri, ki voh orech, kumi oh-ri,

uri, uri, shir daberi, k'vod Hashem olaich nigloh.

Lecho dodi...

Lo sevoshi ve'lo sikal'mi mah tish-to-cha-chi umah te-hemi,

boch yechesu ani-ei ami, venivnesoh ho-ir al tiloh.

Lecho dodi...

Vehoyu lim'shisoh shoi-soich, veroh-chaku kol m'val-aich,

yosis alaich Elo-h-aich, kim-sos choson al kalah.

Lecho dodi...

Yomin usmol tif'rotzi, ve'es Hashem ta-ari-tzi,

al yad ish bein partzi, venis-mechoh venogiloh.

Lecho dodi...

Boi vesholom ateres ba-alah, gam besimchoh uv'tzoholoh

toch emunei am seguloh, boi kalah, boi, kalah;

toch emunei am segulah, boi chalah, boi chalah.

Lecho dodi

Michael struggled with the Hebrew and mostly just hummed. Jonathan was surprised at the robust voice that Saul was displaying with the singing. Jonathan, Michael, and Saul joined hands and began to sing the Shalom Aleichem to welcome the Shabbat angels. Michael asked to recite "A Woman of Valor" from Proverbs 31, a tribute by King Solomon to women. Jonathan was skeptical at first. Michael explained that he did not know the Hebrew form, but could sing the English portion and would very much like to do this part. Jonathan agreed, but stated that all three would sing "A Woman of Valor" in English. Michael started the song and Jonathan and Saul joined in.

A woman of valor, who can find? Far beyond pearls is her value. Her husband's heart trusts in her and he shall lack no fortune.

She repays his good, but never his harm, all the days of her life. She seeks out wool and linen, and her hands work willingly.

She is like a merchant's ships; from afar she brings her sustenance. She rises while it is still nighttime, and gives food to her household and a ration to her maids.

She considers a field and buys it; from the fruit of her handiwork she plants a vineyard. She girds her loins with might and strengthens her arms.

She senses that her enterprise is good, so her lamp is not extinguished at night. She puts her hand to the distaff, and her palms support the spindle.

She spreads out her palm to the poor and extends her hands to the destitute. She fears not snow for her household, for her entire household is clothed with scarlet wool.

Bedspreads she makes herself; linen and purple wool are her clothing. Well-known at the gates is her husband as he sits with the elders of the land.

Garments she makes and sells, and she delivers a belt to the peddler. Strength and splendor are her clothing, and smilingly she awaits her last day

She opens her mouth with Wisdom, and the teaching of kindness is on her tongue. She anticipates the needs of her household, and the bread of idleness, she does not eat.

Her children rise and celebrate her; and her husband, he praises her: "Many daughters have attained valor, but you have surpassed them all."

False is grace, and vain is beauty; a Yaweh-fearing woman, she should be praised.

Give her the fruit of her hands, and she will be praised at the gates by her very own deeds.

At the completion of the song, Saul poured the wine into the Goblet and recited the Kiddush in Hebrew to proclaim the sanctity of the Shabbat.

Yom Ha-shi-shi.

Va-y'chu-lu Ha-sha-ma-yim v'ha-a-retz, v'chowl ts'va-am.

va-y'chal e-lo-him ba-yom ha-sh'vi-i, m'lach-to a-sher a-sa

va-yish-bot ba-yom ha-sh'vi-i, mi-kolm'lach-to a-sher a-sa.

va-y'va-rech e-lo-him et yom ha-sh'vi-i, va-y'ka-deish o-to

ki vo sha-vat mi-kol m'lach-to a-sher ba-ra e-lo-him la-a-sot.

Sav-ri ma-ra-nan!

Ba-ruch a-tah, A-do-nai, E-lo-hei-nu me-lech ha-o-lam,

bo-rei p'ri ha-ga-fen. (Amen)

Ba-ruch a-tah, A-do-nai, E-lo-hei-nu, me-lech ha-o-lam,

a-sher ki-d'sha-nu b'mits-vo-tav v'ra-tsa va-nu,

v'sha-bat kawd'sho b'a-ha-va uv'ra-tson

hin-chi-la-nu, zi-ka-ron l'ma-a-sei v'rei-shit.

t'chi-la l'mik-ra-ei ko-desh, ze-cher li-tsi-at Mits-ra-yim.

Ki va-nu va-char-ta v'o-ta-nu ki-dash-ta

mi-kawl ha-a-mim, v'Sha-bat kawd-sh'cha

b'a-ha-va u-v'ra-tson hin-chal-ta-nu.

Ba-ruch a-tah A-do-nai, m'ka-deish ha-Sha-bat. (Amen)

Michael was obviously lost again and Jonathan chided him about his lack of understanding of the Hebrew language.

Jonathan quietly translated the Kiddush for Michael into English:

The sixth day. And the heavens and the earth and all their complements were finished. And Yaweh finished by the Seventh Day His work which He had done, and He rested on the seventh day from all His work which He had done.

And Yaweh blessed the seventh day and made it holy, for on it He rested from all His work, which Yaweh had created to do.

Attention Gentlemen! Blessed are You, Lord our Yaweh, King of the world, who creates the fruit of vine. Blessed are You, Lord our Yaweh, king of the world, who made us holy with His commandments and favored us, and gave us His holy Shabbat, in love and favor, to be our heritage, as a reminder of the Creation. It is the first of the holy festivals, commemorating the exodus from Egypt.

For You have chosen us and sanctified us from among all the nations, and with love and goodwill given us Your holy Shabbat as a heritage.

Blessed are You, Lord, who sanctifies Shabbat.

Saul, Jonathan, and Michael went to the kitchen and performed the washing-the-hands ritual before eating the bread. Jonathan filled a large cup with water and poured water onto each of his hands three times while reciting a blessing. Saul and Michael did the same, each reciting a similar blessing. All three returned to the table and Saul recited a blessing over the single loaf of challah. He then sliced the bread and dipped it in salt. Saul took a bit and passed the challah to Jonathan and then Michael. Jonathan went and took the chicken and noodle soup from the stove and served Saul and Michael. The three sat quietly while they ate their Shabbat meal. Jonathan had some sadness that their meal did not include some gefilte fish or matzo balls, but they made the best of what they had for the meal. There was no dessert. After the meal, Jonathan offered to discuss the Torah reading for the week (Parshah). Jonathan took out his worn copy of the Torah and turned to Leviticus 16:1-20:27 and began in English so Michael would understand:

---

10. *And the he goat upon which the lot "For Azazel" came up, shall be placed while still alive, before the Lord, to [initiate] atonement upon it, and to send it away to Azazel, into the desert.*

---

11. *And Aaron shall bring his sin offering bull, and shall [initiate] atonement for himself and for his household, and he shall [then] slaughter his sin offering bull.*

---

12. *And he shall take a pan full of burning coals from upon the altar, from before the Lord, and both hands' full of fine incense, and bring [it] within the dividing curtain.*

---

13. *And he shall place the incense upon the fire, before the Lord, so that the cloud of the incense shall envelope the ark cover that is over the [tablets of] Testimony, so that he shall not die.*

---

14. *And he shall take some of the bull's blood and sprinkle [it] with his index finger on top of the ark cover on the eastern side; and before the ark cover, he shall sprinkle seven times from the blood, with his index finger.*

---

15. *He shall then slaughter the he goat of the people's sin offering and bring its blood within the dividing curtain, and he shall do with its blood as he had done with the bull's blood, and he shall sprinkle it upon the ark cover and before the ark cover.*

---

16. *And he shall effect atonement upon the Holy from the defilements of the children of Israel and from their rebellions and all their unintentional sins. He shall do likewise to the Tent of Meeting, which dwells with them amidst their defilements.*

---

17. *And no man shall be in the Tent of Meeting when he comes to effect atonement in the Holy, until he comes out. And he shall effect atonement for himself, for his household, and for all the congregation of Israel.*

---

18. *And he shall then go out to the altar that is before the Lord and effect atonement upon it: He shall take some of the bull's blood and some of the he goat's blood, and place it on the horns of the altar, around.*

---

19. *He shall then sprinkle some of the blood upon it with his index finger seven times, and he shall cleanse it and sanctify it of the defilements of the children of Israel.*

---

20. *And he shall finish effecting atonement for the Holy, the Tent of Meeting, and the altar, and then he shall bring the live he goat.*

---

21. *And Aaron shall lean both of his hands [forcefully] upon the live he goat's head and confess upon it all the willful transgressions of the children of Israel, all their rebellions, and all their unintentional sins, and* *he shall place them on the he goat's head, and send it off to the desert with a timely man.*

---

22. *The he goat shall thus carry upon itself all their sins to a precipitous land, and he shall send off the he goat into the desert.*

---

23. *And Aaron shall enter the Tent of Meeting and remove the linen garments that he had worn when he came into the Holy, and there, he shall store them away.*

---

24. *And he shall immerse his flesh in a holy place and don his garments. He shall then go out and sacrifice his burnt offering and the people's burnt offering, and he shall effect atonement for himself and for the people.*

Jonathan commented on the reading and the references to Aaron being allowed to enter into the Holy of places and how the similarities to the current findings at the excavation site were similar. Saul nodded in agreement that he felt that they were on the verge of something substantial and that he felt a certain increase in his spirituality since finding the walls and the bars. Saul then recited the Grace after Meals. Jonathan suggested the three retire for the evening. As Michael was leaving Jonathan asked if he would be joining them for the shul in the morning. Michael stated that he did not think so but appreciated the offer.

Jonathan was up early, woke Saul up and they attended the shul and reading of the Torah at the local synagogue at the compound. There was a Kiddush buffet after the services and Jonathan and Saul socialized for a while before returning to their cottage. Both decided to take a nap before the evening meal. After the evening meal, Jonathan had checked the time for the end of the Shabbat and, at exactly 2056 hours, he declared to Saul that the Shabbat had ended. Saul and Jonathan then performed the Havdalah. Jonathan placed a glass of wine, some fragrant spices and the special Havdalah candle on the table. Jonathan and Saul recited the four blessings together and this concluded their Shabbat celebration.

"This was one of our best Shabbats here," Jonathan commented after the Havdalah candle was put away until next Shabbat.

Saul was walking back to his bedroom to turn his computer back on and stopped and looked at Jonathan.

"I think we are really onto something," Saul said to Jonathan, "I am not sure what we will find, but I am convinced that these bars and walls are part of Herod's dungeon."

Saul smiled and Jonathan agreed. The discovery of Herod's dungeon would be in and of itself remarkable. However, Jonathan reminded Saul that, if it turns out to be the dungeon beneath Herod's palace, they still had to find evidence that supported their original theory, that the man Jesus was not the Messiah. The smile never left Saul's face as he displayed more confidence in his beliefs than Jonathan could remember seeing in these past three years. Jonathan wanted to believe that this was the discovery that they had been waiting to find. However, he also did not want to be disappointed. Jonathan was fearful that, if they did not produce something of value in the next few months, they would have to return home not only empty handed, but academically ruined.

"Let's not get our hopes up," Jonathan cautioned as he turned out the lights to secure the cottage for the evening.

"Too late," Saul replied with a smile, "I know in my heart we are going to find what we are looking for, I just know it."

Jonathan told Saul good night and returned to his bedroom and also turned on his computer. Jonathan was confused. He should be feeling confident about the discoveries and happy that Saul is so sure. But Jonathan found uneasiness in the calm and peacefulness that Saul was now showing. The Friday before the Shabbat, Saul did not even want to stop digging. Now there is no anxiousness, no urgency, as he displays an uncharacteristic tranquility. Even during the Shabbat celebration, Saul only mentioned the excavation on one occasion. Jonathan was concerned about his mentor and his friend. Jonathan was in deep thought as he hung his formal clothes back in the closet until next Shabbat. He sat on the side of the bed and pulled on his sleeping pants, removed his kippah, then his glasses and placed them both on the bedside table. He heard Saul's voice from the other room. Jonathan listened carefully but could not make out who Saul would be talking to this late in the evening. Jonathan got up and went to the joining door in the bathroom. Jonathan slowly returned to his bed, somewhat embarrassed.

"He's praying," Jonathan said quietly.

Jonathan laid in bed for several minutes, listening to the sing-song rhythm of Saul's voice as he prayed. Finally, Saul was silent and Jonathan could hear the bed creaking as the weight of Saul's body made contact with the mattress. Jonathan thought for a moment longer and then whispered his own prayer:

> *"I will lift up mine eyes unto the mountains: from whence shall my help come?*
>
> *My help cometh from HaShem, who made heaven and earth.*

He will not suffer thy foot to be moved; He that keepeth thee will not slumber.

Behold, He that keepeth Israel doth neither slumber nor sleep.

HaShem is thy keeper; HaShem is thy shade upon thy right hand.

The sun shall not smite thee by day, nor the moon by night.

HaShem shall keep thee from all evil; He shall keep thy soul.

HaShem shall guard thy going out and thy coming in, from this time forth and for ever."

Jonathan finished and he felt an actual peace inside and calmness about tomorrow. He thought it ironic that he, the Masorti Jew, had been taught the true meaning of the Shabbat by Saul, who until this week rarely practiced the Hebrew religion.

"Maybe Saul is right," Jonathan thought, "maybe tomorrow will be our day."

With those words and a feeling of contentment, Jonathan turned out the light and quickly fell to sleep.

CHAPTER 14

It had been four months since Michael had discovered the metal bars. The excitement that Saul and Jonathan felt that Saturday night before returning to the excavation site quickly faded. The mundane task for slowly digging dirt away and filling buckets to remove the dirt became tedious very quickly as no new discoveries were made. Michael quickly lost interest and had resumed his tour of Christian sites. Some of the workers from the Hebrew University of Jerusalem had demonstrated interest at first, but even that waned when there were no new discoveries. Saul carefully continued his dig, searching for more bars, but only the six were found. He had removed dirt approximately six feet down vertically, finding the base of the bars and the floor. Carefully brushing aside the dirt, the floor was found to be large, smooth stones, clearly indicating that this was the floor. In addition, sifting through the dirt, Saul had discovered two assarions and a prutah. These coins were bronze and dated around the time of the man Jesus and definitely Herod. Michael had been excited due to the discovery of the pertutah. While the assarions were Roman coins, the prutah was a Jewish coin. Michael explained his excitement about the

Jewish prutah as the coin most likely referred to in the Christian New Testament as a "widow's mite." Jonathan recalled the story was found in both the books written by Mark and Luke. Michael gave a short lesson to Saul and Jonathan about how Jesus was in the Temple in Jerusalem with his disciples. People were giving large contributions and a "poor" widow gave just "two mites." Jesus used the event as a teaching point that the widow gave more than all because she gave "all that she had." Saul just scoffed at the tale. Jonathan argued that neither of those two writers were "eyewitnesses" to the events and that the story was probably just another fabrication attributed to the man Jesus to enhance his status as a great teacher. Jonathan immediately realized he had made a mistake when he saw Michael carry a bucket of dirt up one ladder, lay it down, and ascend the second ladder and leave without a word. That was two months earlier and since that time Michael had only been involved in the excavation site sporadically.

While Saul had worked clearing the dirt away from the six bars, Jonathan had worked on the other wall discovered. Jonathan had been able to clear large amounts of dirt from the wall surface that would have been inside the bars, but he had been unable to find the outside wall. He had excavated outward from the top edge about four meters out and laterally to the edge of the wall. He and Saul were both confused but finally came to the conclusion that the wall had no other edge as it was built with multiple cut stones placed against a large stone. At the time of construction, placing smaller stones on the wall against the much larger stone made for a secure cell. Jonathan had been able to dig downward to the same level as Saul to the floor on the inside of the bars. When Jonathan and Saul discovered the floor they were able to conclude that the six bars were the door to a prison cell. They basically discovered two edges of what must have been a prison cell.

Saul decided that the discovery of the coins at the level of the floor dated the cell at the time of Jesus, around 25 – 35 AD. Because of the area where the dig was occurring, Saul was convinced that this prison cell must have been part of the dungeon beneath the palace of Herod Antipas at Tiberius. However, according to historical documents, there was a stable for horses on the same level and that had not been found. Jonathan would have felt better if there were more evidence. However, working together they had cleared an area that clearly demonstrated that there was a prison cell.

It was getting late in the day and the sun was starting downward. Saul had placed makers for the day's findings. He had makers at the exact location of where the three coins were found. As Saul placed the markers, Jonathan used the digital camera to record the finds of the day, just as they did every day. When everything was completed, they left the tools where they had been working for the day. Saul and Jonathan ascended the two ladders as they did every day to return to their cottage. No words were exchanged. Jonathan could see the discouragement on Saul's face. On arrival at the top, Jonathan stood on the edge and looked over the site of their excavation. There was enough debris and dirt cleared away that the site was now beginning to look like a prison cell. There was a clear door made of bars, and two walls. The one wall held the door and the other wall at a right angle would have been on the left walking into the prison cell. Jonathan was deep in thought when he heard Saul beeping the horn of the Land Rover. As they drove back to their cottage, neither spoke.

As the Land Rover stopped in front of the cottage, Saul sat with his shoulders slumped forward. Jonathan looked at the Professor who seemed to have aged from just that morning. His long hair was white and matted with dirt on the ends. His beard contained stains and had grown three years of length.

His once sharp eyes looked tired and Jonathan noted that there seemed to be more lines than before.

"Are you okay?" Jonathan asked

Saul nodded in the affirmative.

"I just wonder sometimes if we have wasted three years."

Jonathan had wondered that at the two year mark, but kept his feelings to himself. There had been so much promise four months ago and that enthusiasm had been short-lived. The drudgery of digging daily and finding very little was discouraging and would sap the positive feelings of the most ardent optimist. Saul sighed a long, frustrated sigh and exited the Land Rover. Jonathan did the same and caught Michael out of the corner of his eye coming toward the two at a quick pace.

"Professor Harkman, Professor Weitzman, I need to talk with you both."

Michael did not seem excited, just matter of fact. Michael explained that he had visited all of the Christian sacred sites in Jerusalem several times and was not sure what else there was for him to do.

"Are you wanting to leave?" Saul asked.

Michael stated that he was unsure, but admitted that the thought had been nagging at him for several days. He expressed his disappointment with the excavation site and the progress made. Saul just nodded, which was uncharacteristic. As Jonathan watched the interaction, he was surprised that Saul was so calm, so understanding of Michael's expression of his feelings. Any other time, Saul would have just dismissed Michael as he generally did about everything. However, this time Saul seemed to have empathy.

"I understand, we are going to close up the dig at the end of the month."

It was the middle of August, that would be just two more weeks.

"Hopefully, we can all be home in time for the Fall semester at the University."

Saul asked Michael to stay and help close the site and return with them back to the United States. Jonathan stood with mouth gaping open. He adjusted his kippah and removed his glasses to clean them as Michael agreed to stay and left to return to his cottage.

"See you in the morning at the site."

Jonathan looked at Saul.

"When were you going to tell me?"

Saul looked at Jonathan as Jonathan readjusted his glasses on his face after cleaning. Jonathan could see the sadness in Saul's eyes.

"I think we have done all we can do. I just decided at this moment to close the site."

Jonathan and Saul walked into the cottage and Jonathan sat down on the couch as Saul went to his bedroom to leave his briefcase. He returned and found Jonathan still sitting on the couch.

"We can't dig forever," Saul stated.

Jonathan knew Saul was right, but had never thought about an end date. Now seemed as good a time as any to end the project. Saul outlined the plan for the next couple of weeks. They would clear away the two walls and bars some more. Saul would go to the leader of the Hebrew University of

Jerusalem and see if they wanted to pick up the dig and purchase their equipment. They would make one last trip to Jerusalem to record the coins found with Mr. Goldman and then try to leave by the end of August.

Jonathan listened intently and those details were all fine. However, he was worried about one thing, and that was the Jewish Defense League who had invested so much money with no real return. Jonathan asked Saul about his plans in regards to the financing. Saul explained that it was a risk, just like any other risk and it did not pay the dividends expected. He would just explain that to the Jewish Defense League and that was that. Jonathan was not sure that would be enough but decided not to pursue it tonight. There was still more to do at the site and he could figure out those details later.

After a small dinner where neither Jonathan nor Saul spoke much, the two Professors went to bed early. Jonathan laid in his bed and again heard the low voice of Saul praying again. Jonathan felt strangely at peace with this decision. It was time to go home. He silently said a prayer of thanks for an end to this journey. Jonathan was glad that tomorrow was Friday and another Shabbat. He felt a spiritual break would be beneficial to both of them. He had trouble sleeping as he went over in his mind the past three years and wondered if he and Saul had just wasted their time and more importantly the Jewish Defense League's money.

Jonathan awoke to the sun streaming through his window. He felt he had only been asleep for a couple of hours. He could hear Saul in the kitchen getting ready for their day at the site. Jonathan pulled on his cleanest dirty pants and shirt and joined Saul in the kitchen.

"Good morning," Jonathan greeted Saul as Saul handed him a cup of coffee.

"I just wanted to get started and start wrapping this up," Saul informed Jonathan.

Saul headed for the door, coffee in hand, and Jonathan followed.

"What about the Land Rover?"

Saul explained that they would try to sell it and have whoever bought it take them to the airport. Since Saul never hesitated with an answer in regards to finishing the project, Jonathan felt that he had been considering this option for a while.

Jonathan was surprised to see Michael waiting at the Land Rover. Michael greeted them both and all three piled into the Land Rover as they had done countless times and headed for the excavation site for the day. This time it was Saul who reminded everyone it was the Shabbat and that they would end their work early today.

Little was said as the three descended the two ladders to the site of their excavation. Tools were lying where they had been left. Markers remained in place. Saul suggested that Michael and Jonathan work and try to find the bottom edge of the inside wall. Saul was going to begin trying to find all the tools at the three levels and place them in one area.

Lunch came quickly as the three worked almost in silence. Saul had found just about all of their tools. There were several shovels, trowels, and four sifters now stacked neatly at the level they were digging. Saul announced that after lunch he was going to go to where the Hebrew University of Jerusalem team was digging to discuss plans for abandoning the excavation site and see if they were interested in the tools and the site.

After lunch, Saul started on the first ladder. Jonathan watched while Saul climbed both ladders and disappeared out of sight in the direction of the Hebrew University excavation site. As he turned, he did not realize that Michael was knelt down behind him tying his shoe. Jonathan fell against the wall of cut stone hard. As he reached out his hands to brace himself when he hit the wall, his right hand struck a cut stone and it pushed in slightly. Michael apologized profusely but Jonathan did not hear him. He was focused on the stone that moved when he fell.

"Hand me a small trowel."

Michael went to the pile Saul had made and found the small trowel that Jonathan requested. He watched intently as Jonathan carefully etched around the stone that had moved.

"What is it?" Michael asked.

Jonathan was unsure and at first did not respond. He carefully continued to remove dirt from around the stone, careful not to push the stone forward. The stone was located about chest height and was easy to work around. He explained to Michael that he wanted to remove enough dirt to move the stone outward. Jonathan looked around and found the small flat bladed trowel that was the size of a painter's knife and cautiously removed smaller portions of the dirt from around each edge of the stone. Finally, the flat blade pushed through to the other side. Jonathan could feel his heart pounding. Michael was standing just at Jonathan's right shoulder, eyes transfixed on the stone. Jonathan stopped and took a step backward. He looked at the wall and the stones. Each stone was cut and hued about the same size. The stone that moved was not any different and would not have been noticed had Jonathan not fallen into the wall, and in particular if he had not reached out to catch himself and his hand landed on that particular stone.

"What is it?" Michael asked again.

"I'm not sure if it is anything."

Jonathan carefully worked his fingers into the area of the stone on top and on bottom and gently rocked the stone backwards and forwards while pulling outward. The stone made a scratching sound as it slowly began to respond to the gentle pulling. He stopped.

"Michael, before I remove this stone, take pictures and mark everything."

Michael went to where Saul had left his briefcase and it was not there. Saul had taken the briefcase with him. However, Michael saw the camera sitting on a ledge on the side of the wall that the ladder leaned against. He grabbed the next numbered marker "56" and placed it next to the stone. Jonathan moved away and Michael took the digital photographs.

"Finished," Michael said and quickly removed the marker.

Again Jonathan delicately placed his fingers on the top and bottom margin of the stone. As it was jutting outward about one centimeter equally on all sides, Jonathan was able to grasp the edges more easily. Jonathan pulled the stone slowly away from the wall until he held the stone in both hands. Jonathan noted that it seemed light and he was easily able to hand it to Michael. Michael took the stone and measured it on all sides, recording the measurements, and placed it on the ground with a marker that said "57." He snapped photographs of the same.

While this was being done, Jonathan stared at the hole that had been left. There seemed to be a ledge hollowed out into the solid rock that the wall was built against. It was too dark for Jonathan to see.

"I need a flashlight."

Michael reached into his pocket and handed Jonathan his small penlight. It was not bright enough and Michael looked around for a regular flashlight without success. Jonathan was reluctant to place his hand into the hole where the stone had been without some sort of light. Michael handed Jonathan his cell phone that was now a very bright LED flashlight.

"It's a flashlight app I downloaded," Michael volunteered, "first time I've used it."

Jonathan pushed the cell phone into the hole and illuminated the opened area in the back. There appeared to be an object of some kind in the back of the hole. Jonathan looked more closely and could tell it was a container, such as a jug or vase lying on its side. Jonathan removed the light and reached inside and was able to easily grab the vase and remove it from the hole.

"There is something inside it," Michael exclaimed.

Jonathan carefully looked at the object. It was a jug shaped like a wide vase that would have been used for water. The mouth of the jug was very wide and there was something, as Michael had said, inside the jug. Jonathan was unsure of what to do first. He held the jug with a marker "58" and Michael took several pictures. Jonathan dared not move from the site to preserve the location. He knelt with the jug and peered inside at the object. The object appeared to be round and cylindered, a dark brown in color; the upper edges were frayed. Jonathan wished Saul had returned to help. However, he did not want to wait. He gingerly grasped the frayed edges and pulled the object from the jug. Jonathan and Michael gasped at the same time. It appeared to be a scroll of tightly rolled papyrus paper, darkened by the time bound with a leather strip.

Jonathan placed the number marker "59" on the rolled paper and Michael took more pictures. Neither man spoke a single word. Jonathan examined the scroll and was amazed at the quality of the paper. There did not appear to be any fragmenting of the main body, only the edges. The leather strip that was tied around them was very dried and most likely would crumble if touched. He directed Michael to bring over a sifter. Jonathan placed the scroll in the sifter gently. He turned his attention to the jug. There was nothing special about the jug. The style and material dated the jug at around the same time as the coins, between 25 – 35AD. There was a residue on the inside of the jug that darkened the entire inside. Jonathan suspected that this may have been a weak wine mixed with water that was the standard drink of the time. This aridity of the area with the further preservation of the wine on the inside of the jug safeguarded the scroll from deterioration.

Jonathan set the jug in a separate sifter and knelt down in front of the sifter that continued the scroll. He turned the scroll slowly until the knot of the leather tie was facing upward. Jonathan was suddenly aware that sweat was pouring from his head. He adjusted his kippah, removed his glasses and cleaned them with a dirty handkerchief from his pocket. He reached out and fingered the knot warily.

Michael stood beside him with camera ready. Jonathan suddenly stood up and turned to Michael.

"Go and find Saul now and bring him here."

Without a question, or hesitation, Michael handed Jonathan the camera and scampered up the two ladders and ran in the direction Saul had walked.

CHAPTER 15

After Michael left to find Saul, Jonathan dropped down to both knees beside the sifter. He closed his eyes tightly and prayed, *Baruch atah adonai eloheinu melech ha'olam, hatov vhameitiv.* (Blessed are you, HaShem, our God, King of the Universe, the Good and the Doer of good).

Michael covered the four to five blocks to the center of the city at the site of the mosaic floor that the Hebrew University of Jerusalem had uncovered several years earlier. Saul was talking with two men very intently. Michael hurried to where Saul was standing. He could hear Saul discussing terms of turning over the excavation site to the two men. As they shook hands, Michael finally reached him.

"Professor Harkman, you need to come back with me, Professor Weitzman needs your assistance."

Saul looked at Michael, somewhat annoyed at the interruption. He excused himself from the conversation with the two men. One of the men stated he would talk to Saul tomorrow and the two walked away.

"What did you say?" Saul asked.

Michael again emphasized that Saul needed to return to the excavation site. Saul looked as if he wanted more.

"Professor Weitzman has found something."

Saul was skeptical.

"What, another coin, a horse shoe?" Saul retorted sarcastically.

Michael pulled Saul very close. He looked around to see if anyone was standing near. He tried to whisper in Professor Harkman's ear. Saul drew back and looked at Michael with disgust. Saul was annoyed with this cloak and dagger theatrics.

"Just tell me what is going on," Saul insisted.

Michael hesitated and decided not to tell him at this location, too many ears. He stuck to his story that Professor Weitzman needed him and it was urgent. Saul reluctantly followed Michael back to the excavation site. As Saul reached the edge of the site he saw Jonathan on both knees in front of a stiffer at the second wall. Saul immediately saw the hole in the wall where the stone was removed.

"Out of the way," Saul said as he pushed Michael aside and descended the first ladder.

Jonathan turned and saw Saul coming down the ladder.

"You have got to see this," Jonathan exclaimed.

Jonathan was afraid to leave the scroll unattended and just stood still, waiting for Saul. As Saul came closer, he saw the two sifters. One contained a jug, the other, something dark brown and shaped like a scroll. He rushed toward the dark brown object and Jonathan reached out and grabbed Saul with both hands on his shoulders.

"What have you found?" Saul asked with a level of excitement that could hardly be contained.

"I don't know," Jonathan replied.

Saul knelt down beside the sifter that contained the scroll and Jonathan joined him. They both just stared at the scroll, lying there in the stiffer with the dried leather band around it. Michael joined them on the other side.

Jonathan began telling Saul of the story of falling over Michael. How his hand struck the wall and he felt the stone move. He related how he had worked to remove the stone since Saul had left but did not want to go any further until Saul returned.

"That is why I sent Michael for you."

Saul questioned Jonathan in detail about the discovery.

"You took pictures, numbered everything?" Saul asked.

Jonathan assured him that all was in order. All three men just looked at the scroll for several moments without speaking a word.

"I guess we should open it," Saul finally said, breaking the silence.

Jonathan offered to let Saul open the scroll. He declined, stating that it was Jonathan's find and he should be the one to open it. Saul reminded Jonathan that the entire document could crumble into a million pieces the minute it was touched. Jonathan explained he had used the sifter just in case that happened. Saul directed Michael to convert the camera to video as the scroll was opened to record every second of the event.

Everyone was ready. Michael trained the lens of the camera, now on video at the scroll. Jonathan used great care as he delicately tried to maneuver the strip of leather tie around the scroll. With only the slightest manipulation, the knot on the piece of leather crumpled and the band fell into the sifter, freeing the scroll. Jonathan stopped and waited. The tightly rolled scroll did not open after being disturbed. Jonathan slowly turned the scroll so that it was lying perpendicular to the bottom of the sifter. He rolled the scroll until he found the leading edge. Next, he took the flat blade of the smallest trowel, the one that was as thin as a painter's knife, and very carefully slid it under that edge, beginning at the top. Jonathan suddenly stopped and removed the scroll. Saul looked up at Jonathan and noted he was soaked with sweat. Jonathan adjusted his kippah, removed the dirty handkerchief from his pocket and cleaned his glasses. Saul had seen him do this a thousand times.

"It's okay," Saul reassured Jonathan.

Jonathan placed his glasses back on his face, licked his lips and started again. With the thin edge of the blade he slowly separated the lead page from the scroll. As he reached the end the bundle began to loosen in its entirety. Jonathan and Saul watched, horrified, and held their breath as the scroll loosened from its tight roll and bits and pieces of the papyrus fell into the sifter. Jonathan again used the thin blade to push open the pages of the scroll. He did not want to touch it with his hands and have the acid from his hand destroy some part of it. The scroll slowly opened and more pieces of the papyrus dropped off. Jonathan was sure that the entire scroll was going to crumble into dust. Saul took another small trowel and held the left side open for Jonathan. Jonathan, with painstaking patience, deliberately pushed the roll outward to his right and held it in place. The papyrus was intact thus far. Jonathan saw the writing at the same time as Saul.

"It's ancient Hebrew," Jonathan whispered, terrified that the sound of his voice or the wind of his breath would destroy the parched papyrus.

Jonathan looked at the right upper corner to try and translate right to left. The characters were hand written, some slightly faded, but clear enough to be read. Jonathan spoke the words aloud:

אני ג'ון , קרא המטביל

Saul mouthed the translation and tears formed in his eyes. Jonathan looked at Saul in disbelief. Michael saw Professor Harkman's lips moving but could not make out his words. Jonathan said to read it with greater volume, which did not help Michael as it was in Hebrew.

"What does it say?" Michael asked, trying to video the events.

Saul repeated it as if he could not believe what he read:

אני ג'ון , קרא המטביל.

"Please, what does it say," Michael pleaded.

Tears formed in Jonathan's eyes also. He and Saul ignored Michael. Jonathan let the scroll roll onto itself again. He used the small knife to make sure that the scroll rolled together in a controlled fashion so as little of the parchment as possible was lost. Saul by now had tears streaming down his face. Jonathan turned to Saul and the two men hugged tightly beside the sifter where the scroll now sat rolled back together. Michael stopped recording and joined the two men, although he did not have a clue as to what was happening. He asked again and Jonathan repeated the phrase in Hebrew:

אני ג'ון , קרא המטביל.

"My Hebrew is not that great," Michael pleaded, "what does it say."

Jonathan looked at Saul and Saul nodded in the affirmative that Jonathan should tell Michael.

Jonathan looked at Michael. Michael could see Professor Weitzman's face was streaked with tears as well. Jonathan stretched out his hands and placed his hands on Michael's shoulders. He repeated the Hebrew again

אני ג'ון , קרא המטביל

"It says," Jonathan paused and took a deep breath.

"I am John, called the Baptist."

Michael looked with disbelief at Professor Weitzman and what he had just heard. He questioned Jonathan.

"Are you sure?" Michael asked.

Jonathan repeated the phrase,

"I am John, called the Baptist."

Michael sat down in the dirt, stunned with disbelief. Did this mean that the three of them had found another ancient text? Michael was trying to form words, but nothing was coming out. Professor Harkman and Professor Weitzman were once again sitting and just staring at the sifter that held the scroll.

Saul asked Jonathan what his theory was about the scroll and its origins. Jonathan speculated that this was the dungeon where John the Baptist had been imprisoned by Herod and that somehow John the Baptist had been able to write something while imprisoned. Jonathan guessed from the size of the scroll that it must be twenty to thirty pages thick. He told Saul that, from what he could see, all the pages contained writing on them.

Michael interrupted the two professors. He wanted to make sure he understood correctly that they thought this might be the writings of John the Baptist. Michael reminded them both that in the Christian world there was nothing written about John the Baptist, only what the writers of the four gospels had to say. Jonathan assured Michael that he was very familiar with John the Baptist.

"Maybe there are clues about the man Jesus and the hoax in the document," Saul stated to no one in particular.

Jonathan glanced at his watch, two hours until the Shabbat. He asked Saul about transporting the scroll. Saul sent Michael to the Land Rover, where there was a metal tube that had maps in the back seat. Michael removed the maps and returned with the metal tube. Jonathan was not so sure it should be transported in that manner. He argued that the jug had preserved the documents all of this time and that it might be better to use the same vessel that had housed the scrolls for all these centuries.

"We can't get it out of the country in that jug," Saul exclaimed.

Jonathan reminded everyone that there was only two hours before the Shabbat started. Saul found a piece of oilcloth in the tools that had been used to wrap ropes to keep them moist in the heat. He suggested to Jonathan that the scroll be wrapped in the oil cloth and placed in the metal tube. The jug could be transported separately in a crate that could be manufactured from the pieces of wood lying about. Next Saul did something that Jonathan did not expect. He took the camera, found the video and deleted it from the camera.

Jonathan tried to stop him when he realized what Saul was doing.

"I want no records of this scroll," Saul stated plainly.

He explained to Michael and Jonathan that he had no intention of being required to turn the scroll over to someone else for evaluation and interpretation. No one knew about their discovery except the three of them. Saul forbad them to talk to anyone else about the discovery. Saul stated that he would declare the jug to Mr. Goldman when they closed up the excavation, but was afraid that if the scroll was declared that the Antiquities Commission would confiscate it as a "relic of Israel." Michael pointed out that it did belong to Israel. Saul ignored his comment and began cleaning off the oil cloth. Jonathan explained to Michael that, technically if this was an actual document, written by John the Baptist, it would belong to the Christian community and not the Israelis. Michael thought that was lizard logic but accepted that explanation. Jonathan was not sure that he agreed with Saul in keeping the scroll a secret, but he did not personally want to be left out of any translations. Neither Saul nor Jonathan cared about the discovery; they were most interested in the contents of the scroll.

Saul began giving directions in order to secure the dig and the find. Jonathan would be responsible for transporting the scroll. Saul suggested that all the fragments that fell into the sifter be placed in a plastic bag. Saul directed Michael to build a crate for the jug. Saul walked over to the stone that Jonathan had removed from the wall. Michael and Jonathan watched as Saul lifted it into the hole and replaced it. He next began picking up all the markers.

Michael started building a framed crate for the jug while Jonathan began the task of trying to move the scroll without destroying it. He laid out the oil cloth and, together with Saul, they placed the scroll at the far edge. Just a few flakes fell from the edges. Next, Jonathan began the unhurried task of rolling the scroll in the oil cloth. Saul watched as, without touching the scroll, Jonathan expertly began to roll the oil cloth onto the scroll. After several minutes the scroll was completely covered and Jonathan increased his pace until the scroll was rolled in several layers of the oil cloth. With that completed, Jonathan opened the metal tube and with great care lowered the scroll, now wrapped in oil cloth, into the tube. There was about a centimeter between the scroll and the edges of the tube. Jonathan worried about it banging into the sides and disintegrating.

As Jonathan placed the cap on the metal tube, Michael finished crating the jug. Saul had removed all the markers and left the tools and sifters in a pile. Michael carried the jug up the first ladder, followed by Jonathan with the metal tube containing the jug. As Saul arrived on the upper level, he pulled the ladder up behind him.

"Are we not coming back?" Jonathan asked.

Saul explained that he did not think so. Jonathan countered that there may be more discoveries to be made at the site. Jonathan urged Saul to return at least till the end of the week. He argued that if they abruptly abandoned the site that would raise suspicions. Saul was hesitant, but reluctantly agreed. However, he and Jonathan decided that the scroll would not be removed from the metal tube and oil cloth until they returned to the United States. Jonathan would hide the tube someplace safe in their cottage until they were ready to leave.

When they reached the Land Rover, Michael was in the back with the jug and did not look happy. Jonathan and Saul got into the Land Rover and, after they were travelling in the direction of the cottages, Michael spoke up. Michael was unhappy about the deception of hiding the scroll from the

Israeli authorities. He stated that it was illegal and that it was the same as being untruthful. Jonathan started to try to reason with Michael when Saul interrupted. Saul in no uncertain terms explained to Michael that he had no part in the scroll. He was an employee, who did not deal with the Israeli authorities, whose name was not on any documents related to the excavation site and basically had no responsibility, or authority, and therefore had no say in what or how business was conducted. Saul also reminded Michael that he was very young and did not understand the political issues and corruption that was a part of the antiquities community. Jonathan could see that Michael was obviously hurt by Saul's reaction.

No one said another word until the Land Rover reached the cottages. Jonathan glanced at his watch. They had about thirty minutes before the start of Shabbat. As Michael started to walk away, leaving the jug in the Land Rover, Jonathan invited him to join them for the Shabbat again. Michael declined with a wave of his hand and, shaking his head, continued to walk. Jonathan hurried to catch up to Michael. He acknowledged that Michael was upset. Michael agreed that Dr. Harkman was correct about his status. However, he still felt it was not right. Jonathan looked directly at Michael and asked him if he thought it would be an important discovery for the Christian community if the scroll were written by John the Baptist. Michael agreed it would be important.

"So, do you want to be a part of that, or would you prefer that someone else do it and not even know it has been done correctly, where it may be mistranslated for some political agenda, if translated at all?"

A small smile came to Michael's face as he listened to Professor Weitzman.

"Let me pray on it," Michael responded.

Jonathan assured Michael that he would be doing a lot of praying as well. The two shook hands and Jonathan hurried to get inside. He glanced at his watch and he had just enough time to change and for the start of Shabbat. As he entered the cottage, he was surprised to see Saul at the table, with the candles, eyes closed, praying, and, most importantly, ready for the Shabbat.

CHAPTER 16

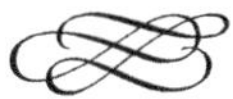

After their meal, Jonathan took the metal tube that now contained the scroll and placed it casually on his desk. Saul watched from the door.

"Is that where you are hiding it?" Saul asked with a challenging tone.

Jonathan explained that if the room was searched and something was found hidden it would bring more attention. He convinced Saul that the best place to hide the scroll was in plain view. This made perfect sense to Saul. He left and went to his room to prepare for bed. Jonathan did the same.

Neither man slept much that night. Jonathan kept thinking of the possibilities associated with interpreting the scroll. Just the first words already indicated who the author must be. He worried that the scroll was like many of the other gnostic documents that had been found after the man Jesus was killed by the Romans. He recalled the fervor over the "*Book of Thomas*" and most recently "*The Gospel of Judas.*" Jonathan realized that there were many books that were part of the apocryphal text not considered by Christians to be part of the "canons" of the Christian Bible. In his study Jonathan had come across these writings but was not familiar with them. Jonathan was worried that the scroll they had found would fall into this category. As he laid in his bed staring at the ceiling, his fears overcame him. He very quietly got out of bed, walked over to his desk, sat down and turned on his computer. The light from the screen of the computer filled his room with an eerie blue glow. Jonathan sat impatiently for what seemed like hours, but was actually only a few seconds while his computer ran through the start program. He immediately went to his *Google* search engine and typed in *The Apocrypha* and waited. Jonathan looked at the results. There were over one million, four hundred and sixty thousand results. Jonathan began to scroll through them, looking for religious or scholarly references. He found a couple of sites and began to read that most of the apocrypha books were thought to have been written between the second and fourth century. Some of the titles were interesting, *"The Gospel of Mary," "The Gospel of Philip"* and so on. Jonathan continued to search and finally found the object of his search, "Nag Hammadi Library."

While in school, Jonathan had studied Gnosticism briefly. From those studies he had remembered that the majority of the books categorized as part of the apocrypha were part of the "Nag Hammadi Library." Nag Hammadi is a city in Upper Egypt. However, it is best known for being the site where local farmers found a sealed earthenware jar containing thirteen leather-bound papyrus codices and pages from other books in 1945. Legend has it that the mother of the farmers burned one of the books and parts of a second. This left twelve books and pages from other books. Jonathan was now even more concerned because the scroll he had found had been in a sealed earthenware jar just as these texts were found. His anxieties were quickly relieved when he found that this Nag Hammadi library was written in Coptic. The scroll

Jonathan found that clearly defined the author as John the Baptist was written in ancient Hebrew, not Coptic. Jonathan breathed a sigh of relief.

"What are you doing?" Saul asked.

Startled by the voice, although familiar, Jonathan nearly jumped from his chair and quickly turned off his computer.

"That was silly," Jonathan thought to himself, "I'm doing nothing wrong."

Jonathan laughed as Saul entered the room.

"Sorry, I didn't mean to scare you," Saul muttered almost inaudibly.

Jonathan turned to Saul and explained what he was doing. They laughed together at Jonathan switching off the computer. Saul explained that he was not worried about the authenticity of the scroll, but about getting it out of the country. He explained that he had been lying awake worried about transporting the scroll to home.

It was about an hour before the sun was to start coming up. Jonathan and Saul entered the kitchen and turned on the lights. As Saul sat down at the table, Jonathan started a pot of coffee and then went to his room and returned with a tablet.

"We need to have some sort of plan," Jonathan stated.

Saul nodded in agreement and the two men sat down at the table together and began to brainstorm what their plan should be. Jonathan argued that they should return to the dig. Saul again wanted to leave right away. Saul asserted that he had already begun talking to the other group that was digging about buying their equipment and/or taking over the dig so it would not be unusual to just leave. Jonathan countered that Saul needed to finish those negotiations and that he and Michael should continue to dig not to raise suspicions.

Both men jumped as there was a knock at the door. Jonathan cautiously approached the door and inquired who was knocking. It was Michael and again Jonathan exhaled in relief.

"I saw the lights," Michael said as he entered the room, "and we left this in the jeep."

Michael had the crated jug in his arms. Michael explained that he could not sleep thinking about the scroll and the three men laughed together. Jonathan poured Michael a cup of coffee. But, before he continued, he asked Michael if he still felt the same way about the scroll belonging to the Israelis as he did last night.

Michael looked down at the floor and did not say anything for a moment. He appeared to Jonathan to be deep in thought, but not conflicted. Michael then looked up first at Jonathan and then turned to Saul.

"The scroll may be the most important discovery to the Christian religion in two thousand years," Michael began, "I believe it is our destiny to find these scrolls and to interpret the writings."

Michaels paused and then shouted, "To hell with the Antiquities Commission."

All three laughed and Michael joined Saul and Jonathan at the table. He listened as both outlined the plan thus far. Saul would continue to talk with archeologists at the Hebrew University excavation site about buying their equipment. Jonathan and Michael would continue to dig and sift for at least a couple of days. After that, while Jonathan and Michael closed up the site, Saul would drive to Jerusalem and close out with Mr. Goldman at the Antiquities Commission. He would declare the jug and the other few artifacts that they had found since the last trip and explain to Mr. Goldman that they were leaving. By declaring the jug as a major find, Saul thought this would avoid raising any suspicions from Mr. Goldman. Jonathan laughed at that statement. He commented sarcastically that they could declare the crown of Herod and Mr. Goldman would not care as long as he received his bribe. Saul laughed as well, but with mention of the bribe he realized that, with funds so short, the sale of the excavation equipment would be critical. Saul also planned to make the trip to Jerusalem in one day so that the three could be ready to leave the next morning. Saul, Jonathan, and Michael discussed the next three to four days for another hour until all three were satisfied with the plan. Michael was given the task of obtaining tickets for travel from the airport in Tel Aviv.

As today was Saturday and not the end of Shabbat yet, they could not start their work until tomorrow morning. However, as Michael was not Jewish, he could begin working on the flight details and purchasing the tickets. Tomorrow was Sunday and everyone would be at the excavation sites again. In planning a timeline, Saul figured that Sunday and Monday would be used for digging, he would leave for Jerusalem on Tuesday, returning Tuesday night, while Jonathan and Michael closed the excavation site. Jonathan would then close out everything at the kibbutz and begin packing. If everything went according to plan, they should leave for the United States on Wednesday. Michael would purchase tickets for the three of them on a direct flight from Tel Aviv to New York. They would leave the Land Rover at the airport in Tel Aviv. Michael suggested that they donate it to someone in the kibbutz and have them drive the three to the airport. Saul was not happy about this idea, but Jonathan thought it was a great idea.

"Do you have someone in mind?" Jonathan asked Michael.

Michael related that he had developed a friendship with a young student named Solomon who lived in the kibbutz and was part of the Hebrew University archeological team as a student. Michael explained that Solomon was twenty three years old, responsible, and would not ask any questions. Saul was still hesitant, but Jonathan reminded Saul that leaving the Land Rover might raise some eyebrows.

"We need to make sure that nothing we do draws any attention to us."

Saul listened to Jonathan's counsel and finally agreed. Michael would discuss this with Solomon on Sunday evening. If Solomon was unable to drive them to the airport in exchange for the Land Rover, Jonathan agreed to leave the Land Rover at the airport.

"Is that everything?" Saul asked more rhetorically than an actual question.

Michael was shaking his head in an affirmative manner. Jonathan suddenly went pale.

"What about the fragments of the scroll I have in the baggie?" Jonathan asked in a panicked tone.

Saul considered for a moment the options and recommended that the baggie with the fragments be placed in the metal tube with the scroll. The three went to Jonathan's room where the metal tube was on his desk amidst all of the other clutter.

"Hiding it in plain sight," Michael quipped, "genius!"

The three stood in front of the desk and stared down at the metal tube. Jonathan found the baggie with the fragments in the pocket of the shirt he had worn the day before. He held the baggie in his hand and handed it to Saul. Before picking up the metal tube, Jonathan adjusted his kippah, removed his glasses and pulled a dirty handkerchief from his pants and cleaned the lens. He slowly placed the handkerchief in his pocket and returned his glasses to his face. He then grasped the tube as if he were holding dynamite. He slowly removed the cap. Ever so gently, Saul placed the baggie containing the scroll fragments in the end of the metal tube. Jonathan carefully replaced the cap on the metal tube and then realized he had been holding his breath. He returned the metal tube to his desk. The three men just stood and stared for a moment at the metal tube which contained the scroll. No one spoke as they left the room together.

When they returned to the kitchen, it was almost 1400 hours.

"I am going to take off," Michael said.

Saul agreed and reminded him that they would leave at the normal time for the excavation site tomorrow morning.

"No unusual behavior to raise suspicions," Saul chided.

Michael returned to his cottage, leaving Saul and Jonathan alone again. Jonathan went to the couch and stretched out on the worn cushion. He was quickly asleep. Saul quietly entered Jonathan's room and returned to the desk when the metal tube was placed. He stood there for several moments, looking down at the metal tube that contained a lifetime of work. He bowed his head and for several minutes repeatedly recited a prayer:

קה נֵר-לְרַגְלִי דְבָרֶךָ; וְאוֹר, לִנְתִיבָתִי.

Thy word is a lamp unto my feet, and a light unto my path.

קו נִשְׁבַּעְתִּי וָאֲקַיֵּמָה-- לִשְׁמֹר, מִשְׁפְּטֵי צִדְקֶךָ.

I have sworn, and have confirmed it, to observe Thy righteous ordinances.

קז נַעֲנֵיתִי עַד-מְאֹד; יְהוָה, חַיֵּנִי כִדְבָרֶךָ.

I am afflicted very much; quicken me, O LORD, according unto Thy word.

קח נִדְבוֹת פִּי, רְצֵה-נָא יְהוָה; וּמִשְׁפָּטֶיךָ לַמְּדֵנִי.

Accept, I beseech Thee, the freewill-offerings of my mouth, O LORD, and teach me Thine ordinances.

קט נַפְשִׁי בְכַפִּי תָמִיד; וְתוֹרָתְךָ, לֹא שָׁכָחְתִּי.

My soul is continually in my hand; yet have I not forgotten Thy law.

קי נָתְנוּ רְשָׁעִים פַּח לִי; וּמִפִּקּוּדֶיךָ, לֹא תָעִיתִי.

The wicked have laid a snare for me; yet went I not astray from Thy precepts.

קיא נָחַלְתִּי עֵדְוֺתֶיךָ לְעוֹלָם: כִּי-שְׂשׂוֹן לִבִּי הֵמָּה.

Thy testimonies have I taken as a heritage for ever; for they are the rejoicing of my heart.

קיב נָטִיתִי לִבִּי, לַעֲשׂוֹת חֻקֶּיךָ-- לְעוֹלָם עֵקֶב.

I have inclined my heart to perform Thy statutes, for ever, at every step.

Saul was amazed that he recalled the passages from the Psalms of David, 119. He felt at peace as he exited Jonathan's room. He could hear that Jonathan was snoring, asleep on the couch, and decided that some rest was not a bad idea. However, he did not want to go to bed, so he joined Jonathan in the living room and sat in the recliner. Saul tilted it back and, within moments, he too was sound asleep.

CHAPTER 17

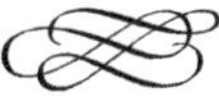

Jonathan and Saul were awoken the next morning by loud knocking on the front door. As Jonathan rubbed his eyes he could hear Michael outside yelling for him and Saul. Jonathan jumped from the couch but saw that Saul was already opening the door. The sunlight rushed into the room as Michael came in past Saul.

"We should have been at the dig an hour ago," Michael fumed, "remember, no attention."

Saul and Michael looked at their watches and went to their respective bedrooms to gather their things and go to the site of the dig. Michael waited in the den somewhat impatiently. Michael grabbed his cleanest dirty shirt, slipped it on over his dirtier T-shirt, picked up his kippah and placed it on his head. He looked at the metal tube just sitting on his desk and reached to get it as well. As he walked from the room he ran into Saul in the hallway.

"Why do you have the scroll?" Saul asked.

Michael explained that he did not want to leave it here and thought it could be left in the Land Rover during the day. Saul did not like this idea.,

"Leave it on your desk," Saul urged, "we have not lost anything in this room to thieves in the three years we have been here. It will be alright."

Jonathan hesitated but knew Saul was right and returned the metal tube to his desk.

"Come on," Michael shouted as he bounded out the door for the Land Rover.

As Saul and Jonathan closed the door of their cottage, Michael quietly mentioned that he had purchased the tickets for the three of them to fly out from Tel Aviv to New York on Wednesday afternoon.

"What about Solomon?" Saul asked.

Michael explained that he had not seen Solomon yet but reassured Saul that it would not be a problem as the three took their familiar seats inside the Land Rover. Not a word was spoken until the three arrived at the dig site as they had each morning for the past three years. It was true, they were later than usual, but this would not be noticed. As Jonathan pulled the Land Rover to a stop, Saul finally spoke.

"Everyone clear on the plan?" Saul asked.

Jonathan and Michael both nodded their heads to affirm that they understood. Saul immediately headed toward the center of Tiberias where the excavation site of the Hebrew University students and their faculty stood. Jonathan and Michael approached the first ladder at their excavation site. Jonathan watched as Saul quickly traversed the distance between the Land Rover and where the Hebrew University students and faculty were digging. Michael was descending the ladder.

"Are you coming?" Michael asked.

Jonathan followed Michael downward to the first level, and again down another ladder to the second level and the site where the scroll had been discovered. Jonathan felt as if he was moving in slow motion. He saw all the tools gathered together and reached for a small trowel.

"Let's see if we can find anything else along the base of the wall," Jonathan suggested.

As Jonathan and Michael bent over to begin the appearance of working, that was just what was happening. Jonathan could not stop thinking about the discovery of the scroll. Michael was whistling and scratching dirt away from the wall where the scroll had been found. Jonathan again felt he was moving in slow motion. He was annoyed that Michael was so happy while he cleared the dirt.

"Why are you so happy?" Jonathan asked.

Michael looked at his Professor as if the question was too stupid to even reply. Michael stood up and Jonathan stood up and walked over to where Michael stood. The two men looked at each other, student and teacher. Michael laughed.

"You don't get it... we are going home!" Michael exclaimed, "and with a treasure of unknown value and full of mystery."

Jonathan looked at Michael and his exuberance and suddenly felt much older. He smiled, adjusted his kippah, removed his glasses, took the handkerchief from his pocket, cleaned the lenses and placed the glasses back on his face. Slowly his somber face cracked into a large smile as he realized what Michael had said—the obvious. After three years they are going home, and they are going home with a great discovery.

"You're right," Jonathan laughed and repeated, "you're right," let's get back to pretending to work."

Jonathan slapped Michael on the back and they both went back to moving small amounts of dirt away from the wall.

While Jonathan and Michael were digging at the excavation site, Saul looked for the two men with whom he had been talking the day Michael interrupted him for the discovery. Saul could see that the excavation was coming along for the Hebrew University. He admired the support the University provided. There must have been at least fifty people at the excavation site. Saul saw the men he was looking for under a canopy looking at charts.

"Good morning, Dr. Zimmerman, Dr. Silverstein," Saul shouted as he approached the canopy.

Both men looked up and immediately called Dr. Harkman by name and turned to walk toward him with a similar greeting.

"What brings you over this morning?" Dr. Zimmerman asked.

"I wanted to talk to you and Dr. Silverstein about some equipment," Saul replied.

Dr. Zimmerman complained that this was much too formal. He introduced himself as "Levi" and Dr. Silverstein as "Abraham."

"I am Saul."

Saul, Levi, and Abraham entered the canopy and stood around the tables with the charts. It took some effort for Saul not to study the charts. Abraham left for a moment and returned with three coffees. Saul thanked Abraham and after some pleasantries, Levi went right to the point.

"What brings you to our site this morning Saul?" Levi queried.

Saul asked Levi and Abraham if they recalled the conversation from two days ago about selling some equipment. They both acknowledged that Saul had mentioned this possibility. Saul began his tell that he had rehearsed in his mind several times in order to prevent suspicions from being raised in the two Professor from the Hebrew University. Saul outlined briefly the past three years, casually mentioned the discoveries, downplaying them all, and alluded to the finances being stopped. Levi and Abraham looked at each other as Saul wove his tale of woe about how their backers had stopped sending money and they were basically just living on their meager salaries from the University for the past three months. However, now, the University was requiring him and his partner, Dr. Weitzman to return or take unpaid leave.

"Neither of us are wealthy men, we live on teachers' salaries," Saul laughed.

The two professors laughed with Saul and acknowledged that teachers' salaries were not much.

"But how can we help?" Levi asked again.

Saul then explained that there was not enough money for the three to purchase tickets to get home. Levi and Abraham listened as Saul told them that he and Dr. Weitzman planned to abandon the excavation site and return to the United States. However, they cannot afford to take all of their equipment with them.

"I would ask if you would be interested in buying our equipment," Saul finally asked.

Levi and Abraham looked at each other. Levi asked what type of equipment. Saul was prepared and pulled out a list from his pocket that inventoried the shovels, pick axes, ladders, lanterns, sifters, trowels, all to the tools they had brought with them or purchased since arrival. Abraham and Levi took the list from Saul and studied the items with serious faces. Finally, Levi inquired how much Saul wanted for the equipment. Saul suggested 3,000 American dollars. Abraham whistled and had a look of pain on his face. Levi studied the list once again. He and Abraham walked a little away from Saul and were whispering. Saul tried to make out what was being said but was unable to hear anything. Finally they both returned and Levi apologized for the private conference.

"Saul," Levi began, "we have no need for this equipment. The Hebrew University supplies us with everything we need. However, there may be an arrangement."

Saul listened as Levi outlined that he and Abraham believed that the excavation site Jonathan and Saul started was in the stables of Herod's palace. They wanted to expand their excavation site into the same area. However, because of the Antiquities Commission, Jonathan and Saul held the rights to the sight and any discoveries for another eight months. Levi offered to give Saul 2,000 American dollars for the equipment and the rights to the excavation site. Saul thought for a moment about the possibility of something else to be found. He quickly decided that he, Jonathan, and Michael could finish searching for anything obvious today. He countered with 2500 dollars. Levi and Abraham looked at each other, Abraham nodded yes and the three shook hands.

"We will be out of the sight today," Saul advised both men.

Abraham departed to a tent for several moments and returned with 2500 American dollars in cash. Levi explained that, when Saul checked out with the Antiquities Commission, he could simply sign a transfer for the remaining eight months of the excavation site over to Drs. Levi Zimmerman and Abraham Silverstein.

"Don't you mean the Hebrew University?" Saul asked.

"Saul," Levi laughed, "we get paid teachers' salaries as well."

Saul understood that the two professors thought that there might be more money in the excavation and they did not need the University's money to purchase the site. Their books would show that the 2500 dollars was spent to buy equipment. Saul was not impressed with their deception but at this point did not care. The three said their good-byes and Saul hurried back to the excavation site.

When he arrived, he found Michael and Jonathan haphazardly scraping at the base of the wall. Jonathan saw him first.

"How did it go?" he asked.

Saul explained the negotiations and the amount of money that was paid. Jonathan was pleased but was curious as to why the two professors from the Hebrew University would want the excavation site. Saul theorized that there may be more here and suggested that instead of the small, slow process of scraping away small amounts of dirt, the three began looking to make sure there was nothing else significant to be found.

"There is one catch," Saul said and Jonathan's face fell, "we need to be out of here by today, not Monday as planned."

"But the tickets to leave are for Wednesday," Jonathan explained.

Michael quickly pointed out that when he got back to the cottage tonight he could easily change the tickets to Tuesday. This would require Saul to go to Jerusalem tomorrow.

"The only catch will be Solomon as he had planned to drive us on Wednesday. I will see him tonight and hopefully he can make the change also," Michael injected.

"Then we better get this site ready," Saul quipped and began moving toward Jonathan.

Jonathan agreed and the remainder of the day was spent searching for loose stones in the wall, trying to see into the hole where the water jug with the scroll had been found, and moving large amounts of dirt. The three found a couple more coins and pieces of iron, but nothing of real value.

About 1700 hours Saul directed that all the tools be stacked neatly on that level. Just as they were finishing, Dr. Zimmerman and Dr. Silverstein appeared at the rim of the excavation site.

"Are you guys finished?" Levi asked.

Saul began an ascent of the ladder, followed by Jonathan and Michael. When the three reached the top, Saul shook the hand of Levi and Abraham.

"We are finished," Saul said to both men, "the site is yours."

With some sadness Saul, Jonathan, and Michael walked back to the Land Rover for the last time from this excavation site. Jonathan heard one of the men on the radio ordering someone to come to the site to get the equipment. The three climbed into the Land Rover and, after traveling about two miles, a large smile simultaneously came over the three men.

"We are on our way," Saul exclaimed as the three slapped their hands together in a high five.

Dust flew up behind the Land Rover as Saul, Jonathan, and Michael returned to their cottages. Saul and Jonathan knew that the real challenge lay ahead, getting the scroll out of the country and back to the United States. The Land Rover pulled into the front of the cottage occupied by Saul and Jonathan and came to a stop.

Before anyone stepped out of the Land Rover, Saul reminded everyone of their plan. Michael needed to speak to Solomon tonight. Tomorrow, Michael would help Jonathan pack up the cottages.

"While you two are packing, I will drive to Jerusalem to check out with Mr. Goldman at the Antiquities Commission," Saul reminded everyone.

Saul was comforted in the fact that he had 2500 American dollars for a bribe, which should make things very easy and quick at the Antiquities Commission tomorrow. Michael started for his cottage and Jonathan and Saul reached their front door.

"Get a good night's sleep," Jonathan shouted, "it's a big day tomorrow."

Michael waved his hand to acknowledge Jonathan's salutation and hurried off to find Solomon.

CHAPTER 18

Saul and Jonathan were both up early on Monday morning. Saul was preparing to leave for Jerusalem and reviewing last minute details with Jonathan over breakfast.

"We need to make our exit with as little attention as possible," Saul cautioned Jonathan.

Jonathan had difficulty sleeping thinking about the scroll. He desperately wanted to begin the translation but knew that was not possible while still in Israel. He had laid in his bed for hours imagining what was in the scroll, what new information or secrets would be revealed. He knew that Saul hoped that it would finally expose the man Jesus as just another man and do away with this Christian myth that he was the Son of God. Jonathan's hopes were not that lofty, but he did hope that new information would be shed on exactly who this man Jesus had been. At breakfast he was half-listening to Saul. Michael's familiar excited knock on the door brought Jonathan back to reality.

Michael walked in without waiting for either Saul or Jonathan to extend an invitation. Saul asked immediately about Solomon. Michael explained that Solomon would meet them around 1000 hours on Tuesday.

"That late?" Jonathan asked, a little shocked at the late hour. He had hoped to be gone with the rising sun.

Michael explained the travel arrangements. The three would fly out of Tel Aviv on British Airways Flight 164 that departed at 1640 hours. The flight landed in London for a twelve hour lay-over and then departed the next day to JFK. To allow for the hour and forty-five minute drive to Tel Aviv and then the need to be at the airport two hours before departure for an international flight, he thought noon would give plenty of time. Jonathan acknowledged that Michael was right and Saul just chuckled in the background. He was continuing his preparation for his two hour drive to Jerusalem to meet with Mr. Goldman. He pulled a worn black leather pouch from his back pocket and asked Michael to count the money contained inside. Michael announced a total of four thousand dollars. Saul advised that this included the money for the excavation site and equipment. The airline tickets had been paid for on Saul's credit card. Saul explained how he hoped to get away with a bribe of just two thousand dollars, leaving the remainder for the three to travel. Jonathan thought that was ambitious but agreed that Saul should at least try. Jonathan and Saul had agreed previously to just give Mr. Goldman American dollars and not try to exchange for the Israeli shekel.

Saul finished packing his backpack with documents and placed the leather pouch with the money back in his back pocket.

"Let's get going," Saul said and walked out the front door. Jonathan and Michael followed as Saul went straight to the Land Rover.

Saul reminded both men of the importance of packing up everything in the cottages in order to depart the Kibbutz. He left it to Jonathan to go to the director of the Degaina Bet Country Lodge and make sure everything was in order for their departure tomorrow.

"I just want to leave the keys in the room and leave," Saul reminded Jonathan.

Jonathan countered that it might speed things up if Michael went ahead and checked out of his cottage completely and just slept on the couch of their cottage. Saul agreed and Michael thought that was a great idea. Satisfied that everything was going as planned, Saul climbed into the Land Rover. As he backed out onto the road, he waved good-bye to Jonathan and Michael. As Saul drove away he looked in his rear view mirror and saw Jonathan adjust his kippah, remove his large round glasses and pull the handkerchief from his pocket. Saul smiled at the familiar sight and turned the Land Rover onto the road that led to Jerusalem.

Michael and Jonathan watched until the Land Rover was out of sight.

"We need to get started," Jonathan spoke these words to no one in particular and he returned his glasses back to his face and brushed a thick lock of his black hair out of his eyes.

Michael took off at a quick pace toward his cottage, exclaiming he would meet up with Jonathan around lunch time. Jonathan returned to his cottage, walked in the front door and surveyed the living room. The majority of the work was to throw away everything that was not going to be taken back to the United States. This included cleaning the refrigerator and the bathroom. Jonathan found the suitcases, his two and the two for Saul. He carried Saul's suitcases to his bedroom and returned to his room. He let his hands fall onto the metal tube which contained the scroll. The temptation was very strong to open the tube, but Jonathan resisted. He busied himself with packing away the clothes he wanted to take back with him. He made two piles, one to pack, one to throw away. He realized very early that he probably would only need the one suitcase as he was not taking back as much as he brought with him. He left out a pair of brown khaki trousers, his best pair, a change of underwear, and a blue shirt. He planned to throw away the clothes he was wearing in the morning. Satisfied that his clothes were packed, he then proceeded to pack his backpack with his laptop, pencils, pens, a couple of magazines, and the book Thomas Jefferson: The Art of Power by Jon Mecham. A friend had sent it to him from the United States. Jonathan had not had time to start the book and had decided that the airport and layover would give him time to read. He placed the metal tube inside the backpack with about twelve inches sticking out of the top. He again gently moved his hands over the top of the tube and slightly twisted the cap clockwise to remove it, but resisted and turned the cap counterclockwise and tightened it snuggly. He found a few artifacts, pieces of iron and about two dozen Roman coins from the dig and threw these into his only suitcase and closed it tight. He lifted the suitcase to make sure it did not exceed the fifty pound limit. Satisfied that the suitcase would not cost any overweight fees, Jonathan gathered all of the unneeded clothes, trash, and other unnecessary items and placed them in a large, green trash bag to be taken to the dumpster behind the office. He looked around his bedroom for the past three years and was satisfied that he had all he wanted. Jonathan turned and started toward the kitchen to clean out the refrigerator. He laughed to himself as he did not think that either he or Saul had cleaned the refrigerator since their arrival.

Saul covered the distance to Jerusalem quickly. There was little traffic and he arrived after only about an hour and a half of driving. Saul found a suitable parking spot for the Land Rover about two blocks from his destination. Saul grabbed his backpack and started his walk to the Antiquities Commission. Saul reached the steps and, with a bounce in his step, took two at a time and entered the state building that housed the Antiquities Commission. He walked down the hall that led to Mr. Goldman's office, hoping for the last time. As Saul entered he immediately saw Mr. Goldman in the same place behind the desk too large for the room. Mr. Goldman was picking at a sore on his bald head and smoking his cigarillo with a long ash hanging fire.

"Good morning Dr. Harkman," Mr. Goldman announced as he acknowledged Saul's arrival.

"What can I do for you today?" Mr. Goldman asked as he pushed his glasses from the tip of his nose back onto his face.

Saul watched as the ash from the end of the cigarillo fell onto the large desk. Mr. Goldman just pushed it aside and waited.

Saul outlined for Mr. Goldman the plans to leave Israel and transfer the permit to dig at Tiberias to Dr. Zimmerman and Dr. Silverstein. Saul inquired about the transfer paperwork. He also explained that he had some artifacts to declare.

"You are leaving us?" Mr. Goldman exclaimed, genuinely sounding shocked.

Mr. Goldman expressed his fondness for Saul and Jonathan and his sadness at their departure. He then inquired as to what artifacts were to be declared. Saul listed the additional Roman Coins found, some pieces of an iron gate, and the water jug. Mr. Goldman seemed most interested in the water jug. Mr. Goldman reminded Saul that the artifacts belonged to Israel and could not be removed from the country without the expressed written consent of the Antiquities Commission. Saul inquired about the transfer. Mr. Goldman explained that it could take days, even weeks to prepare the paperwork. He smiled at Saul through yellow teeth and crushed out his cigarette.

"When did you plan to leave?" Mr. Goldman asked.

Saul explained that they were scheduled to leave in the morning. Mr. Goldman started to express his sympathy that the departure would be delayed when Saul interrupted.

"I have a sizable donation for a charity of your choice, Mr. Goldman," Saul continued, "that I would be happy to leave with you if the paperwork could be completed this afternoon."

Saul passed an envelope containing the two thousand dollars to Mr. Goldman. Mr. Goldman felt the thickness and his eyes widened. For the first time that Saul could recall, Mr. Goldman actually looked in the envelope.

"Yes, yes," Mr. Goldman stated idly, "come back in one hour, the paperwork will be completed."

Saul asked about the transfer and Mr. Goldman asked for the full names for Dr. Zimmerman and Dr. Silverstein so that the papers could be done correctly. Saul thanked Mr. Goldman and turned to exit.

"You will certainly be missed," Mr. Goldman said and grinned as he placed the envelope containing the two thousand dollars into his desk drawer.

Saul went down the street and ate some lunch and returned after an hour. True to his word, Mr. Goldman had everything prepared. Saul signed the transfer order and asked for a copy to give to Dr. Zimmerman and Dr. Silverstein. Mr. Goldman was happy to accommodate. Within half an hour, Saul was outside the Antiquities Commission for the last time and walking to the Land Rover. As he reached the Land Rover and turned to start the journey back to Tiberias, he tried to have good thoughts, but his resentment towards Mr. Goldman was too much.

"Good riddance," Saul shouted as he drove in the opposite direction of the Antiquities Commission with his hand out the window and middle finger raised in a last act of bitterness.

Saul brought his hand back inside the Land Rover with a sense of satisfaction at his act of defiance. A small smile ran across his lips and he stroked his beard as his thoughts wandered to the scroll in the tube. He had not declared it as an artifact and soon he, Jonathan, Michael, and the scroll would be on a jet to London.

"To hell with Mr. Goldman and the Antiquities Commission," Saul shouted as he sped out of Jerusalem.

Mr. Goldman counted the two thousand dollars again and placed the envelope in the left inside pocket of his jacket. He thought carefully about his next actions and picked up the telephone, quickly dialing a number he knew by heart.

"Joseph," Mr. Goldman stated, "This Dr. Harkman and Dr. Weinstein are leaving tomorrow. I think that there is something going on that should be investigated."

Mr. Goldman explained to his friend Joseph, who was in charge of the National Treasures division of the Israel Antiquities Authority, the situation. He informed Joseph that Dr. Harkman and Dr. Weinstein were staying at the Deganina Bet Kbbutz and planned to leave tomorrow.

"I will meet you at 0900 in the morning and we will head out there," Mr. Goldman stated on the phone, "I would bring three or four officers, just in case."

Mr. Goldman hung up the phone. He could care less about the Roman coins, but if a water jug had been found, maybe Dr. Harkman had other things he was not declaring.

“We will see what tomorrow brings,” Mr. Goldman said with a chuckle and patted his coat at his left breast, smiling at the thickness of the money he had placed there. Reassured the money was secure, he rose from his desk and walked to the only window in his office. It looked out over the street. Mr. Goldman watched with great interest as the Land Rover sped away from the building.

“What are you hiding, Dr. Harkman?” he whispered quietly to himself, “what indeed.”

CHAPTER 19

Saul arrived back at the cottages just as Michael was walking up to the front door with his suitcase in hand and a loaded backpack over his shoulder. Jonathan came outside and saw the large smile on Saul's face.

"It went well?" Jonathan asked.

Saul explained that the money was more than adequate for Mr. Goldman. All paperwork was completed for the transfer of the site, and all antiquites declared save one.

Michael shook Saul's hand and congratulated him on a successful "mission." Michael reported that he had spoken to Solomon to finalize a noon departure tomorrow. Michael related that he had not mentioned the deal with the Land Rover and thought it best to deliver this good news to Solomon at the airport after their departure.

"I think we will encourage him to stay until we board our flight. We can give him the keys as we are boarding. That way, if he is suspicious, it will be too late and we will be on our way home!" Michael said to both Saul and Jonathan with a large grin on his face.

The three entered the small cottage together. Michael picked up his suitcase and backpack as the three crossed the threshold. Saul was shocked at the work that had been done. Michael confirmed that he had checked out and would be staying the night on the couch.

"Just left to you to pack," Jonathan said to Saul with excitement.

"Where is the scroll?" Saul asked anxiously.

Jonathan picked up his backpack and showed Saul the metal tube sticking out of the top. Saul admitted to himself that it did not appear to be suspect in any manner.

"What about the airport?" Saul suddenly asked aloud, "we will need to get through security, they will open the tube!"

Jonathan smiled and calmed Saul, "Relax, I placed folded maps inside over the scroll, if they pull those out, the scroll will just look like another map."

Saul was somewhat relieved but still skeptical.

It was already late evening, the sun slowly setting in the western sky. As Jonathan and Michael began preparing their last meal before departure in the morning, Saul went to his room to begin the task of packing. He surveyed his room, his closet. He looked at the large green trash bags that Jonathan had left empty on the floor. Methodically, Saul placed his suitcase on the bed, opened it, went to the closet, took out two pairs of pants and two shirts and placed them in the suitcase. He went to his drawer and took out two days' change of underwear and added them to the contents of the suitcase. He decided he would place his toiletries in the suitcase tomorrow morning. He went to his desk, set aside his laptop, a few papers with quickly written notes, a couple of pencils and pens. He thought for a minute, placed those items in his backpack and reached for an empty, large, green trash bag. Holding the bag open, Saul raked the remaining items on his desk into the trash bag, pulled the drawers of the desk open and dumped the contents of all three into the same bag. He hurriedly went around the room filling trash bags with clothes, equipment, trash, everything except for the bed linens, the contents of his suitcase and his backpack. After about an hour he surveyed an empty room, save those items. On the floor were four large green garbage bags filled with three years of living in the kubitz. He asked for the help of Jonathan and Michael and the three men carried three years of Saul's life to the dumpster. There they unceremoniously tossed the four garage bags into the dumpster.

Without a moment of sorrow or regret, Saul turned around and said to the other two, "Let's eat."

Back at the cottage the three men talked excitedly about returning to the United States while they ate a modest meal of heated beans, unleavened bread, and flat wine. The discussion centered around the scroll and how best to go about translating the language. There was concern expressed by Johnathan that they would crumble and be useless.

"Let's pray not," Saul stated solemnly.

Michael expressed his faith that the scroll would support that Jesus was the Messiah, the Christ. Jonathan and Saul looked at him, a bit shocked and then laughed heartily.

"Very doubtful," Saul explained, "everything we have found thus far does not indicate that this man Jesus was a Messiah, Christ or anything."

Jonathan added his doubt, "But what if..."

"No," Saul shouted, "it is not possible."

Saul offered that the scroll most likely would shed light on how the myth of Jesus as the Messiah got started. The three discussed various theories of the scroll and what they would say as they finished dinner. All of Michael's theories centered around Jesus as the Messiah, Saul's, the exposure of the myth, and Jonathan vacillated between supporting Saul and expressing just a little concern that they could be wrong.

By the time they were finished with dinner, it was late, and the sun was gone. Saul suggested that the three get to bed early, up early and have the Land Rover packed and ready to go at 1000 hours when Solomon arrived. They all agreed, Saul and Jonathan departed for their rooms and Michael made himself comfortable on the couch. No one said "Goodnight," as each were in their own deep thoughts about tomorrow.

Jonathan did not sleep during the night and was awake when the sun began to rise. Saul was the same and they both entered the kitchen fully dressed and ready to go about the same time. Jonathan glanced at the couch and Michael appeared to be sleeping soundly.

As if Michael could hear their thoughts he exclaimed, "I couldn't sleep either."

The three men laughed. Jonathan glanced at his watch, noting it was almost three hours before they could leave.

"There is that small restaurant just a couple of miles up the road, we have been here for three years and never eaten there. Why don't we have a good meal and cup of coffee before we leave?" Saul suggested.

Michael and Jonathan eagerily agreed and the three loaded into the Land Rover and headed out for breakfast. They were completely unaware that, in Jerusalem, Mr. Goldman and his friend Joseph Levenson, the head of National Treasures division of the Israel Antiquities Authority, were finishing their breakfast, while outside a group of six soldiers waited in an olive drab Humvee transport. Mr. Goldman and Mr. Levenson were discussing their plans for the day over breakfast as well.

On arrival back at the cottages, Jonathan immediately went to the office to pay his and Saul's final bill. Saul and Michael went into the cottage to obtain the gear and load the Range Rover. Jonathan paid the bill and joined the other three. They exited the cottage with the three suitcases, each carrying a backpack. They loaded the suitcases into the rear of the Land Rover. Michael carefully carried the crated jug out and loaded it last, making sure it would not bounce around during the ride.

"Who is that?" Michael asked, pointing at the cloud of smoke rising from the road on the horizon.

Saul glanced at first, "Probably Solomon," he said flaty.

Then Saul stood erect and held his hand over his eyes to see better.

"Those are military vehicles," he said with some trepidation, "I believe they are coming for us."

Saul saw the panic in Jonathan and Michael's eyes.

"Stay calm, stick to the plan, we have done nothing wrong," Saul reassured.

Jonathan started to take the metal tube from his backpack, but hesitated as the vehicles came clearly into view.

Saul could see Mr. Goldman riding in a jeep with another man driving. Behind was a Humvee with several soldiers. Saul could not see how many soldiers but this could not be a good sign.

The jeep pulled in front of the Land Rover, blocking any exit, and the Humvee slid in behind, trapping the Land Rover between the two vehicles. Dust swirled around everyone as the vehicles came to a stop.

"Let me do the talking," Saul quickly said to Jonathan and Michael.

Joseph Levenson stepped from his jeep in military olive drab clothing. He was a very short man,

"Stubby," Saul thought to himself.

Saul watched as Mr. Goldman exited the Jeep behind the stubby short man.

"Good morning Dr. Harkman," Mr. Goldman shouted, "this is my friend Mr. Joseph Levenson. He is Head of the National Treasures division of the Israel Antiquities Authority. He has some questions."

Jonathan and Saul were quickly surrounded by six armed Isreali soldiers as Mr. Levenson walked up to Saul and stuck out his hand, smiling.

"Just a friendly visit before you depart from our country," Mr. Levenson said.

Saul noticed the gap between his yellow-stained teeth and smelled the strong odor of cigarettes.

"Does everyone get this type of sendoff?" Saul inquired.

Mr. Levenson and Mr. Goldman laughed large belly laughs and then Mr. Levenson's face became very serious. He looked at Saul, Jonathan, and Michael sternly.

"There is reason to believe that you are trying to exit our country with artifacts that belong to the National Treasures division of Israel Antiquities," Mr. Levenson stated matter-of-factly to Saul and the other two.

"I declared everything," Saul responded.

"We shall see, we shall see," Mr. Levenson replied and, with a snap of his fingers over his head, the soldiers went into action.

Two of the soldiers ushered Saul, Jonathan, and Michael away from the Land Rover and stood in front of them. The other four began pulling the luggage from the back and opening each suitcase. They were not gentle or caring, throwing the contents onto the dirt, tearing the linings from the suitcase. The few Roman coins and assorted iron nails fell into the ground. All the while, Mr. Levenson and Mr. Goldman stood and supervised. One soldier pulled the crated jug carefully from the Land Rover. Saul thought that this was deliberate, that Mr. Levenson had known about the water jug. The soldier walked the water jug over the jeep and placed it carefully into the back.

"That belongs to Israel," Mr. Levenson stated as a matter of explanation.

When the soldiers were finished tearing through the suitcases, they started on the Land Rover. Jonathan could see they were experts. The sides of the doors were removed, as well as all the seats. The Land Rover was stripped down inside to bare metal.

"Nothing," Mr. Levenson muttered under his breath as he walked around the empty Land Rover.

Saul saw Mr. Goldman whispering something to Mr. Levenson but could not make out what was being said.

"Search the backpacks," Mr. Levenson ordered to the soldiers.

Saul gave a quick glance at Jonathan who appeared panicked as the soldiers roughly removed his backpack. Michael handed his backpack over without incident and Saul did the same. The soldiers proceeded to pull out the contents of each backpack under the careful eye of Mr. Levenson. Mr. Goldman was leaning against the front of the jeep, watching, cigarillo hanging between his lips.

The soldier that took Jonathan's backpack dumped all the contents on the ground including the metal tube containing the scroll. Jonathan's papers, iPod and assorted writing instruments along with his laptop and the metal tube landed in the dirt. As the soldier picked up the metal tube, Jonathan adjusted his kippah, removed his glasses and pulled a dirty handkerchief from his pants and cleaned the lens very quickly. Saul could see the bits of perspiration building on Jonathan's forehead. The other soldiers quickly finished with the contents of Saul and Michael's backpacks and stood back, waiting for instructions. The other soldier with Michael handed the metal tube toward Mr. Levenson.

"What's in this?" Mr. Levenson asked Jonathan as Jonathan placed his handkerchief back in his pocket.

Saul waited anxiously, hopeful that Jonathan could remain calm. He let out a sigh in relief as he listened to Jonathan's quick response.

"Just some maps, not really anything," Jonathan said, looking directly at Mr. Levenson.

"Open the tube," Mr. Levenson ordered the soldier.

The soldier removed the cap and took out the fold maps from the top.

"Hey, what's going on?"

Everyone turned and looked as Solomon came riding his bicycle into the group.

"Did they do something wrong?" Solomon continued.

"Who is this?" Mr. Levenson directed at Saul.

As Saul explained that Solomon was a friend of Michael's and was driving them to the airport, Jonathan noticed that the soldier had placed the maps back in the tube and screwed the cap back into place. The soldier was holding the metal tube by his side. Michael was watching also.

Mr. Levenson seemed satisfied with Saul's answer. He looked around at all of the personal belongings lying on the ground surrounded with the seats and door panels from the Land Rover.

"Dr. Hartmann, we will not charge you for trying to take the antiquities from this country, we will simply confiscate them for the Israeli museums," Mr. Levenson instructed.

Mr. Levenson then ordered the soldiers to take the Roman coins, nails and other artifacts found in the suitcases. The soldier with Michael dropped the metal tube and scoop up the Roman Coins on the ground.

Saul protested, "We declared all of these with him," and pointed to Mr. Goldman.

Mr. Levenson explained that Mr. Goldman was not the final authority on what leaves Israel in terms of antiquities.

"If you would like to file a protest, we can go back into Jerusalem," Mr. Levenson offered.

From the corner of his eye, Saul saw the metal tube on the ground, he slowly bowed his head and nodded in the negative.

"I did not think so. Enjoy your flight home," Mr. Levenson shouted as he dropped behind the steering wheel of the Jeep. Mr. Goldman, laughing, climbed into the passenger's seat. The soldiers did the same, returning to the Humvee, leaving the metal tube lying on the ground at Jonathan's feet.

As the convoy pulled away, Saul whispered, "wait until they are out of sight."

Solomon looked perplexed and queried Michael as to what this was all about. As Michael explained things to Solomon, Saul rushed over Jonathan who had knelt down on one knee. Jonathan gingerly picked up the metal tube just as Saul joined him.

"That was close," Saul exclaimed.

Jonathan did not say a word. He slowly placed the metal tube back in his backpack, drew a heavy breath and looked at Saul. Saul could see tears in Jonathan's eyes.

"It's okay," Saul reassured in a low voice, "they are gone."

Jonathan stood up, holding his backpack with the metal tube against his chest with his left hand. With his right hand, Jonathan adjusted his kippah, removed his glasses and pulled a dirty handkerchief from his pants and cleaned the lens. He replaced his glasses and placed the handkerchief in his pocket. Saul saw a large grin run from each corner of Jonathan's mouth to cover his entire face. Saul began laughing, holding Jonathan by both shoulders. Solomon and Michael joined the men and the laughter, although Solomon was not sure where the humor was in the situation.

"What a mess," Solomon observed.

The men just kept laughing as they began the task of repacking their suitcases and backpacks. Solomon helped put the Land Rover back together. The four men were packed and off to the airport a little before noon.

On arrival at the airport Saul parked in short-term parking. Solomon did not say anything as the four entered the airport. Saul checked the flight to London and advised the other three that British Airways Flight 164 was on time. Michael asked Solomon to join him for lunch, which kept Solomon with the three until the flight departed as planned. The next hurdle was getting through security.

After lunch there was about an hour before the flight departure. Saul, Jonathan, and Michael stood at the entrance to airport security and said their good-byes to Solomon, thanking him for the ride.

"What about your Land Rover?" Solomon asked.

"It's yours," Saul said gleefully and threw Solomon the key.

Michael walked over and handed the title to Solomon, completely signing the vehicle over to the young man. He gushed thank you repeatedly and, as Saul was first to show his identification to airport security, Solomon left.

"Phase 1 completed," Saul thought.

All three breezed through the identification process and placed their backpacks on the conveyor belt for security. The metal tube stuck out of Jonathan's as it entered the x-ray scanner. Jonathan could feel himself sweating again as he passed through the metal detector. On the other side, Saul, then Jonathan, then Michael retrieve their backpacks. Nothing was said, no additional security checks were made. They walked to a table, replaced their shoes and belt, put on their watches and headed to their gate for departure.

"Really?" Jonathan said in the form of a question, "really?" he repeated.

After about 30 minutes they heard the words, "Now Boarding British Airways Flight 164 for London Gate 25." Saul, Jonathan, and Michael got into line and boarded the jet. Saul and Jonathan placed their backpacks in the overhead compartment and Jonathan held out the metal tube with the scroll to keep with him in their seats. They took their seats, Jonathan and Saul together, Michael behind them.

Just as Saul and Jonathan looked at each other and smiled, Michael exclaimed "Oh NO!"

Saul and Jonathan watched in horror as four Israeli Airport Security Police boarded the plane and pushed back through first class. They were coming right at Saul and Jonathan. Jonathan tightened his eyes together and slid the metal tube down between the seat and bulkhead of the plane. He heard shouting. The Israeli Airport Security Police stopped beside Saul and Jonathan.

"Come with us, please," the officer stated firmly in perfect Hebrew.

The man in the aisle next across from Saul got up and was escorted off the plane by the Security Police. Jonathan realized he was not breathing again. Saul looked at Jonathan; he was pale as a sheet. The Security Police left with the man, the Flight Attendant closed the door, and the plane began to be pulled from the gate.

As British Airways Flight 164 left the runway en route to London, Saul looked at Jonathan and the men slapped their hands in the air together in a high five. Michael leaned over the seat and joined each of them in his own high five.

"Phase 2 completed. We are on our way home," Saul said softly.

Jonathan gripped the metal tube tightly, settled back into his seat, placed headphones over his ears and simply said, "Thank God!"

CHAPTER 20

Saul, Jonathan, and Michael arrived at JFK airport after an uneventful flight from London. Jonathan held onto the metal tube containing the scroll as if it were filled with gold. After retrieving their luggage, Saul and Jonathan said goodbye to Michael, who planned to return to Boston for a few weeks to visit with family.

Saul and Jonathan decided that Jonathan would keep the scroll in the metal tube until they returned to the University. Saul would set up a workshop for them to begin translation between their classroom responsibilities.

"I'll see you Monday at the University," Saul said to Jonathan.

After three years together, it was difficult to part. Jonathan and Saul hugged each other and kissed each other's cheek. The two separated for the first time in three years. Jonathan, clutching tightly to the metal tube, hailed a cab to take him to his apartment. Saul did the same. No other words between them were spoken.

Monday arrived and Saul was first to be at the University. He went straight to his office only to find another name on the door. He was dismayed and went straight to see the Dean of Religious Studies.

"Your back,," Dean Lewis said, a little shocked.

"I wrote to you that I would be back," Saul responded, "and Dr. Weitzman is coming also. Has his office been given to someone else, too?"

Dean Lewis explained that after a year they needed the space. However, the University had provided an office on the fourth floor for Dr. Harkman.

"We need a lab as well, I wrote to you about that," Saul said anxiously, "and where is Dr. Weitman's office to be?"

Dean Lewis was a bit miffed that there was no gratitude. After all, the University was under no obligation to give him a job teaching, let alone offices and a lab. However, Dr. Harkman had a long history with the University and he was technically on a University sponsored trip for the first year, and then sabbatical. But Dr. Weitzman did not even have tenure and had been gone for three years. Dean Lewis explained to Dr. Harkman that Dr. Weitzman no longer had a teaching position at the University.

"He was fired?" Dr. Harkman asked in a challenging tone.

Dean Lewis explained that Dr. Weitzman had resigned after the first year in Israel to continue working in Israel. He told Saul he was not fired and quickly followed up that there currently were no openings for a Professor in Ancient Hebrew, even one as distinguished as Dr. Weitzman. Saul explained to Dean Lewis that they had found something important at the dig site and that he would need Dr. Weitzman's assistance to translate and interpret what was discovered. Dean Lewis pushed Saul to reveal what was found. Saul would not do that.

He and Jonathan agreed that no one except Michael would be privy to their discovery until the scroll was translated.

"I will be entitled to a graduate assistant," Saul asserted.

Dean Lewis acknowledged that was true and Saul informed him that it would be Dr. Weitzman. Dean Lewis argued that the pay was very little and meant for a student, not someone with a Phd.

"Do you have a job for him to teach?" Saul asked.

"No, I have already told you there are no positions," Dean Lewis responded, exasperated.

"Fine, then he will be my assistant. He will have an office in the lab on the fourth floor. It is settled," Saul confirmed, turned and left the Dean's office to go to the fourth floor.

"Jonathan will not be happy," Saul thought as he entered the elevator and the doors closed to take him to the fourth floor.

Saul walked to the door at the end of the hallway and saw the familiar sign, "Saul P. Harkman, Phd, Professor, Ancient Hebrew. He suddenly drew open the door. The office was much smaller but all of his books appeared to have been moved in. The desk had just a small, very thin layer of dust. Saul took his index finger and slowly wrote "clean me" in blocked letters. He noted a yellow legal paper with the words "Class Schedule" at the top and days of the week, times and room numbers for his teaching. He noted that the first class was not until Wednesday. The chair, covered in similar dust, was pushed beneath the desk. Saul sat his briefcase down, pulled the chair out, took a handkerchief from his pants pocket and beat the seat of the chair until the dust disappeared. Just as he sat down he heard a rap on the door.

"So this is your new office."

It was Jonathan and in his hand was the metal tube. Saul was very happy to see him.

"Why didn't you tell me you gave up your job?" Saul asked as he walked over to the doorway to greet Jonathan.

"Would it have made a difference, two years ago, in Israel?" Jonathan replied and they both laughed.

Jonathan explained that he had spoked to Dean Lewis and understood that he would be the new "graduate" assistant for Saul. Saul was concerned Jonathan would be insulted. But that was the least of Jonathan's concerns. There was enough graduate assistant money to pay his rent and that he would be able to work on the scroll full time.

"Does Dean Lewis know about the scroll?" Jonathan asked.

"No one knows but you, me, and Michael," Saul replied, "Let's go look at our lab."

Saul and Jonathan walked into the hallway and halfway down the hall on the left hand side was a door with an opaque window and the words "Private" written in the center. They opened the door to a small room, about 8 feet by 8 feet with a solitary light above, no furniture. There were windows all along the farthest wall.

"This is perfect," Jonathan observed, "a long table and chair, something to store supplies, no phone, just perfect."

Saul suggested that the windows be darkened to avoid light hitting the scroll when laid out. He also wanted at least three padlocks on the outside of the door.

"We can get the supplies tonight and have things set up tomorrow," Saul said, "I don't have my first class till Wednesday, so I can help you set up. Let's get a cup of coffee and come up with a plan."

Jonathan and Saul actually had two cups of coffee. They divided the list of supplies needed and agreed to meet in the morning to set up the room.

Saul asked, "have you looked at the scroll?"

Jonathan replied, "No, I have not seen it since we placed it in the metal tube in Israel, but it never leaves me, I take the metal tube everywhere.

The next morning, the two professors began setting up the lab. They had purchased two long tables to fit end to end. The University provided some lighting and chairs. Jonathan placed a small four drawer cabinet against one wall to keep supplies. He had purchased several pens, pencils, tablets, magnifying glasses, and assorted weights to hold the scroll in place. While Jonathan was putting things away inside the room, Saul was installing the padlocks on the outside. Three locks, three different keys, two sets of keys, one set for Jonathan, one set for Saul. Saul knew the scroll would need to be left on the tables when Jonathan left each day and he did not want any "accidents" or prying eyes. Next, Saul installed a padlock on the inside of the door, so when working no one could come in expectantly. Since Saul had to teach, the bulk of the translating would be left to Jonathan with Saul helping as he could. For Jonathan's part, this would be his job as graduate assistant, translating the scroll.

It was late evening before the room was finished and the proper security in place. Saul had some time to set up his office. The University installed a telephone during the day which was helpful. Saul noted that Jonathan had placed the metal tube with the scroll in one of the drawers in the cabinet. He was not surprised to see that there were two padlocks on the side of that drawer.

"Here is your set of keys to the door," Saul said as he handed Jonathan three keys.

"And here is your set to the cabinet," Jonathan replied.

They discussed a strategy for beginning the work in the morning. Saul commented that his first class was not until 10 am so he could help Jonathan get started. The two men left and agreed to begin at 0800 the next morning.

Saul arrived first and unlocked each padlock, beginning at the top. He opened the door and went inside.

"I'll need another chair," he thought.

He was going to get one from another office when Jonathan arrived. He had the metal tube containing the scroll as he always did. When Jonathan entered the room, Saul closed the door and hooked the inside padlock through the lock but did not lock it. Dr. Harkman and Dr. Weitzman stood looking at the metal tube, now lying on the table.

"It's now or never," Jonathan let out a long breath, then he adjusted his kippah, removed his glasses and pulled a dirty handkerchief from his pants and cleaned the lens of his glasses, returning the handkerchief to his pocket.

Both Jonathan and Saul took cotton gloves from the top drawer of the supply chest and pulled them over their hands to protect the document from the oils on their fingers. Jonathan removed the cap of the metal tube and removed the maps. The baggie containing the few fragments was extracted next. With great care, as if cradling a perfect snowflake, Jonathan removed the scroll from the metal tube, the oil cloth still wrapped gently around the scroll to protect it. As Jonathan removed the oil cloth, a few fragments fell onto the table but the scroll was intact. Very slowly, Jonathan unrolled the scroll, carefully taking the scroll and rolling it onto the table. The scroll was dark brown, and the ink used was even a darker brown. Some areas were faded. Saul took weights to hold down each of the four corners. Jonathan grabbed a ruler to measure the width and length. The scroll was 30 centimeters high and 75 cm long. Saul documented the dimensions and the appearance of the scroll on a yellow pad. Next Jonathan took a camera and made multiple digital photographs on the scroll from several angles. Jonathan and Saul were satisfied with recording the superficial qualities of the scroll.

Jonathan sat down in the only chair and pulled a magnifying lamp with a built in light over the first section of the scroll to read the lettering:

אני ג'ון , קרא המטביל

"I am John, called the Baptist," Jonathan stated aloud for Saul to hear and then he took a leather bound notebook and in blue ink wrote the same on the first line of the first page, "I am John, called the Baptist."

"It begins," Saul said, weeping.

CHAPTER 21

For several months Jonathan and Saul worked on the translation of the scroll. After translating just the first few paragraphs, Jonathan had declared with certainty that the author was John the Baptist. Saul continued teaching Ancient Hebrew, but when he could he would assist Jonathan. Primarily, he would review Jonathan's work for the day to make sure that it was correct in terms of translation. To date, Saul had not had to make any corrections. Because the language of the scroll was ancient Hebrew, hand-written translation was painstakingly slow at times. Sometimes Jonathan would spend several days on a single sentence. However, both Jonathan and Saul agreed that the translation had to be right.

Michael returned from Boston about two weeks after the translation work began. He did not speak, read, or understand ancient Hebrew. However, he was helpful in providing history that provided context for the text. Michael's knowledge of the New Testament helped Jonathan determine time lines regarding the content. Michael would also spend time in the library, researching documents regarding John the Baptist. He looked at both theological documents, as well as other writers such as Josephus. Jonathan and Saul were very familiar with Josephus and his writings, but not so much with the details regarding John the Baptist. Michael explained that the historian Josephus essentially corroborates the accounts of John the Baptist found in the Christian "New Testament" first four books.

"The Gospels," Michael added for clarification.

Michael found the account of John the Baptist is the *Antiquities of the Jews* (book 18, chapter 5, 2) by Flavius Josephus (37–100).

> "Now some of the Jews thought that the destruction of Herod's army came from God, and that very justly, as a punishment of what he did against John, that was called the Baptist: for Herod slew him, who was a good man, and commanded the Jews irate, both as to righteousness towards one another, and piety towards God, and so to come to baptism; for that the washing [with water] would be acceptable to him, if they made use of it, not in order to the putting away [or the remission] of some sins [only], but for the purification of the body; supposing still that the soul was thoroughly purified beforehand by righteousness. Now when [many] others came in crowds about him, for they were very greatly moved [or pleased] by hearing his words, Herod, who feared lest the great influence John had over the people might put it into his power and inclination to raise a rebellion, (for they seemed ready to do anything he should advise,) thought it best, by putting him to death, to prevent any mischief he might cause, and not bring himself into difficulties, by sparing a man who might make him repent of it when it would be too late. Accordingly he was

> sent as a prisoner, out of Herod's suspicious temper, to Macherus, the castle I before mentioned, and was there put to death. Now the Jews had an opinion that the destruction of this army was sent as a punishment upon Herod, and a mark of God's displeasure to him."

However, there was little found regarding the early life of John the Baptist.

As the months passed, Michael's research discovered many conflicting histories of John the Baptist. The Church of Jesus Christ of Latter Day Saints (LDS) teaches that John the Baptist appeared on the banks of the Susquehanna River near Harmony Township, Susquehanna County, Pennsylvania as a resurrected being to Joseph Smith and Oliver Cowdery on May 15, 1829, and ordained them to the Aaronic Priesthood. According to LDS doctrine, John's ministry has operated in three dispensations: he was the last of the prophets under the law of Moses; he was the first of the New Testament prophets; and he was sent to confirm the Aaronic Priesthood in our day (the dispensation of the fullness of times). Mormons believe John's ministry was foretold by two prophets whose teachings are included in the Book of Mormon: Lehi and his son Nephi.

Jonathan was fascinated by the many references to John the Baptist by other religions. As a student of Ancient Hebrew he was aware that John was considered a prophet by the Jewish people, as well as a priest. The baptism described in the New Testament would be consistent with the Jewish ritual of Mikvah, a form of baptism. As a priest or prophet, John would have practiced this ritually cleaning through immersion. As an Orthodox, Jew he had seen the special baths called ritualariums constructed for the purpose of baptism or immersion. Through contact with women who are ritually unclean or through the violation of other tabus, a man may also become polluted (Lev. 11-15; Nums. 19). As a means of cleansing or purification and sanctification, a ritual of total immersion is required for him. So Jonathan had always considered John the Baptist a prophet or at the very least a priest who foretold the coming of the Messiah. But Jesus was that Messiah. For that to be true, Jonathan knew that John the Baptist would need to be the reincarnation of Elijah the Jewish Prophet. He hoped the scroll would shed light on exactly where John the Baptist fit in Christian and Jewish theology.

Michael also found that John the Baptist is a part of Islam and the Muslims and is considered a prophet of Islam. He is believed by Muslims to have been a witness to the word of God, and a prophet who would herald the coming of Jesus. His father Zechariah was also an Islamic prophet. Islamic tradition maintains that John was one of the prophets whom Muhammad met on the night of the Mi'raj, his ascension through the Seven Heavens. It is said that he met John and Jesus in the second heaven, where Muhammad greeted his two 'brothers' before ascending with archangel Gabriel to the third heaven. John's story was also told to the Abyssinian king during the Muslim refugees' Migration to Abyssinia. According to the Qur'an, John was one on whom God sent peace on the day that he was born and the day that he died. Michael brought this information to both Jonathan and Saul. Saul was more troubled about the prominence of John the Baptist in the Islam religion than Jonathan. Michael explained that, in the Qur'an, John was exhorted to hold fast to the Scripture and was given wisdom by God while still a child. He was pure and devout and walked well in the presence of God. He was dutiful towards his parents and he was not arrogant or rebellious. John's reading and understanding of the scriptures, when only a child, surpassed even that of the greatest scholars of the time. In Islam, John was a classical prophet who was exalted high by God for his bold denouncing of all things sinful. Furthermore, the Qur'an speaks of John's gentle pity and love and his humble attitude towards life, for which he was granted the Purity of Life: Michael found that John is also honored highly in Sufism as well as Islamic mysticism, primarily because of the Qur'an's description of John's chastity and kindness. Sufis have frequently applied commentaries on the passages on John in the Qur'an, primarily concerning the God-given gift of "Wisdom" which he acquired in youth as well as his parallels with Jesus. Although several phrases used to describe John and Jesus are virtually identical in the Qur'an, the manner in which they are expressed is different. Michael found it fascinating that the Qur'an and the New Testament accounts of John the Baptist were so similar. He questioned Jonathan many times as to why the Jews do not discuss John the Baptist except in Josephus even though he admittedly was the son of a Jewish High Priest, Zachariah. Jonathan did not have an answer but always listened intently on the research that Michael would bring to the room. All of the different stories, traditions, history, and writings from Josephus to the Qur'an were helpful in translation of the scrolls. With each line translated, each paragraph, each page, each passing month a clearer picture was painted of John the Baptist by his own hand.

After fourteen months of work, Jonathan walked into Saul's office late one evening and handed him two leather bound notebooks. As Saul took them from his hand, Jonathan flopped down into the chair across the desk from Saul.

"Is it finished?" Saul queried cautiously.

"Yes," Jonathan said in a low whisper, "it is finished."

Saul began at page one, line one,

"I am John, called the Baptist."

Jonathan sat as Saul slowly turned each page, eyes darting from side to side as he intently read and absorbed each line of translation. Sometimes he would turn back a page and re-read it in order to make sure that he understood the subsequent line of thinking. Jonathan sat quietly for three hours until Saul finished by placing both of the notebooks together on his desk. He leaned back in his chair and placed the fingertips of both hands together and brought them to his face.

"Do you believe this?" were Saul's first words to Jonathan.

"I do," Jonathan replied plainly.

The two men who had worked so long and so hard sat staring at each other without a sound for what seemed like hours. Finally Saul stood up and took the two notebooks and handed them back to Jonathan.

"We are not finished," Saul stated.

Jonathan started to protest and Saul held up his hand to stop him before Jonathan was able to utter a single word.

"You must write this like the Christian Bible, the same form, verses, chapters," Saul said solemnly.

Jonathan nodded his head in the affirmative and then asked, "Do you believe it?"

Saul responded, "I am not sure. I will need to think about this for a while."

Saul sat back into his desk and sighed heavily.

"Tomorrow, carefully roll the scroll and protect it with oil cloth and place it in an airtight metal tube. We will secure it in a vault later tomorrow, then begin the re-writing of the translation in the Christian Bible form."

Jonathan stood up, looked down at his feet, then directly into Saul's eyes, and he adjusted his kippah, removed his glasses and pulled a dirty handkerchief from his pants and cleaned the lens of his glasses, returning the handkerchief to his pocket. Taking the notebooks with him, he turned, looked back again at Saul and headed down the hallway, past the lab, and, standing in front of the elevator he pushed the "down" button. Glancing down the hallway, Saul's door was still opened. Jonathan could see Saul in the dim light and he appeared to be kneeling. He appeared to be praying.

CHAPTER 22

Jonathan returned the next day but could not get the image of Saul's prayer from his head. He fumbled with the keys as he opened the three padlocks to enter the room where the translation had taken place. In his hand were the two notebooks containing the words translated from the scrolls over the past fourteen months. Once in the room, he closed the door and inserted the padlock through the clasp. He did not lock the padlock, but once he was sure no one could get into the room, Jonathan began to remove the weights that held the corners down of the fragile scroll. He went to the top drawer of the supply cabinet and took out a pair of cotton gloves, slipping them onto his hands. He then carefully began to roll the scroll back to its original size. Small fragments from the edges fell onto the table. Jonathan would go back and place those in a baggie after the scroll was secured. When finally rolled, Jonathan placed the oil-cloth carefully around the scroll. Walking as if he were carrying a flickering candle that would blow out any second, he transported the scroll to the supply cabinet. On top was the metal tube used to transport the scroll from Egypt. Jonathan carefully placed the scroll in the metal tube. He placed the tube cautiously back on top of the supply cabinet, not wanting to make any sudden shaking or dropping to cause more fragmentation. Satisfied that the scroll was safe, Jonathan returned to the table and, piece by piece, he picked up every fallen fragment and placed them in a baggie. He placed the baggie in the top of the metal tube, secured the cap and then placed the metal tube into his backpack. He reasoned it had been transported safely from Israel to the lab in his backpack and would be safe there until it could be locked into a vault.

Completing this task, Jonathan took out his laptop and placed it on the table. He powered the laptop up and opened his word processing program. He placed the first notebook to the left of the computer and adjusted his glasses forward on this nose to see the words better. He started to open the notebook when there was a light knock at the door.

"Must be Michael," Jonathan thought.

He went to the door and removed the lock from the inside clasp. Before opening the door he asked the identity of the person knocking.

"It's Michael," Michael responded, a bit frustrated, "who did you think it would be?"

Jonathan opened the door and allowed Michael into the room.

"Where's the scroll?" Michael asked.

Michael had gone back to Boston for the weekend and had no idea the translation was finished. He had mostly helped Saul with classes, grading exams, and the graduate assistant duties that Jonathan would have done if he had been a real graduate assistant. He had read small portions of the translation, but only bits and pieces.

"I have placed it back in the metal tube, we are finished with it for now," Jonathan responded quietly.

"You finished the translation?" Michael inquired further.

Jonathan told Michael to sit down. He picked up the books and passed them to Michael.

"Read the translation for yourself, Saul read it last night." Jonathan instructed, "I will go out for coffee, lock the door behind me."

With those words, Jonathan gave the two notebooks to Michael and left the lab. Michael replaced the lock into the claps as Jonathan headed for the elevator. Michael then sat down with the notebooks and opened the first page.

"I am John, called the Baptist."

Michael quickly began to read the translation. He could not read the words fast enough.

"Can this be true?" Michael thought to himself, as he turned each page, "it can't be," he kept repeating.

Jonathan was gone intentionally for about an hour to give Michael time to read the translation. He knocked on the door and when he saw Michael he could see that he had been crying.

"Are you okay?" Jonathan asked.

"This is so hard to believe, so hard," Michael said with a touch of sadness mixed with joy, "but it must be."

"Yes, it is hard to believe," Jonathan agreed, "not anything that we expected or set out to learn."

"What are you going to do now?" Michael wanted to know.

Jonathan explained that Saul had recommended that the translation be transcribed in the same form as the Christian New Testament Bible, in chapters and verses to make it easier to read. Michael thought that was a great idea.

"That will make it easier to read and give it so much more meaning," Michael exclaimed.

Jonathan agreed. He explained that he was just sitting down to begin the task when Michael arrived.

"What about the scroll?" Michael asked.

Jonathan explained that Saul would be by later that afternoon to place it in a vault that was specially designed and climate controlled for artifacts. Michael explained that was not what he meant.

"This needs to be published, the discovery, the translation, all of it, the world needs to know," Michael exclaimed.

Jonathan had not considered what to do with the information. He was not sure that Saul had thought much about it either. However, Michael was right.

"Can you handle that while I work on converting the translation to Biblical form?" Jonathan asked with hesitation.

Michael was thrilled and considered it a tremendous honor to be allowed to be involved in publishing the story of the scrolls.

"Do you have a name for it yet?" Michael asked.

Jonathan thought deeply for a minute, holding his chin in his hand. He closed his eyes. Michael waited anxiously.

"The Gospel of the Baptist," Jonathan finally said.

Michael repeated "The Gospel of the Baptist."

Michael thought the title was perfect. He began listing the journals he would contact. He needed to write a synopsis of the discovery, of course, but the scroll itself was the story. He told Jonathan he could use the pictures Jonathan had taken before starting the translation. Jonathan was amazed at Michael's enthusiasm.

"Well, let's get to work," Jonathan advised.

Michael agreed and informed Jonathan he would go to the library and work on the publication of the discovery so Jonathan could work alone. Michael exited and Jonathan replaced the clasp on the lock.

Jonathan placed the notebook to the left of his computer, pushed his glasses to the end of his nose, opened the first page and began to move his fingers across the keyboard, transforming the translation literally into Scripture form.

"The Gospel of the Baptist"

CHAPTER 1

[1]I am John, called the Baptist.

Jonathan's fingers quickly began pushing the keys with the letters, adding verses and chapters. Without a break, he worked, and when he heard the knock at the door, it startled him. He heard a voice. It was Saul.

"Jonathan, you in there?" Saul asked.

Jonathan looked at his watch, it was nearly 1630, he had been working non-stop for almost six hours. He had not stood up, he had not stopped typing, he had not looked up, he had not stretched, he simply continued to take the words of the translation and place them into the form of a Gospel from the

Christian New Testament. He stood up, stretched, hit save on the word processing program and let Saul into the room.

"We need to secure the scroll," Saul instructed.

Jonathan agreed. He turned off his computer and retrieved the backpack with the metal tube containing the scroll.

"Yes, let's do that quickly," Jonathan responded, somewhat distracted.

The two left the room and Jonathan secured all three locks. Saul did not ask about the progress. He knew Jonathan would provide him with information as he felt necessary. Jonathan was glad Saul did not question him about the progress. Once in the elevator, Jonathan updated Saul on Michael's plans to try and have the discovery published. Saul laughed at himself that he had not thought about that. However, he thought it was a good idea. Finally, as the elevator reached the ground floor, Saul asked,

"How long?"

"Maybe two more days," Jonathan said, "maybe three."

The two professors headed onto the sidewalk into the night air. Both men were deep in their own thoughts. Saul hailed a cab and Jonathan took the metal tube from his backpack and held it in his lap as they got into the cab. Saul told the cab driver to take them to the Federal Reserve Bank of New York on Liberty Street. Saul then explained to Jonathan that the Federal Reserve Bank of New York had a vault 80 feet below street level and 50 feet below sea level. Saul told Jonathan he had a friend at the bank who was in a position to allow them the use of a safety deposit box in the vault large enough for the metal tube containing the scroll.

"It was, by far, the safest place for it," Saul said with a sense of security.

Over the next two days, Jonathan continued to work diligently, frequently late into the night. Michael returned with possibilities with the *Archeological Survey of Israel*, the *Biblical Theory Bulletin*, and Sage Publishing *Archeology Biblical Review*. All three were very interested in the publication of the archeological findings, but only the *Archeology Biblical Review* did not demand to see the scrolls. Saul opted to publish with the Sage Publishing journal primarily for that reason.

Finally, at around 1800 on the third day, Jonathan hit save for the last time on his word processor. The conversion to a Scripture format was finished. He inserted a flash drive and made a secure copy. He re-saved the document and added a security password to the thesis and to the copy on the flash drive. Saul and Michael had left for the day. Jonathan turned off his laptop and placed it in his backpack. He took the original notebooks and placed them inside the backpack as well. He would need Saul to lock the notebooks into the vault with the scrolls. He picked up the backpack and left the lab. He only placed one padlock on the door. After all, there was really nothing left in the room to secure. He departed by the elevator and walked across campus to the library where he had access to a printer. Once in the library, he inserted the flash drive into a printer and made three copies of the manuscript, one each for him, Saul and Michael. After making the copies, he left the library and went quickly to an office supply store and had the copies bound in a manuscript format. He then went outside, took his cellphone from his pocket and called Saul first.

"I will see you at 0800 in the morning in your office. The conversion is finished and in manuscript form," Jonathan informed Saul.

Jonathan called Michael and advised the same.

That night Jonathan could not sleep. Although he was relieved the work was finished and thrilled with the results, his heart was very heavy at the words contained in the scroll. He had many questions left unanswered, questions about his faith, and questions about Christianity. Across town, in his apartment, Saul knelt beside his bed and prayed for guidance, for answers to some of the same questions that Jonathan wondered about. And finally, Michael was not tossing and turning, but sitting with his Pastor discussing theology, the early teachings of Jesus and, in particular, that of John the Baptist. Michael and his Pastor had been having this discussion for the past four hours with Michael questioning the very foundations of his Christianity.

By the time Jonathan arrived at Saul's office the next morning promptly at 0800, Saul and Michael were already there, seated, sipping coffee and waiting. There was no talking, no discussion, just looking into space, waiting. Jonathan broke the silence when he arrived. He shut the door to Saul's office behind him and sat his backpack on the desk. He reached into his backpack and removed three manuscripts, giving one each to Saul and Michael.

"This is it," Jonathan said flatly.

The other two men just nodded, took the manuscripts from Jonathan's hand and sat back down with the papers lying in their lap. Each seemed hesitant to open the document. Saul sat behind his desk, hand lying flat on the manuscript, stroking his finger nail across the cover. Michael's eyes were closed as he held the manuscript tightly between his hands. Jonathan could see Michael's lips moving rapidly and Jonathan knew he was saying a prayer. Jonathan suggested that they begin together. They all agreed and each turned to page 1 of the manuscript and read the following: "The Gospel of the Baptist"

CHAPTER 1

[1]I am John, called the Baptist, I am imprisoned in the dungeon below the palace of Herod Antipas, son of Herod the Great who killed the children of Bethlehem trying to kill the infant Jesus; in the city of Tiberius. I have been imprisoned for many months.

[2]In the seventh month, when my disciples visited, I sent them to ask of Jesus if he was the Christ, the Messiah.

[3]These men did not return. In the evening while I lay sleeping, a presence was felt. I awakened and saw Jesus standing in my cell.

[4]He told me many things which will be described later. He told me to write down everything starting that very night. He said my time was short.

[5]I told him I had nothing to write with or on.

[6]My guard, a Jew who was my follower in secret provided the parchment and writing instrument that morning.

[7]In obedience to Jesus I now write what I have seen in my life as a testament that Jesus is the Christ, the Messiah.

CHAPTER 2

[1]I am John, the son of Zacharias and Elizabeth. Zacharias was a High Priest, Elizabeth was the cousin of Mary the Mother of Jesus.

[2]Zacharias and Elizabeth were advanced in years when Elizabeth conceived. I was born in the hill country of Hebron six months before Jesus.

[3]At my birth, my right leg was twisted and my foot deformed and I was to be raised a Nazarite.

[4]Zacharasis was killed by Herod the Great for daring to condemn Herod for his sinful acts in killing the children of Bethlehem.

[5]In fear Elizabeth fled into the wilderness of Judea where I was raised. Here my mother taught me to read Hebrew and to write my letters.

[6]I struggled to walk, using a crutch as the deformity of my leg prevented walking unassisted.

[7]When I was twelve years old, my Mother and I as was the custom traveled to Jerusalem for the feast of the Passover. We travelled with Mary, Joseph and Jesus who was also twelve.

[8]When leaving, about a day's journey from Jerusalem, Mary approached Elizabeth fearful as Jesus could not be found.

[9]Together we returned and Jesus was found in the Temple talking with the Priest.

[10]Mary and Joseph spoke their concern to Jesus, Mary asking "Why have you treated us in this way."

[11]Jesus responded "Do you not know that I am about my Father's business."

[12]I was standing a little off to the side and listened to Mary and Jesus. After they spoke Jesus approached me.

[13]Jesus said, "It is now the time John," and he touched me and my leg straightened and immediately the strength returned and I did not need the crutch.

[14]Jesus said "Since birth you, John, have been chosen to prepare Israel for My coming. You have been filled with the

Holy Spirit since you were in the womb. No wine has touched your lips, no strong drink. Your hair has not been shorn and you will not shave your beard for you are a Nazarite.

15You shall go before your Lord in the spirit and with the power of Elijah in order to make ready the people for the coming of the Lord."

16Mary and Elizabeth witnessed this and said not a word. Jesus said nothing more and I returned to Judea and Jesus to Nazareth.

CHAPTER 3

1After two years in the desert of Judea, in my fourteen year, my mother, Elizabeth passed on from this earth and I was alone.

2I did not know how to care for her and had nothing to prepare her for burial.

3While I knelt by her body weeping, a mist appeared and came down to the earth. I heard the voice of Jesus. "I have heard your weeping for your Mother Elizabeth," Jesus said, "I bring help to the burial of your Mother."

4From the mist the Angels Gabriel and Michael appeared. They were wearing metal breastplates with the stones of the twelve tribes inset. At Michael's side was a sword the length of a man with a blade that glistened. Both were white as snow and gave off a soft, white light. Michael and Gabriel dug a grave. Mary, Mother of Jesus was also with Him and washed Elizabeth's body and prepared the body for burial. When all was completed, the Angels Gabriel and Michael placed the body in the grave and covered it making the sign of the cross on the covered grave. Gabriel and Michael departed into the mist without a word spoken.

[5]As I knelt beside the grave of my Mother Elizabeth weeping, Jesus and Mary comforted me for seven days. At the end of seven days Jesus said to Mary, "Let us now go to the place where I may learn and proceed with my work." The Virgin Mary wept over my loneliness and pleaded with Jesus for me to go with them.

[6]But Jesus said, "This is not My Father's will. John will remain in the wilderness until his showing to Israel. John must prepare the way to fulfill the words of the prophet Isaiah who said 'A voice is calling, Clear the way for the YHWH in the wilderness; make smooth in the desert a highway for our God.'"

[7] "And also the prophet Malachi who foretold 'Behold, I am going to send My messenger, and he will clear the way before Me.'"

[8]As Jesus and Mary moved upward away the mist surrounded them. I followed after and asked "What am I to do, I am alone, here in the desert."

[9] Jesus replied, "Where is your faith, you are filled with the Holy Spirit, My Father will provide."

[10]With those words, the mist was gone, and I was alone with my Mother's grave. I knelt beside the grave until the sun began to fade.

[11]Evening came and I had no food, no water. I was alone in the wilderness with no one to comfort or help me.

[12]Rembering the words of Jesus I began to pray asking God to relieve my hunger, my thirst. I did not fear for dying as I knew that was not the plan of God for me.

[13]As I prayed, my faith increased, my hunger left me, and I thirsted no more. I prayed for some time until I fell asleep by my Mother's grave.

[14]My Mother appeared to me while I was in a dream saying, "My son, you are chosen by God to prepare Israel for the coming of Jesus, fast and pray for three days and He will answer your prayers."

[15]The next morning I awoke, tired, hungry again. I looked around and found the desert alive, the movement that could not be seen. In the distance there was a small tree. I walked only a short distance to the tree where there was shade.

[16]I knelt beneath the tree and prayed until the sun was low in the sky again. I rested. I hoped that I would have some company in my dreams, but I awoke alone as I was when my eyes closed in sleep.

[17]On the third day, there was a slight breeze to cool, the pangs in my stomach were too much to bear at times. My lips were parched, cracked and bleeding, I would not make spittle to give relief. With effort I knelt to pray.

[18]I did not remember the nightfall, or falling to sleep, but that night in my dreams the Angel Gabriel appeared to me. He told me that God was pleased and that morning would bring new life.

[19]In my dream, Gabriel bathed me in cool water, gave me figs to eat and honey to drink. I saw myself sleeping in my dream.

[20]Gabriel softly awakened me, "Get up, John, your new life begins."

[21]I opened my eyes from the dream, looking at the leaves of the tree softly moving with a breeze.

[22]I no longer hungered, my lips were soft as rose petals, my skin moist and unmolested from the dryness of the desert air and heat from the sun.

[23]I stood easily feeling the strength flow into my body. I surveyed the horizon and saw a figure in the distance.

[24]As I watched the figure come closer I could see it was a man, very aged. He walked with a staff.

[25]As he approached I could see he wore camel skin with a leather girdle to tie the halves together, a pouch on his side. Although aged, he walked with strength, with authority.

[26]He walked now looking straight at me. When a few strides from where I stood he spoke,

[27]"Are you the one called John, son of Zachariah the Priest and Elizabeth, cousin to Mary, Mother of Jesus?"

[28]I nodded and said, "I am John."

[29]"Gabriel has sent me for you," the man replied.

CHAPTER 4

[1]The man turned to walk away and I followed.

[2]"I am Nathan," he said, while walking, "descendant from Zadoq, son of Eleazar, son of Aaron, brother to Moses and father of all Priests of Israel."

[3]No additional words were spoken and Nathan walked and I followed. We walked all day through the desert and in the evening, about an hour before the sun set, Nathan stopped.

4He spoke for the first time since he told me his name, "First we pray, then eat, then pray, then sleep."

5I looked around, there was no shelter and Nathan only had his pouch by his side. He did not spread out a cloth or take any additional steps, he knelt where he was standing and began to pray silently.

6I could see his lips moving, but I could not hear his words. I too knelt and began to pray. When prayers were finished, Nathan opened his pouch and took out locusts and honey and offered the same to me.

7Nathan did not speak during our meager meal. Little as there was to eat and drink, I felt satisfied and without hunger when we were finished.

8Nathan knelt again and prayed, I did the same. After prayers, we slept and the next morning repeated the same from the evening before. A meal of locusts and honey, no words exchanged.

9After the morning meal, and morning prayers, Nathan finally spoke, "We have half a day travel to reach to Qumran. At Qumran you will begin your studies for the path God has set for you."

10I started to ask a question, but Nathan held up his hand, "Everything will be revealed with time at Qumran."

11As we walked, a small plateau could be seen in the distance rising from the Judea Desert. On the horizon I could see a body of water in the distance.

12Without the question asked, Nathan said, "The Dead Sea's Northwestern shore," and kept walking.

13Walking a single trail upward to the plateau, caves could be easily seen with men walking about. I could not hear any sounds. The plateau was isolated with a single entrance and departure that Nathan and I now followed.

[14]We entered into a large open area that was full of men walking about. I counted at least twelve caves in the surrounding area. I saw what appeared to be a dam holding water and a large that carried water into a plastered pool. There were men lowering and rising from the water and walking from the pool.

[15]It was mid-day when we arrived. Nathan pointed to a structure built of stones for us to enter. On entering there was a large room with multiple stone benches aligned as if for a meeting.

[16]We entered into a smaller room that contained hooks on the wall with various pieces of clothing and some pouches hanging on those hooks. This led into another very large room where there were three long stone tables with men sitting in silence on stone benches.

[17]Food was present on all of the tables and the men ate in silence. No one stood to greet us, no words were spoken. There were two empty spaces at the third table, Nathan pointed to one space for me and he took the other.

[18]He looked at me and brought his finger to his lips to tell me to remain silent. He bowed his head in prayer, I did the same.

[19]The meal was meager, consisting of figs, goat meat, and a container of water. The meal lasted a short time with no spoken word. I finished before Nathan and waited for him to finish.

[20]Without speaking, he rose and motioned for me to follow. Opposite from where we entered the room, we passed through a door that opened into another large room.

21 In this room were several benches and tables where scrolls of parchment and papyrus were being written and copied.

22 I strained to see what was written, some were in Hebrew and I made out the word "Psalm," as we passed, the others parchments and papyrus were in words I did not understand.

23 Nathan took me through this room into a hallway with small rooms on each side. We walked to the end of the hallway and Nathan gestured for me to enter.

24 "You will sleep here, pray here, study here," Nathan explained, "Tomorrow early when the sun rises, you will begin, first you will be purified with the waters and then you will take your vows and begin your studies."

25 Nathan departed and I examined my room. There was a small patch of fresh straw on one side, a small table and stool on the other; some opening had been left in the sides of the wall. The ceiling was also made of stone.

26 After the events and the long journey, I was very tired. I knelt beside the straw and prayed thanking God for bringing me to this place. I then laid down and quickly fell asleep.

CHAPTER 5

1 Nathan arrived to retrieve me just as the sun was rising and smiled to see that I was already prepared for the day.

2 Nathan took me to a large open area where a number of men all dressed in camel's hair cloaks stood around a pool with steps down into the water.

[3]I was taken before a man who was on his camel hair and wore the breastplate of a priest.

[4]The breastplate was attached to an ephod of gold chains/cords tied to the gold rings on the ephod's shoulder straps, and by blue ribbon tied to the gold rings at the belt of the ephod. There were twelve jewels placed in the breastplate with the names of the twelve tribes of Israel inscribed on each stone. On the man's shoulder were two black stones. I recognized this man as a High Priest for I had seen my father wear the same breastplate.

[5]Nathan spoke, "High Priest Joshua, I present to you John, son of Zachariah and Elizabeth, descendent from the tribe of Levite, and of Zadoq, Eleazar, and of Aaron, brother of Moses. He has been chosen by God to prepare the way for his Son and sent to us by Gabriel, the Angel of the Lord."

[6]Joshua was very old, his hair hung well over his shoulders and his beard almost as long as his hair was white. I stood waiting as Joshua looked at me and spoke."

[7]"John, son of Zachariah and Elizabeth, descendent of Zadoq, Eleazar, and of Aaron of the tribe of Levi, are you the one to prepare the way of our Lord?"

[8]"I am," I replied and with those words the Holy Spirit descended into our midst in a cloud and a voice said, "Behold, this is My messenger, and he will clear the way before Me and he has been sent to show to you that My covenant with Levi may continue."

[6]When the cloud disappeared, Joshua asked, "Do you renounce worldly pleasures, immoral activities, and commit yourself to the Lord?"

[7]"I do," I responded.

8Joshua continued, "Strip off your clothes and descend in the water for purification."

9I removed my clothing and stepped into the pool of water with Joshua following behind, the water darkening his camel hair as we stood waist deep in the cool water.

10"Do you confess your sins to God and beg his forgiveness, do you believe in God the Giver of Life and the redemption of his Son, the Messiah?"

11I responded again, "I do," and with those words, Joshua placed his hand over my mouth and nose and lowered me into the water, completely immersing my body.

12Bringing me up from the water, he announced "This is John, sent from God to prepare the way."

13As I exited the pool, Nathan handed me a camel hair cloak, leather girth and pouch. There was no excitement among the men watching, they simply turned and went back to their duties.

14Nathan told me, "Your studies begin today after our morning meal. There is a lot for you to learn. You will purify yourself in this pool daily to remove the sins of the world and remain a Narzirite to the Lord."

15Nathan continued as we were walking, "you are forbidden from swearing oaths and from sacrificing animals. You are to control your temper and serve as a channel of peace, only carrying weapons for the protection against robbers. You are not to possess slaves but serve others always…"

16Nathan continued to teach as we walked into the large room where other men dressed the same way sat with parchments and papyrus, writing or copying.

[17]As we walked around the large room, I could read, written in Hebrew, the words "Books of Moses," "Judges," "The Books of the Kings," the "Book of the Prophets," and many others in a different language I did not recognize. I questioned Nathan about this language.

[18]"These are the books of the Israelites, the Jews, written in Hebrew, which you can read, and Aramaic, which you will learn," Nathan explained.

[19]Nathan pointed to a stone bench with a small table for me to sit down. He brought over a collection of scrolls and placed them on the table in front of me. I read the title, "The Five Books of Moses."

[20]"Begin here, each day from the rising of the sun till the setting of the sun you will study and learn all of the books of the Jewish nation. After your evening meals, I and the other elders will assist you with understanding what you have read," Nathan advised and left me to my studies.

CHAPTER 6

[1]I spent every day reading the books and the evenings discussing the content with the elders. In addition, in the evenings I was taught the language of Aramaic so that all could be read.

[2]I moved through the Five Books of Moses, to the Judges, the Kings, and finally the prophets.

[3]As I read I saw that the prophecies of the Messiah were being fulfilled. And they were being fulfilled by one man, Jesus.

[4]The first of these prophecies by Moses in Genesis 3:15: "I will put enmity between you and the woman, and between your offspring and her offspring; he shall bruise your head, and you shall bruise his heel."

[5]I traced Jesus' roots and he is descended from the tribe of Judah, Jacob and Isaac, and Abraham as described in Genesis and Numbers. He also is a descendant of King David from the Second Book of Samuel 7:12, 13: "When your days are fulfilled and you lie down with your fathers, I will raise up your offspring after you, who shall come from your body, and I will establish his kingdom. He shall build a house for my name, and I will establish the throne of his kingdom forever."

[6]I found the foretelling of the Virgin birth by the prophet Isaiah in Chapter 7, 14: "Therefore the Lord himself will give you a sign. Behold, the virgin shall conceive and bear a son, and shall call his name Immanuel." And Micah describing the birthplace of Bethlehem; Micah 5:2: "But you, O Bethlehem Ephrathah, who are too little to be among the clans of Judah, from you shall come forth for me one who is to be ruler in Israel, whose coming forth is from of old, from ancient days."

[7]Even the details of Herod killing the male children two years or under was predicted by the prophet Jeremiah 31:15: "A voice is heard in Ramah, lamentation and bitter weeping. Rachel is weeping for her children; she refuses to be comforted for her children, because they are no more."

[8]I realized that the prophets had foretold this event, and that the escape of Jesus into Egypt was prophesied by Hosea; Hosea 11:1: "When Israel was a child, I loved him, and out of Egypt I called my son."

9 In the evenings the Elders would discuss all that I had studied. Nathan in particular expressed interest in the prophecies about Jesus. "You are sure this man that you know, the son of the carpenter Joseph, is the one the prophets foretold?" he asked. But his questions were more statements to query my certainty than his.

10 As my studies reached a new phase, I now was copying the books like the priests in the great hall. I would transcribe each book onto a new scroll. As the book was finished, the scrolls would be placed and sealed in an earthen jug and stored in one of the numerous caves.

11 One day as I was transcribing the book of Malachi, Nathan approached as I sat on the stone painstakingly writing the words onto a new scroll. I had just finished the second chapter and started the third.

12 "Read me the next words," Nathan said.

12 I straightened my back and read the words, "Behold, I send my messenger, and he will prepare the way before me. And the Lord whom you seek will suddenly come to his temple; and the messenger of the covenant in whom you delight, behold, he is coming, says the Lord of hosts."

13 "Do you know what this means, who this is?" Nathan asked.

14 I explained that I had read, written and heard the words many times and understood that they were thought to be me, "But I am not this man," I said to Nathan. He just nodded his head and moved away.

15 For the next fifteen years I studied at the Qumran with the elders. I was celibate, remained pure, being baptized daily in the waters for purification. My knowledge increased and I understood that Jesus was the Messiah.

16I also understood how He would die for our sins, that He would be betrayed, beaten, and be crucified. But also that He would be raised from the dead and sit at the right hand of God. The Psalmists were clear, Psalm 16:10-11: "For you will not abandon my soul to Sheol, or let your holy one see corruption. You make known to me the path of life; in your presence there is fullness of joy; at your right hand are pleasures forevermore." Again in Psalm 49:15: "But God will ransom my soul from the power of Sheol, for he will receive me." Finally, Psalm 68:18: "You ascended on high, leading a host of captives in your train and receiving gifts among men, even among the rebellious, that the Lord God may dwell there."

17I knew that Jesus was the Messiah, the Salvation of the World, yet I was still not clear about my role, my relationship to Jesus, even after fifteen years of study.

18Until the night of my twenty-ninth year, as I slept the Angel Gabriel appeared to me.

19"It is time," Gabriel said, "you will go into the wilderness, first to Ein Kerem, and then all about the country of Jordan and preach the baptism of repentance for the remission of sins and prepare the way of your Lord. You will baptize all who seek forgiveness and tell them the coming of the Messiah. The Messiah will come to you to be baptized and then He will increase and you will diminish."

20I awoke and immediately went to Nathan's room and before I could speak he said, "You know it is you and it is time." I nodded. "Go back to your room and prepare, when morning comes you will start."

21The next morning Nathan and the elders led me to the entrance to the desert and the valley of the Jordan River.

22I had nothing except the camel hair garment and leather girdle and pouch that I had worn for those past fifteen years. Saddles on my feet and a staff for the long walks. I needed no food as I had been taught to live on wild locust and honey.

23It was in the fifteenth year of the reign of Tiberius Caesar, Pontius Pilate, governor of Judaea, and Herod, tetrarch of Galilee, and his brother Philip, tetrarch of Ituraea and of the region of Trachonitis, and Lysanias, the tetrarch of Abilene, that I would begin.

24I began walking to Ein Kerem where I was born, near the city of Bethlehem as the Angel Gabriel had instructed.

CHAPTER 7

1In Ein Kerem no one recognized who I was. I remained outside the city walls and began to shout at those walking on the road.

2"Repent," I would say, "repent of your sins, the kingdom of God is at hand. Repeat, and prepare yourself for He who comes after me will baptize you with the Holy Spirit."

3As I repeated my message, a crowd of people formed and listened as I spoke of forgiveness, the coming of the Messiah, and the need for repentance.

4A young man stepped forward from the ground, "I wish to be baptized," he said with tears in his eyes.

5"What is your name?" I asked.

6"James," he replied and pointed, "and this is my brother John, we are sons of Zebedee."

7I was standing by a pool and the crowd watched as John entered the pool with me, I asked, "Do you repent of your sins and follow the laws of God?" John nodded and I placed him under the water and raised him up, "You are now cleansed by the water of Baptism, sin no more and await the Messiah to baptize you with the Holy Spirit."

8I followed with baptizing his brother James in the same manner. In addition on that day, thirty four others were baptized.

9As the crowd moved away, James and John remained, John ventured, "We would like to travel with you, to learn from you about the Messiah."

10"I have nothing, want nothing, no possessions, you must leave everything and come with just what you have to follow me," I replied.

11James and John were the first of many disciples who would remain with me. The following days we grew with Simon, who had been a Zealot fighting the Romans, Jude, Thaddeus, and Judas.

12During the day I would preach the repentance of sin and the coming of the Messiah, at night I would teach these men about the scriptures and the prophecies and that the Messiah was near.

13After sometime in Ein Kerem, when I had baptized all those who desired, I began to walk to the desert outside of Bethabara along the Jordan River. This would provide a central location for Jerusalem, Judea, and the region of Jordan.

14I would stand on the bank of the Jordan, teaching those who followed, and people would come from the region and crowds would increase. This happened daily and each day many more were baptized.

15As the crowds departed a very young man approached. He was dressed in military attire and Simon intercepted him due to fear that he had come to do me harm.

16"I wish to speak to Elijah," the boy said.

17I motioned for Simon to release him and I told the boy I was not Elijah, nor the Messiah, but simply a messenger.

18"I am Caleb," he said, "a member of the army of Herod. I wish to be baptized."

19"Why do you wish to be baptized?" I asked.

20Caleb responded, "I wish forgiveness of my sins and eternal life through salvation of the Messiah."

21I was impressed by the boy's response. I motioned for him to come into the Jordan River with me and there asked, "Do you repent of your sins and follow the laws of God?" Caleb barely said "yes" where it could be heard. I placed him under the water and raised him up, "You are now cleansed by the water of Baptism, sin no more and await the Messiah to baptize you with the Holy Spirit."

22Caleb exited the water and I asked if he wanted to stay with us.

23"I cannot," he replied, "I must return to my duties. But I must warn you that the Pharisees and Sadducees are not happy and will try to do you harm."

24The others looked at me for a response, I just laughed, and said, "I am the Messenger of God and teach only the forgiveness of sins, there is nothing here for these Pharisees and Sadducees to fear unless they are evil men."

25Caleb advised that he just wanted to make sure I was aware and departed.

26I was surprised that the Pharisees would take issue with my message. After all, they believed that God controlled all things, and they believed in the resurrection of the dead. Also, they were very knowledgeable of the scripture and should understand my message.

27However, the Sadducees were the High Priests and the Chief Priests and also understood the words of the Prophets and Moses. I could not see where there would be conflict with these men.

CHAPTER 8

1When I awoke from my sleeping, James and John were waiting for me as I finished my breakfast.

2"John," James said, "The Sadducees and Pharisees are here for you. They wish to question you."

3As I approached the Jordan River where I stood each morning, the crowds were much larger than usual. In the distance, Herod's soldiers stood to insure no problems occurred. I could see Caleb standing with them.

4I started to speak when I saw some of the Pharisees and Sadducees approaching. I recognized Annas with his son-in-law Caiaphas, the High Priest.

5As they reached the Jordan River I pointed to them and said, "You brood of snakes! Someone must have warned you about the judgement to come. You should not think that you do not have to repent as these others because you are descendants of Abraham.

6 I tell you this, God is able from these stones to raise up the children of Abraham. Even now, if your actions do not bear fruit, do not show your love of God, you will be cut off and thrown away, descendants of Abraham or not."

7 Caiaphas responded, "Who do you think you are, what authority do you baptize for remission of sins?"

8 I responded, "I baptize you with water for repentance, but there is someone else coming after me. He is mightier than me and I am not worthy to even carry his sandals. He who is coming will baptize you the Holy Spirit.

9 He will separate those who believe and repent from those who think that because they are descendants of Abraham that is enough. Keep thinking that, Caiaphas, and you will burn in unquenchable fire.

10 Annas spoke, "Caiaphas is mad, but harmless, leave him to his followers." The two high priests turned and walked away.

11 The crowd drew near and I preached repentance and forgiveness of sins and continued to baptize all those who asked.

12 Many asked me the same question, "What shall we do after we are baptized to avoid the unquenchable fire?"

13 I told them that whoever has two coats, share with someone who has none and do the same with their food."

14 Tax collectors who were despised by the people came. James and John attempted to prevent them from entering the water for baptism, but I reminded them all were welcome.

15They asked, "What should we do?" And I told them to collect no more than was due from the people.

16Caleb approached and introduced more of Herod's soldiers, many of whom had been there every day listening to me preach.

17The soldiers asked me, "What can we do, we are just soldiers," I told them not to take money or threaten others for their own gain by making false accusations, to be content with what they were paid.

18One man in the crowd shouted, "I keep God's Commandments, I do not steal, do not take the Lord's name in swears, do not covet, do not kill. Why do I need forgiveness? I have not sinned."

19The man had garnered the attention of the crowd with his question, and they turned from him and back to me awaiting my answer.

20I asked the man this question, "A young man was caring for his elderly father who was very sick. They were both very poor. It was very cold and the father was freezing. The son had no coat to give his father.

21The son went to several merchants and people begging for a coat. No one would help and he became desperate. His father was dying.

22While a merchant's back was turned, the son, without paying, took a coat for his father. Did the young man commit a sin?"

23The man in the crowd responded, "Of course, the law of Moses is clear, 'you should not steal.' " And the crowd nodded in agreement.

[24]"I say this," I responded, raising my voice, "The son did not sin for there was no sin in his heart, just the love of his Father. Sin is in the heart, not in the act, and only God knows the heart, knows your heart. If you know that your heart is without sin, then you do not need repentance."

[25]The crowd fell silent, the man who asked the question looked down at the ground for a moment.

[26]When he raised his head, there were tears in his eyes and he said, "I wish to be baptized for repentance of my sins."

CHAPTER 9

[1]I could feel that the people were questioning if I was the Messiah, the Christ. I held up my hands and repeated, "I baptize you with the water of repentance, but the Messiah will baptize you with the Holy Spirit. I am not even worthy to strap his sandals."

[2]There were many people approaching, but I could feel the presence of something, someone.

[3]I surveyed the crowd and in the distance I could see Him, standing with the people, waiting for his turn.

[4]Although distracted, I tried to continue to baptize all who asked.

[5]And then Jesus stood in front of me. He had become a man, as I had, yet I still recognized him immediately.

[6]"John," Jesus said, "I come from Galilee to be baptized."

[7]I protested, "It is I who should be baptized by you."

8 Jesus said, "Let it be so for now, that I fulfill all righteousness."

9 I started to protest again, but Jesus looked directly into my eyes and my heart knew this was to be.

10 I walked a little ways into the Jordan River with Jesus, as was my custom, in order to immerse completely under the water. I did not ask Jesus if he repented of his sins, for I knew he was sinless. I simply baptized him as I had others.

11 When Jesus exited the water, a light shone down upon him and a dove descended. Then a voice said, "This is my Son, with whom I am well-pleased."

12 As Jesus walked from the water onto the shore, I looked about and could see that those that followed me had heard the voice, but the crowd did not.

13 I remembered the words of Isaiah, "And the Spirit of the Lord shall rest upon him, the Spirit of wisdom and understanding, the Spirit of counsel and might, the Spirit of knowledge and the fear of the Lord."

14 And the words the voice used recalled words from Isaiah, "Behold my servant, whom I uphold, my chosen, in whom my soul delights; I have put my Spirit upon him; he will bring forth justice to the nations."

15 I knew as I saw Jesus walking out into the wilderness that my time was done. I must now fade away so that he might rise up for the people.

16 I called my disciples to me as Jesus walked away. I pointed to him, "He is who you should follow now."

17 I was not questioned by anyone. Each one, James, John, Jude, Simon, Thaddeus, and Judas all gathered their meager belongings and walked after Jesus.

18"I am done," I said to myself as I watched my disciples quicken their pace to catch up to Jesus.

19That night as I slept, Gabriel appeared to me. He directed that I go to Macherus which was near the mouth of the Jordan River in the region of Perea. There I would confront Herod about this adulterous marriage to his brother's wife, Herodias.

20When I awoke, I began my journey. I did not question my task although I was certain that my message would not be received well by Herod.

CHAPTER 10

1As I walked, James and his brother John found me on the road to Macherus and joined me.

2"I sent you with Jesus," I said to them both.

3John and James explained that Jesus entered into the wilderness too fast and He asked that they join him in Galilee.

4Shortly Jude and Judas joined us on the road to Macherus. They reported the same instructions from Jesus, they were sent away to meet him in Galilee in a few days.

4I explained to the four men that I was on my way to Macherus to offer Herod forgiveness of his sins of adultery with his brother's wife Herodias.

5Judas was the first to question the wisdom of this journey. "You will surely evoke the anger of the King."

6 I assured Judas and the other three that I was not afraid, that God was with me.

7 "The angel Gabriel appeared to me and sent me on this journey," I said to reassure the group.

8 Jude offered to go to Macherus with me, and the others made the same offer. They would also preach to the people about Herod's adultery and confront Herod.

9 Judas said, "The people love you John and if Herod imprisons or harms you, they will rise up against him and the Romans."

10 I laughed and responded, "Judas, always looking for a fight."

11 "Always trying to rid us of the Romans," Judas responded.

12 The others agreed with Judas and then as we walked asked about Jesus.

13 There was a small hill to my left, so I walked a little ways up and sat down. James, John, Jude and Judas sat around me and waited for me to speak.

1 "He is the One I have preached about for two years, He is the One that comes after me, the Messiah, the living Son of God," I said solemnly.

15 James and John accepted this without question, Judas and Jude voiced some skepticism.

16 I explained further, "He was born of the Virgin, Mary, in Bethlehem, just as the prophets foretold." I reminded them of the words of the Prophet Isaiah: "And he said, "Hear then, O house of David! Is it too little for you to weary men, that you weary my God also? Therefore the Lord himself will give you a sign. Behold, the virgin shall conceive and bear a son, and shall call his name Immanuel."

17Jude asked how I knew the Messiah would be born in Bethlehem.

18"Remember," I said, "the prophet Micah said 'But you, O Bethlehem Ephrathah, who are too little to be among the clans of Judah, from you shall come forth for me one who is to be ruler in Israel, whose coming forth is from of old, from ancient days.'"

19"A King," exclaimed Judas, "to rid us of these Romans."

20I started to protest when Judas quoted Isaiah also, "For to us a child is born, to us a son is given; and the government shall be upon his shoulder, and his name shall be called

Wonderful Counselor, Mighty God, Everlasting Father, Prince of Peace. Of the increase of his government and of peace there will be no end, on the throne of David and over his kingdom,

to establish it and to uphold it with justice and with righteousness from this time forth and forevermore."

21I tried to explain to the four that Jesus would be a King, but a heavenly King. They looked confused so I did not try to explain further.

22"Tell us more," John said, "you think he is the Messiah?"

22"I believe he is the Christ, the Son of God, born of the virgin Mary in order to become man and save us from our sins. Do you remember the killing of the infants by Herod's father, Herod the Great?"

23All of them nodded to indicate they remembered. I explained that this affected Jesus and was part of the prophecy of Jeremiah regarding the coming of the Messiah. Jeremiah said, "Thus says the Lord: 'A voice is heard in Ramah, lamentation and bitter weeping. Rachel is weeping for her children; she refuses to be comforted for her children, because they are no more.'"

[24]Jude asked, "How does Jesus fulfill this prophecy?"

[25]I explained that Jesus and I were both infants and fled to Egypt to avoid being killed. "Our parents were both told by Gabriel to flee. Jesus fled from Nazareth to Egypt and this fulfilled the prophecy of Hosea, 'When Israel was a child, I loved him, and out of Egypt I called my son.'"

[26]The four men looked at me with confusion, finally John said, "So this Jesus is the Christ, the Messiah?"

[27]"I believe he is," I responded. And with those words I stood up and went back to the road. The four men followed.

[28]"You should go to Galilee and wait for Jesus as He instructed," I told them, "I will be okay in Macherus alone."

[29]Reluctantly the four men left me to go to Galilee. I wanted to go with them and be with Jesus as well, but I knew that this could not be.

[30]God had sent His Angel Gabriel with His instructions and I must not question, I simply obey.

[31]Arriving in Macherus late at night I found I was recognized by many and asked if I was going to preach and baptize in Macherus. I assured the crowd gathering that I would begin in the morning.

[32]One kind follower offered me lodging. I would stay just one night and, when morning came, I planned to go to the palace of Herod and begin preaching. I would sleep there at the palace so that no one would be hurt by Herod for helping me.

[33]I learned later that the crowd gathering around me had alerted Herod to my presence.

CHAPTER 11

[1]I awoke early to avoid any crowds, but this did not work.

[2]As I made my way to Herod's palace, I was followed by a large number of people. Many asked when I was going to preach. Some asked if I would baptize them.

[3]When I reached Herod's palace I began to preach to the crowd, "Repent, the Kingdom of God is at hand. Repent of your sins and be baptized."

[4]Herod came to the balcony of his palace above where I was preaching. He seemed to be interested in my words.

[5]I looked up at Herod and pointed, shouting to him, "Repent of your sins!"

[6]Herod asked if I was Elijah raised from the dead. I responded, "I am the voice crying in the wilderness, repent of your sins."

[6]At that moment Herodias joined Herod on the balcony.

[7]"Listen to the law of Moses," I cried out, "You shall not uncover the nakedness of your brother's wife; it is your brother's nakedness. If a man takes his brother's wife, it is impure. He has uncovered his brother's nakedness; they shall be childless."

[8]I continued, "Herod, you have committed a horrible sin, you have divorced your wife to marry your brother Phillips wife, Herodias, you and she have committed adultery. You have violated the law of Moses, 'You shall not commit adultery.' Herodias is an adulterous woman and you an adulterous man."

9The crowd began to shout at Herod and Herodias, "Adulterer, adulteress; adulterer, adulteress," pointing at the balcony where Herod and Herodias stood.

10"Herod, you and your wife Herodias are in violation of the law of Moses, you should be stoned as the law is clear, 'If a man is found lying with the wife of another man, both of them shall die, the man who lay with the woman, and the woman. So you shall purge the evil from Israel.' Because you are King, are you above the laws? As King David, you have sinned against the Lord," I shouted upward toward the balcony as the crowd continued to chant, "Adulterer, adulteress," over and over.

11Herodias said something to her husband and turned and left the balcony.

12"You speak too much," Herod said to me, "take care of your words."

13The people continued to shout up at him and drowned out any more that he said. He also left the balcony.

14Although Herod and Herodias were off the balcony, they still were in the palace and I continued to preach to the crowd from the law of Moses regarding adultery. I told the story of King David and Bathsheba.

15How King David had seen Bathsheba bathing and wanted her and had her brought to him and he laid with her until she conceived. The crowd quieted as they listened to the story.

16King David had Bathsheba's husband Uriah the Hittite killed in battle. I repeated the parable of the prophet Nathan to the crowd.

17"There were two men in a certain city, the one rich and the other poor. The rich man had very many flocks and herds, but the poor man had nothing but one little ewe lamb, which he had bought. And he brought it up, and it grew up with him and with his children. It used to eat of his morsel and drink from his cup and lie in his arms, and it was like a daughter to him. Now there came a traveler to the rich man, and he was unwilling to take one of his own flock or herd to prepare for the guest who had come to him, but he took the poor man's lamb and prepared it for the man who had come to him. Then David's anger was greatly kindled against the man, and he said to Nathan, 'As the Lord lives, the man who has done this deserves to die, and he shall restore the lamb fourfold, because he did this thing, and because he had no pity.' Nathan said to David, 'You are the man!'"

18The crowd was silent as they listened intently. I then reminded them of Nathan's words to David when he cried that he had sinned against the Lord, "The Lord also has put away your sin; you shall not die."

20I said to the crowd, "God did this because David confessed his sin. You must confess your sins and beg forgiveness from God and be baptized.

21Many came confessing their sins and requesting to be baptized. There was no river, only a well near the palace. I took the bucket and lowered it into the water.

22As I said, "I baptize you with water for forgiveness of your sins, there is one greater coming who will baptize you with the Holy Spirit," I would pour the bucket of water on their head for purification.

23That day, I baptized at least one hundred souls. While I was about my business, preaching and baptizing, Herod and Herodias left Macherus for their palace in Tiberias.

24They must have decided that they were not in favor with the crowd and that I would return the next day.

25 After I had baptized all those who desired, I prayed to the Lord, thanking Him for the day and the words given to me to move the people.

26 I slept in an entrance way to the palace. I planned to be up early in the morning and to travel to Tiberias to speak again to Herod about repentance.

CHAPTER 12

1 I awoke early the next day to begin my journey. It would be a four day journey from Macherus to Tiberias.

2 I began my travels that morning with several people following after me. My direction was toward the Jordan of Jericho.

3 After a day's journey, I arrived at the Sea of Salt just south of the city of Jericho and returned to the city of Bethabara where I had baptized Jesus.

4 Many came out to see me and that evening, standing in the same place where Jesus had come to me to be baptized, I preached and baptized at least forty more for the remission of sins.

5 On the morning, as I prepared to depart and follow the River Jordan to Tiberius, I saw a familiar face. It was Judas.

6 "I am surprised to see you here, I was coming to Macherus to find you," Judas said.

7 I asked why he needed to find me.

8 "I did as you said," Judas responded, "I waited with James, John and the others for Jesus. We waited forty days for Him

to return."

9 I nodded as I listened and encouraged Judas to continue.

10 Judas looked at the ground for several moments, dragging his foot into the door. He stooped over and picked up some of the dirt and allowed it to seep out of his closed fist.

11 Finally he spoke, "Are you sure He is the One?" Judas asked, "the One to fulfill the prophecies, to sit on the throne of David?"

12 "Judas," I said, "why do you doubt?"

13 "He does not look like a King, not a King at all, but more of a beggar. He does not talk of uprisings or defeating the Romans, just of love, hope, caring for others," Judas said with some note of sadness.

14 "Judas," I said, "He is the One, His Kingdom is not of the world, and He is the Christ, the Messiah. You should return to Him and follow him."

15 "He is in Galilee, He has chosen James and John to follow him, and a man named Peter and his brother Andrew," Judas replied.

16 "And you?" I asked.

17 "Yes, and He talks of community and that we all share. He has asked me to care for His and the other's money," Judas offered.

18 I responded, "Judas, son of Simon, how do you doubt? I know your past. I know you were a siqari'im and member of the Zealots, but you have been baptized, those sins are forgiven. He has chosen you to be one of His followers. He has trusted you with the important task of keeping the money. You should return to Him this day."

19"Come with me," Judas pleaded.

20"My path takes me to Tiberias where I am sent by God," I responded, "Perhaps I will see Jesus in Nazareth, as it is close on my journey."

21This seemed to satisfy Judas and he wrapped his arms around me and pulled me tight against his chest, "I will return," and he released me and headed toward Galilee.

22As I watched him leave I felt an uneasiness. I hoped that he would eventually understand that Jesus was here to establish His Heavenly kingdom.

23Judas had been a very good disciple for me, quickly understanding the teachings of the prophets, being one of the first to be baptized, even before James and John.

24However, he struggled with his anger toward the Romans and I knew it was difficult for him to forgive the Romans and "love his enemy," as Jesus had taught him. I hoped this anger did not bring him trouble.

25As I watched Judas walk out of sight in the direction of Jericho, I started on my journey again. I had at least two, maybe three days remaining to Tiberias.

26There were no crowds following me as I began. It was a day's journey to the Jabboth River where Jacob and Esau met and Jacob wrestled with the Angel of the Lord. It would be a good place to rest.

CHAPTER 13

1At the point where the Jabboth River empties into the Jordan, I forded across much like Jacob did on his way back to Canaan from Charan. I recalled how Jacob had spent twenty years in Charan working for his uncle Laban.

2 When I reached the other side of the Jordan, there was a large crowd of people waiting for me.

3 "Are you Elijah, raised from the dead?" one asked.

4 "Or are you the Christ?" another asked.

5 I was pressed by others to explain who I was and I delivered the same message I had before.

6 I explained that I was the Messenger of the One that is coming after me and stated, "You are all sinners and need to be purified through baptism for forgiveness of your sins."

7 "Do you forgive sins, that is blasphemy," someone shouted.

8 "It is not I, but God who forgives your sins," I responded, "I will simply purify you with water to wash those sins and renew your soul. The One coming after me will baptize you with the Holy Spirit."

9 "Who is this who you speak of?" another yelled.

10 "The one foretold by the prophets, by Elijah, Hosea, Micah, Ezekiel, the one called the Christ," I exclaimed.

11 The crowd quieted and I motioned for everyone to sit on the shore. Standing in the shallows of the Jordan River I preached forgiveness of sins and the coming of the Christ in detail, quoting the prophets frequently.

12 All listened quietly as I spoke and then I announced, "Those wishing to be baptized, come to me, confess your sins and receive purification through baptism."

13 Many came and I baptized all of them. Torches were lit as I continued to baptize into the night.

[14]As I traveled to Tiberias many people followed. At each stop, the same occurred with people wanting to know how to be forgiven of their sins.

[15]I spoke of the coming of the Christ to all who would listen. I knew if He were in Galilee that these people would eventually become His followers too.

[16]I finally arrived at Tiberias and sought out the palace of Herod. Again I stood on the steps with a large crowd behind me.

[17]"Herod Antipas, you have sinned a great sin against God and your people. You have entered into an adulterous relationship with your brother Philip's wife, Herodias. Repent, repent and be saved," I cried.

[18]I could see Herod standing inside the door of the balcony above me.

[20]"You are King of this region at the service of God, but you have forsaken the laws of God, you are an adulterer and your wife Herodias and adulterous. Though your sins are great, there is forgiveness through confession," I continued.

[21]Herod appeared, "Watch your tongue, Baptist, who are you to judge?"

[22]"I am the messenger of God, God judges you. Adulterer, admit your sins," I responded.

[23]Suddenly the doors of the palace opened and Herod's soldiers surrounded me. The people began to throw stones and charge against them.

[24]Herod shouted, "Tell them to stop or they will die."

[25]I shouted, "He will not hurt me. Herod knows I am a prophet of God, he will not harm God's messenger."

26The people retreated and the soldiers took me into the palace, down several stairs into the dungeon.

27There was no one else there. I was taken to the last room with heavy bars. The door was opened and I was tossed inside, landing on my front into the dirt.

28Without any words to me the soldiers left but not before slamming the heavily barred door shut behind them.

29"Guard him," an order was given to someone in the shadows. As the guards left, I saw a familiar face.

30I stood up and reached through the bars to touch him, "Caleb!" I shouted.

CHAPTER 14

1I was happy to see Caleb and I asked how he came to guard me.

2Caleb stated that he was a member of the palace guard and that he volunteered. "Most of the guards fear you are Elijah, risen from the dead," Caleb explained.

3"And who do you think I am?" I asked.

4"You are the voice crying in the wilderness to bring the good news of baptism for the remission of sins," Caleb paused and then said, "and to prepare the way for the Messiah, the Christ."

5"This has been revealed to you," I exclaimed, "you are chosen of God."

6Caleb explained that Herod was unsure of what to do with me. There was a large crowd gathered at the palace entrance demanding my release.

7"I do not think this will happen," Caleb offered, "the Queen is very angry and does not want you on the streets, condemning the King and their relationship. You may have gone too far."

8I misjudged Herod's anger as I remained in his dungeon below the palace for several months. Caleb was always there, bringing food, water, and providing some news of the outside world.

9My prison was deep beneath the ground of the palace, no windows and the other cells were empty. I was provided a bucket each day for my daily needs. Caleb would empty the bucket and bring it back each day.

10I received only one meal a day of unleavened bread and a pitcher filled with fresh water. Caleb would bring me occasional fruit, but did so at great risk.

11After about seven months, Caleb came in the morning as always but was very excited, "Jesus is near," Caleb reported, "in the city of Magdala."

12I asked how far, and Caleb reported less than a morning's walk. Caleb described how Jesus had spoken for three days and over four thousand people remained all three days.

13"When he finished speaking," Caleb reported, "they say he took some loaves of bread and fishes and fed them all."

14I listened as Caleb described that after all of the people had been fed the disciples collected seven baskets of food remaining.

15"He is truly the Messiah," Caleb stated with awe in his voice.

16 I slumped against the far wall and recalled the young boy in the temple so many years ago. I did not notice that there were others now standing with Caleb.

17 "John," James called out.

18 I jumped with joy to see James, John, Judas and Simon the Zealot standing with Caleb.

19 "Caleb told us you were here," James said as he reached through the bars to hold my arms.

20 I asked if Jesus was with them and they replied he was not. Judas stated that He was in Magdala and while there had been questioned by the Pharisees and Sadducees.

21 "He asked who we thought he was," Judas said, "and Peter said He was the Christ, the Son of the Living God."

21 The others confirmed Judas' story and Judas added, "This sort of talk will get us all killed."

22 I could see by their expressions that James and John disagreed, but Simon nodded in agreement with what Judas had said.

23 I wanted to see Jesus so I asked the four to ask Him this question, "Are you the Messiah, foretold by the prophets, or are we to look for another?"

24 "But Peter said that He was the Christ, the Son of the Living God, and Jesus acknowledged that He was and told us to tell no-one," John argued, "Now you want us to ask him again?"

25 I explained that they were specifically to tell Jesus that the question was from me. I hoped that when Jesus heard the question that he would come to visit me as he was so close.

[26]We visited a while longer and the four disciples left saying that Jesus would only remain in Magdala a few days.

[27]As they departed, Judas remained, "I fear I will not see you again," he said with tears in his eyes.

[28]"The people want me freed," I told Judas, "Herod will not dare harm me and anger the people, do not worry."

[29]Caleb left with the four and I was alone again. I knelt in a corner and prayed that Jesus would come to visit me while so close.

CHAPTER 15

[1]In had been several days since the disciples had left and Jesus had not come.

[2]Caleb had reported that Jesus had left Magdala and gone to Caesarea Philippi with the disciples. This was the opposite direction from Tiberias.

[3]My hopes that Jesus would visit were dimmed and I was saddened. I tried to be hopeful, knowing that Jerusalem and Nazareth were nearby. As each day passed, the realization that He would not come was upon me.

[4]I continued my daily prayers, sometimes several times a day. I found little comfort and it seemed that God was no longer with me. My sleep became fitful and I would waken frequently.

[5]The next morning, when Caleb came with my rations for the day, I declined them except for the water.

6"I will fast," I explained to Caleb, "bring nothing but water and then leave me to pray in solitude."

7Caleb complied and brought only fresh water each morning and then would sit some distance away to leave me alone while I prayed.

8I lay prostrate on the dirt of my cell, praying quietly to God, asking for forgiveness and for direction and understanding. My prayers were the same.

9On the sixth night of my fast, while I was sleeping I felt a presence.

10I opened my eyes and there was a bright light in my cell, so bright I shielded my eyes.

11Then I heard the voice of Jesus, "Peace be with you, John."

12I removed my hand, "My Lord," I said and knelt on the ground at his feet.

13Jesus stood in the center of my cell, bathed in white, flowing robes, and reached out to lift me from kneeling.

14"John," He said, "do you question that I am Christ, the living Son of God, foretold by the prophets?"

15"I do not," I replied, "the blind see, the deaf hear, lepers are cleansed, the dead rise, You are the Christ, the Son of God."

16"But, John, there are questions," Jesus replied.

17I looked around. Caleb was sleeping, and there was no one else around.

18"They are all in a deep sleep so that I may talk with you. My Father has heard your cries and prayers," Jesus said.

19"John, why are you troubled? You know the prophecies better than any man, you have said that you know that I am the Christ, the Son of God, and yet you are troubled," Jesus continued.

20With hesitation, I explained, "It is true, I know the prophecies and therefore know that You have fulfilled those prophecies of the Messiah, but there are other prophecies."

21"I am the Bread of Life, I am the Light of the World. Before Abraham was I AM. I am the Good Shepherd, the Resurrection and the Life, I am the way, the Truth, and the Life," Jesus said, "and you believe these things."

24"Yes," I said, "but if you have fulfilled the prophecies, then you will fulfill them all?"

25"John, you are blessed among men, there is no prophet as great as you, My Father has heard your prayers, and I am here to answer," Jesus said.

26"The prophet Zechariah foretold, 'Be full of joy, O daughter of Zion; give a glad cry, O daughter of Jerusalem: see, your king comes to you: he is upright and has overcome; gentle and seated on an ass, on a young ass.' Have you entered Jerusalem?" I asked.

27"I have not," Jesus responded, "I still have more to do, but the Pharisees and Sadducees are not happy and are turning the people against Me. The High Priest Caiaphas fears I am a Rebel and will bring down Rome and their Priesthood."

28"From Daniel," I quoted, "Have then the certain knowledge that from the going out of the word for the building again of Jerusalem till the coming of a prince, on whom the holy oil has been put, will be seven weeks: in sixty-two weeks its building will be complete, with square and earthwork. And at the end of the times, even after the sixty-two weeks, one on whom the holy oil has been put will be cut off; and the town and the holy place will be made waste together with a prince; and the end will come with an overflowing of waters, and even to the end there will be war; the making waste which has been fixed. And a strong order will be sent out against the great number for one week; and so for half of the week the offering and the meal offering will come to an end; and in its place will be an unclean thing causing fear; till the destruction which has been fixed is let loose on him who has made waste."

29 Jesus looked at me, into my eyes, and waited, with no word spoken.

30 Finally, I said, "Then you will die?"

31 "John, you know the prophets, what do they say?" Jesus responded.

32 "That one of your followers will betray you, the Psalmist said, 'Even my dearest friend, in whom I had faith, who took bread with me, is turned against me,'" I responded.

33 "Thirty pieces of silver will be the price, Zachariah said, 'And it was broken on that day: and the sheep- traders, who were watching me, were certain that it was the word of the Lord. And I said to them, If it seems good to you, give me my payment; and if not, do not give it. So they gave me my payment by weight, thirty shekels of silver."

34 I did not want to continue as Jesus did not dispute the prophets. "You are to be taken before the Priests and accusations made and you will not defend yourself," I said, "Isaiah foretold, 'Men were cruel to him, but he was gentle and quiet; as a lamb taken to its death, and as a sheep before those who take her wool makes no sound, so he said not a word.'

35I continued, "Isiah said you will be beaten, scourged, and crucified, 'I was offering my back to those who gave me blows, and my face to those who were pulling out my hair: I did not keep my face covered from marks of shame, But it was our pain he took, and our diseases were put on him: while to us he seemed as one diseased, on whom God's punishment had come. But it was for our sins he was wounded, and for our evil doings he was crushed: he took the punishment by which we have peace, and by his wounds we are made well. We all went wandering like sheep; going every one of us after his desire; and the Lord put on him the punishment of us all. Men were cruel to him, but he was gentle and quiet; as a lamb taken to its death, and as a sheep before those who take her wool makes no sound, so he said not a word. And the Lord was pleased... see a seed, long life, will do well in his hand, made clear his righteousness before men... had taken their sins on himself."

36Jesus listened to me and finally said, "All that has been prophesied is true and much more you have not said."

37"So you will die?" I asked, angered.

38"John, you have studied the prophets so well, you have learned so much, have you forgotten the reason I will die?" Jesus said to me.

39I thought for several moments and recalled the Psalmist, "For you will not let my soul be prisoned in the underworld; you will not let your loved one see the place of death. You will make clear to me the way of life; where you are joy is complete; in your right hand there are pleasures forever and ever. Death will give them their food like sheep; the underworld is their fate and they will go down into it; their flesh is food for worms; their form is wasted away; the underworld is their resting place forever. But God will get back my soul; for he will take me from the power of death."

[40]I suddenly realized what Jesus was saying. I exclaimed, "You will die for the sins of the world and be resurrected from death; You must die for the world to live."

[41]"John, this has been revealed to you by My Father and the Holy Spirit. Those that follow will desert Me when My time has come. You, John, you who know the teachings of Moses, the Judges, the Kings, and the Prophets, you are the only one who knows what is to come," Jesus said.

CHAPTER 16

[1]I knelt again and wept at Jesus' feet. I knew that His fate was to be the saving of the world but did not want to accept that He would die.

[2]"Do not weep for me, John," Jesus said, "it was written by Moses, 'And there will be war between you and the woman and between your seed and her seed: by him will your head be crushed and by you his foot will be wounded.' All of the prophecies will be fulfilled as My Father so loves the world that He will give Me up to death on the cross for the salvation of the world."

[3]"John, let us break bread together," Jesus said. "In just a few days I will break bread in this manner with my disciples and then one of those at the table with Me will betray me. I wish to break bread with you, John, tonight."

[4]I sat up across from Jesus; He took unleavened bread, said a prayer, and broke it saying, "This is my body, which is given for you," and he handed me the bread.

[5]Jesus then took wine, and, after saying a prayer, handed the chalice to me and said, "Take this and drink from it, for this

is the chalice of my Blood, the Blood of the new covenant which will be poured and for the world for the forgiveness of sins."

6 I took the chalice and drank it and handed it back to Jesus.

7 "John, you were foretold by the Prophets also and have done all that God has asked of you," Jesus said to me.

8 "Your time is done, My Father has prepared a place for you John, I will be there with you soon with My Father," Jesus continued.

9 I realized what Jesus was saying but to be sure I asked, "Am I to die in this place?"

10 "Soon," Jesus responded, "but I and My Father have one more task for you. You must write down all that you have seen, all that you know, so that those coming afterward will know that I am the Messiah, the Christ, the one foretold by the Prophets, the living Son of God."

11 With those words, Jesus took my face in His hands, looked into my eyes and kissed me.

12 I felt such peace, such love, I closed my eyes and when I opened them the cell was dark, there was no one around. Jesus was gone. Caleb still slept in the corner.

13 When morning came, Caleb brought my bread and fresh water. I spoke to him solemnly, "Caleb, I need you to bring me something for me so that I might scribe."

14 Caleb departed and returned almost immediately with parchment, a rush plant was cut to a flat chisel-like shape and ink made from crushed berries. Not unlike what I had used at Qumran.

15 With these tools I began to write everyday while there was light. I poured the water from my jug into a cup and, at the

end of the day, rolled the parchment, placing it inside the jug.

[16]Caleb had provided a sharp tool and I had scraped away the mortar from around one of the stones on the East wall of my cell until I could remove the stone and place the water jug behind it.

[17]I have now written until the present time. In the morning Caleb brought disturbing news.

[18]"Herod is returning to Macherus in the morning, you are to go and be imprisoned there," Caleb reported.

[19]I thought I would die in Tiberias, but it will be in Macherus.

[20]I am awaiting my departure. I have risen early to write my last words before being taken to Macherus. I will not be able to take the parchment with me and will leave it in the jug before the stone wall.

[21]I have told Caleb that it will be there for him to retrieve and deliver to the disciples of Jesus when I have died.

[21]I have now lived thirty three years and have served God unto my death.

[22]In all of my studies of Moses, the Judges, the Kings and the Prophets; in all that I learned while studying at the Qumran, I have the following profession of faith:

[23]I believe in one Lord, Jesus Christ, the only Son of God, eternally begotten of the Father, God from God, Light from Light, true God from true God, begotten, not made, of one Being with the Father.

[24] Through him all things were made. For us and for our salvation he came down from heaven: by the power of the

Holy Spirit he became incarnate from the Virgin Mary, and was made man.

25In accordance with the prophets, He will suffer death and be buried. On the third day He will rise from the dead.

26He will ascend into heaven and be seated at the right hand of the Father. He will come again in glory to judge the living and the dead, and his kingdom will have no end.

27I believe in the Holy Spirit, the Lord, the giver of life, who proceeds from the Father. With the Father and the Son he is worshiped and glorified.

28He has spoken through the Prophets.

29I acknowledge one baptism for the forgiveness of sins. I look for the resurrection of the dead and the life of the world to come.

30These things are written that whoever reads them will come to believe that Jesus is the Christ, the Son of God, and that through this belief the people of the world will have eternal life in His name.

CHAPTER 23

Michael finished first. Without a word spoken, he got up from his chair and left the room. Jonathan noticed as Michael was leaving that there were tears streaming down his face. Jonathan started to call after him but decided against it. Although he was not finished, Jonathan closed his copy of the manuscript. After all, he had translated the documents, written them out and then placed them in their current form. Jonathan was very familiar with the manuscript and knew what he had to do. He waited for Saul to finish.

Jonathan only waited about five more minutes when Saul closed the manuscript and just kept looking downward. Saul did not speak.

"Are you okay?" Jonathan asked.

Saul remained silent, staring at the bindings of the manuscript.

"Saul," Jonathan ventured again, "everything alright?"

Saul sighed a very deep, long sigh. He stood up and looked down at Jonathan.

"Unbelievable," Saul whispered under his breath, "just unbelievable."

"I know," Jonathan replied, "but there is no doubt, I checked and rechecked my translation multiple times, it is what happened."

Saul paced back and forth behind his desk, pushed his fine, thin hair from his face and stroked his beard with his other hand. Jonathan could tell Saul was in deep thought. Jonathan waited quietly, but with a sense of urgency to do what he knew he must do.

Finally Saul spoke, "I must leave, Jonathan, I have somewhere I need to go."

"Now?" Jonathan questioned.

Jonathan could see that Saul was agitated, yet he noted Saul's eyes were moist with tears, tears that had not yet filled his lower lids and spilled onto his cheeks. As Saul rushed by, Jonathan stood up to follow. Saul had the manuscript in his hand. As they exited the office, Saul was startled to a stop and Jonathan almost ran into the back of him.

"Whoa, where are you going in such a hurry?"

Jonathan recognized the voice of Shelley from the Jewish Defense League, a voice that he had not heard in a long time.

"What do you want?" Saul had a tone of contempt.

"Professor, we invested ten million dollars in your little adventure, now rumor has it, you have something of value, something the Jewish Defense League might have an interest in," Shelley explained.

Saul was first concerned about how the Jewish Defense League learned about their discoveries. Jonathan also was thinking the same and hoped that Saul would question Shelley as to his source. Jonathan was surprised by what happened next.

"Yes," Saul offered, "we did find something," and handed Shelley the manuscript. "This should be everything the Jewish Defense League needs and could hope for."

Shelley was obviously surprised. However, before Shelley could say something, Saul was moving down the hallway at a rapid pace for the stairs.

"What does he mean by that?" Shelley directed to Jonathan.

"Read it," Jonathan responded rapidly, "and have them read it."

With those words, Jonathan tried to catch up to Saul, but the elevator doors closed just as Jonathan arrived. Jonathan quickly burst through the stairway exit door and began to move down to the ground floor. When he arrived just as he came through the door he saw Saul through the glass getting into a cab.

Jonathan was not sure what to do next. He was concerned about Saul and then he heard Michael's voice.

"So, it is all true," Michael said.

Jonathan looked around and found Michael sitting on a bench in the entrance. Jonathan sat down beside him. He could see that Michael had been crying.

"Why are you so upset?" Jonathan asked.

"I am not upset," Michael replied, "these are tears of joy. My faith has always been strong, but there was this bit of doubt with the scriptures being written as such, but now, proof that the events are true."

Michael stood up, Jonathan stood up as well. Michael reached out and grabbed Jonathan in a big bear hug, pulling Jonathan close and squeezing him till his glasses dislodged from his face."

"Thank you," Michael exclaimed, "it is truly a miracle, all this time, hidden in a water jug behind a wall."

Michael released Jonathan and gushed a tearful goodbye, explaining that he had to go to see his pastor and was returning home to Boston.

"We must wait until this is published before we release this to the world. You have no idea the impact, the scrutiny, the criticisms that you and Dr. Harkman will have to endure," Michael said with a tone of concern.

Jonathan just nodded and wished Michael well. The two men hugged each other and Michael departed. Jonathan was left alone. He thought for a few moments about what he had to do. He was puzzled, took out his phone, did a quick search, and returned the phone to his pocket. He went out the door of the building of the University and walked several blocks before hailing a cab. Jonathan got into the cab and gave the driver the address 22 Barclay Street in the middle of downtown New York City. Jonathan was very apprehensive as the cab pulled out into traffic, but this had to be done.

On the other side of town, an older man in brown canvas trousers, light colored shirt, and a jacket with patches at each elbow made his way up the steps of the Neo-Gothic church that he had seen so many times opposite Rockefeller Center. This was the first time Saul had walked up the steps. He went to the first door and was surprised to see that it was opened. It was just after 6 in the evening and the Church had about one hundred people scattered in the pews. Saul was in awe of the inside, so expansive, so large with beautiful stained glass windows. The people were standing and filing into the center aisle where two men Saul assumed were Priests were passing out something that the people were eating. Saul's heart leaped when he realized that this was a bread much like Jesus had given to John the Baptist while imprisoned. Saul's excitement was reaching a fever pitch when the service ended. A young man dressed in black robes walked to the back of the Church and approached Saul.

"May I help you?" the young man said.

Saul did not speak at first and the Priest thought perhaps he had some sort of mental illness. He decided to try again.

"I am Father James, a Priest at Saint Patrick's, is there something I can do for you?"

Father James could see the tears now flowing down Saul's face. Father James placed his hand on Saul's shoulder. Saul collapses onto one knee with the Priest kneeling beside him.

"I am a sinner," Saul cried, "I need the forgiveness and baptism of Jesus Christ."

Father James could barely understand Saul through his crying, but offered a prayer for him and encouraged him.

"You have made the first step toward salvation," Father James said with reassurance and helped Saul to his feet. "Let's go to my office."

Only five miles on the other side of town, Jonathan was getting out of his cab at 22 Barclay Street. Jonathan looked up at the large columns in front of one of the oldest Catholic Churches in New York, Saint Peter's. He quickly ascended the steps and walked inside. The Church was empty except for a Priest kneeling at the front, obviously in prayer. Jonathan very quietly approached until he was behind the priest. He waited for him to stand.

"Hello," Jonathan said timidly.

The priest turned, a little startled.

"Well hello," the priest replied, "may I help you?"

Jonathan introduced himself, "My name is Jonathan Weiztman, a Professor of Ancient Hebrew at the University. I would like to talk with you."

"You are Jewish?" the Priest said, more of a statement than a question and pointing to Jonathan's kippah.

"Yes, I am Orthodox," Jonathan replied, "and I would like to talk to you…"

"I am sorry, I am Father Andrew," the Priest said.

Father Andrew surveyed Jonathan and deemed he looked harmless. He was wearing thick glasses, dressed much like a Professor.

"Let's go to my office." Father Andrew pointed the way and Jonathan proceeded.

Once inside the office, Jonathan was amazed at the size, and there were books everywhere along the wall. Father Andrew sat down behind a very large, ornate desk and pointed to one of two chairs on the other side for Jonathan to sit.

"Please," Jonathan pleaded, "I have just one question," and he continued to stand.

Father Andrew waited and watched as Jonathan brushed a thick lock of his har from his eyes, adjusted his kippah, then removed his large round glasses. He then pulled a handkerchief from his pocket and cleaned the lens. He returned the glasses to his face and drew a deep breath.

"Father Andrew," Jonathan said softly, "I believe that Jesus Christ is the Messiah, the Son of the Living God, that he was crucified, dead, and buried, on the third day he arose from the dead and sits at the right hand of God."

Father Andrew stared in shock at what Jonathan had said, but his next statement was a miracle.

Jonathan continued, "What must I do to be saved?"

THE END

ACKNOWLEDGMENTS

Writing a novel for me involves many hours of research, seclusion, missed meals, late nights. There are so many to thank as each part of my life journey has contributed to my being.

First and foremost, my wife, Donna, and her tireless patience with an obsessive perfectionist; she was fearless in her support and objective criticism, as always, of any of my work.

To Charlotte Warren, High School English teacher, who had the patience to teach a cynical teenager how to write; I am forever grateful.

To my many Sunday School teachers, preachers, nuns, and priests, including Fathers Moquin, Don and Tracy. These inspired me to always question the truth until I was satisfied it *was* the truth.

And finally, to God, for giving me everything necessary to write such a book and for always reminding me how insignificant I really am.

ABOUT THE AUTHOR

Christopher Laurent is a retired Navy Captain and active health care professional. He has been published in multiple professional journals and has an extensive public speaking history. Laurent's prior seminary training provided some of the foundations for his first novel, *The Gospel of the Baptist.* He and his wife Donna reside in the White Mountains of New Hampshire where they enjoy the privacy and seclusion of the Great Northwoods.

www.ingramcontent.com/pod-product-compliance
Lightning Source LLC
Chambersburg PA
CBHW060617310726
48982CB00003B/593

* 9 7 8 1 6 3 7 7 7 1 2 8 0 *